In The Middle Distance

A NOVEL BY

Nicholas Delbanco

William Morrow & Company, Inc., New York   1971

In The Middle Distance

A NOVEL BY

Nicholas Delbanco

William Morrow & Company, Inc., New York   1971

1605838

For Elena, my wife
With all my love

Necessite faict gens mesprendre
E faim saillir le loup des boys

François Villon

I

OCTOBER 6

Far smoke furled; I studied it, was glad. Chestnuts abounded, and hazelnuts, and the seckel pear tree had begun. Nothing ends, I think, nothing terminates—it's all backasswards, life. Barbara gesticulated, a stick figure, at the pond. All summer nothing but that. This. Sneaking off to the shed. Misshapen. Carrying grief like a placard: Eat at Nick's. Heartbreak Ham. Charity Stew. Contemplating a prick like a navel, winking at Eve. Calling this a novel. That.

II

Nicholas Delbanco was forty-eight years old. He had been inoculated against typhus ("There's some medical question," the doctor said, "whether this works."), typhoid, smallpox, and cholera. "That only lasts," the doctor said, "for six months." He had received a tetanus booster and a shot for yellow fever, effective for ten years. His passport number was G1199613, and his passport had been issued in 1967, in New York. He did not plan a trip but readied himself for departure nonetheless. "You won't die of cholera," the doctor said. "I can fill you up with glucose and a saline solution. If it comes to that."

Nicholas had traveled widely, and he had enjoyed it. He was familiar with Europe and Japan and the Caribbean and, to a lesser extent, with North Africa. He had not traveled to South America or to the Near East. He liked to consult the atlas and his visas and a globe that he kept on his desk; he would spin the globe and stop it at random, fingering the spot he planned to visit next. Seven out of ten times, however, he fingered the sea.

He had been married eighteen years. His wife was named Barbara, his daughter Eve—though her true name was Evelyn—and he had one dead son named Michael. Michael had been named after Barbara's cousin; Barbara's cousin, too, was dead.

Nicholas wore double-breasted pin-stripe suits and, sometimes, a stickpin in his tie and, when it became the fashion, he bought necklaces. He liked tapered shirts. He had a weight problem and a large bald spot. His eyes were blue and good, though recently he had had trouble, when driving, with advertisements and road signs. FLY B.O.A.C. had seemed BIVOUAC, and Slippery When Wet, on the Taconic, had been illegible. He kept both eyes open in the Snellen Test.

He was a partner in the architectural firm of Boos, Letterman, Sperry and Johannson, and he had hoped to have his name on the letterhead. He would take it up, he promised Barbara, with Alexander Sperry soon. He wore sideburns and had been engaged to build a memorial theater for his school; by May eleventh, he had worked on the project two weeks. His bid had been tentative though informed with nostalgia; the principal, for whom the theater was to be named, had been a generous man. He had worn brown suits and walked with a cane and had had his hearing impaired, the story went, by shrapnel in the first world war.

Nicholas had not been happy at Fieldston. He had been battered by ambition and insecurity and a sense of class displaced. His parents were poor and had been immigrants from Spain. His mother, twenty-two years younger than his father, died when Nicholas was seven, and they had lived in the Bronx. One of the boys at Fieldston was a Bronk. "My family used to have a place north of Manhattan," he said.

Nicholas blamed their poverty on the Depression and told

friends that his father had been born in a house with three up-stairs maids. "My grandmother lived," he said, "in a room the size of what her bathroom used to be." His father bought a 1930 Plymouth in 1936. Nicholas told friends the Cadillac was in the garage for repairs.

Returning to Fieldston, therefore, he chose anonymity. Thirty years had elapsed, and his teachers were retired or were dead. He was five-foot-nine and had never been sizable for his age but had, inexplicably, been excellent at the broad jump. He was adequate at the high jump and the hop, skip, and jump, but had been the varsity broad jumper for three years. He had broad-jumped nineteen feet six inches, and that was a school record, and he walked to the gym wing to see if the record still stood. That soaring, easeful leap, and the gathering of legs to belly in air, the final reach and curl and impact that would propel him forward—such flight had been and would remain his notion of success.

He found the plaque and hunted for himself. Bill DuBridge had leaped twenty-one feet three and one-half inches in 1968. Nicholas's record had stood, however, for twenty-seven years and he remained, starred, on the plaque. He breathed Ajax and Vitalis and Old Spice and the air beyond; he opened the doors to the track and felt the door spring's sucking release, and was gratified.

He had found, in his father's desk, this letter to his father.

9/22/36

Dear Papaito,
How are you? I am great. Everything is simply won-derful. Mrs. Menendez is coming around very well considering the operation. Andrea has a big wasp sting under her leg but it is getting much better. We miss you in Cuba and wonder what it's like. Fieldston is wonderful! My teacher is Mrs. Landry, the lady who interviewed me. She is very, very nice. I have two good

friends already, Allen "Red" Harris and Bob Shelterling, we all sit together. There are twenty people in our class.

Clarry Beelan our coach is the greatest guy, he's really terriff. I have art and cooking for the first part of the year and ceramics and shop for the other semester. Our teacher Mr. Mall who teaches art is very nice. Everyone recognizes me on sight because I won at ping-pong yesterday. Even Gary the locker room man knows that. Everything is wonderful.

How is your trip? I sure wish you would hurry and bring me sugar cane. Give my regards to everyone.

Love,
Nicky

P.S. That article about the statue was in all the New York papers. The Tribune said "Nude Stolen" and the Times, "Statue Stolen!"

Nicholas had moved three times since his marriage to Barbara. First, they had lived on West End Avenue and Eighty-first Street. Next, with the children old enough for school, they moved to Pinebrook Boulevard in New Rochelle. Teresa Brewer lived near them, and her garage was painted with alternating pink and white squares. He took Eve tricycling to Beechmont Lake, and Michael fished there fruitlessly. They would ice-skate on the lake in the winter, and he planted a boxwood hedge for the front and the back yards. They had a poodle called Zozo and he called Eve Mother Pamplemousse.

When Nicholas was made a partner, his salary was increased by seven thousand five hundred dollars. He earned, in 1958, thirty-seven thousand and five hundred dollars a year. "That's a respectable wage," he would announce. "That's all we need."

Barbara liked New Rochelle and wanted to join a club

there, and to buy a boat. "We could get a catboat," she said. But Nicholas hated commuting; he felt claustrophobic and did not take the train. He drove to Eastchester each day and then took the Cross County Parkway and the Henry Hudson Parkway and got off at Fifty-seventh Street. His office was at Fifty-fifth Street and Park Avenue; he had to leave Pinebrook Boulevard at seven in order to be at his office by nine. This infuriated him, since the trip should not have taken, he told Barbara, more than forty minutes. "It's either too hot," Nicholas complained, "and the cars boil over, or too cold and they stall."

He listened to WCBS and WINS; he liked Alfred Drake's version of "Stranger in Paradise" better than he liked Tony Bennett's, and he admired the entire score of *Kiss Me Kate*. Michael found "Oh! My Pa-pa" and played it every night; Nicholas was embarrassed but proud. He did not like the "Listen to Lacy" jingle but liked the songs that Lacy played; "In Our Mountain Greenery" was his favorite.

He rarely reached home by seven. He told Barbara, "This is ridiculous. It's costing us an extra car and I don't get to see the kids, and if we're going to live in the country we should live in the country. And if we're going to live in town we should live in town."

"Let's do both," she said.

They moved, therefore, to Eighty-first Street and East End Avenue, and he sent Michael and Eve to the Midtown School. They hunted for a "property," and, with his brother-in-law's legacy, he bought the farm outright. His building went co-operative and, as he was about to mortgage himself for the money, he was promoted again and transferred to Boston, to head the branch office there. He completed Fieldston's theater and was asked to join Baltimore's city-planning commission, but declined.

His children went to the orthodontist and had braces fitted but seemed to have no other problems; he was, he told friends, too lucky for words. He put in a bid for the State Capitol complex at Portland, and lost. He offered preliminary drawings for the Bennington College Science Building, and Fine Arts Center, and lost. His secretary married, and quit; he suspected Michael of homosexual tendencies; both Eve and Michael refused to attend Sunday School. He forced Michael to go, as a trial, for one month. "If you don't like it," he said, "you can quit. I promise. We'll say no more about it. All right?" Michael agreed and, after the first Sunday, Nicholas went to collect him and found Michael playing football in the Sunday School's front hall.

He gained eight pounds and drank and Barbara feared cancer of the left breast. They removed the growth, and it was non-malignant, but Nicholas could feel only disgust and compassion, not love. He had seen *J.B.* in New York, with Christopher Plummer and Raymond Massey and Pat Hingle, and he wondered if he were not equally some sort of Job. " 'Things fall apart';" Barbara recited, " 'the center cannot hold.' " She read Yeats often and particularly liked the line, "The foul rag and bone shop of the heart."

He traced his allergies to oysters and had strep throat, and the firm's Boston branch did not break even for three years. "You've got to give us time," he argued in New York, "to get established. There's fierce competition in that town."

"I think we ought to close it up," Henry Letterman said. "I think we ought to face the fact it's costing us more than it's worth."

"Give me one more year," Nicholas asked. "That's all I ask. We're going to get that shopping center. The one in Mattapan. And there's the condominium and shipyards and it does, I can only repeat it, take time."

"Three years?" Henry Letterman asked.

Barbara was inchoate, wanted mink, and she drank gin and bitters by noon. Nicholas dreamed of camels disporting themselves on his driveway, with seven days of urine spilled on what were Perma-press sheets, and everything aflame but that, and his houses crumbling and the upstairs curtains crumbling and Eve and Barbara crumbling and Michael, mostly Michael, crumbling.

He drove from New York to Boston with his new secretary, Ruth. He chose secondary roads.

"That meeting didn't go badly," she said. "You mark my words. They'll give us another year, you'll see."

He offered her rum from his glove compartment, and they had a slice of apple and Camembert cheese.

"Maybe you're right," Nicholas said. "Why not? We deserve it."

She loosened her seat belt and kicked off her shoes. "I'll drive," she said, "if you'd like."

They exchanged places, and Nicholas had a second drink from the flask. It was leather and embossed with his initials and had a small deck of cards in the pouch. Ruth overtook a trailer, and he admired her legs. She overtook a second truck and was directly in front of a wrecker. She attempted to slip in between the two, but Nicholas shouted, "Don't. Pull over to the grass!" She swerved off the road to the grass and braked too suddenly and the car spun around and drifted slowly back onto the road, and the wrecker hit them, headlong, sideways, tearing the hood off and shearing through the engine block. The hood flew fifty yards. Ruth was unhurt and Nicholas, the doctor said, had a hematoma on his left shin. He had a bad bruise on his stomach where the seat belt had caught and retained him; his ribs hurt; he had been, he realized, in shock.

He drew plateaus; his life had been, he told Barbara, first, rise and, second, decline. "Everything was together," he said. "That's just the way it was."

"I hate the phrase," Barbara said. "I hate your faddish expressions."

"What do you mean?"

"What do you think I mean? Together."

"Come off it," he said. "Things are pretty scattered now. They're not together, that's all."

"Don't," she said, mimicking him, "make me uptight about it, dig? Everything's together, dig? It's groovy, man."

He wanted to fuck Ruth, and fire her, and wondered when it would be fashionable to shave skulls. He joined the Peace Offensive Group on Beacon Hill. "What we've got to realize," he said, "is that Middle America, you know, that great unwashed electorate, also has its rights."

"You're the only manic-depressive I know," Barbara said, "who's depressive all the time. Congratulations."

"You're the only sadomasochist," he countered, "who's only sadistic. Congratulations right back."

"Darling," she said, "let's not fight. Especially not now."

"Why not now?" he asked. "Now's as good a time as any. I can't move my leg."

"Now, on Michael's birthday," she said, contrite. "You can't have forgotten. Not yet."

She had no love of ceremony, and he wanted to accuse her of using death as leverage for life. "That's not fair," he said. "That's cheap."

"Darling," she said, "I'm being honest for once. Honestly. Even if I've been a rotten nurse. We need a change, and rest; we don't need to squabble like this. It's June now, and you could take the summer off."

Ruth's insurance premiums went up; she asked for a raise. "It happened," she said, "on company time. In a sense."

The cardboard turned to ash, he dreamed, crepitant,

wreathed to itself. The camels, their humps become pyres, were equally aflame; he squinted at the shadow's substance, was not hot. Richard Nixon's teeth fell out and sprouted and Nicholas covered the country with salt. Soft snow coalesced to teeth, congealed, and the deer that came to lick were Henry Letterman's servants. The New Rochelle Fire Brigade came and put the fire out, handling the hose-whip like antlers, but with authority. Firemen vaulted the teeth. Even the Japanese maple, with Michael's swing affixed to it, was aflame and crumbling. Barbara slept on her side, her breasts away from him, hands crossed.

Nicholas left Beacon Hill for Cossayuna on June fifth. Barbara and Eve would follow in ten days; they would take a Greyhound bus when Eve completed school. He drove to Cossayuna slowly, traffic-shy, stocking groceries. He turned on the radio and attempted harmony with the commercials. "You've got a lot to live," he sang, and ". . . When you're having more than one."

He drove a yellow Pontiac Catalina convertible, Barbara's car. It had automatic transmission but a console shift. He stopped the car near a closed roadside stand and relieved himself behind it, attempting to spell PEPSI-COLA in the dust. He spelled the first word with precision but was emptied by the o and dribbled, at the o's turning, away. The stand would offer garden produce soon; he had laid in turnips and carrots and lettuce with Eve the previous spring. "How's our thistle patch?" he would ask Eve each morning. "How did the rabbits eat last night?"

He had taken one month's vacation, with a provision for more. "In order to reconnoiter," he told Henry Letterman, "in order to decide priorities."

Henry had agreed. "Particularly after the accident," he said. "Meantime, don't worry yourself. We can use Ruth in New York."

Barbara would see to the packing. "You go ahead," she said. "You need this time."

He took his typewriter; it was in his dressing closet, under ski boots and Frank Sinatra albums and a raccoon coat. He was at ease with her, and comforted, but he felt her patience willed. "You're piling up points," he said. "You're being better to me than you feel like being."

"Don't be paranoid," she said.

"Who's being paranoid?" he asked. "Help. The paranoiacs are after me."

For seven nights running, he had slept in Michael's room. He did this for fear of strangling Barbara; he lay, arms folded, hands under his armpits, on his side. He did not sleep at all, or woke to find the pillow soaked. He ate only baby food, and little enough of that for a man of his bulk. He evolved some remedies: a glass of wine would calm him, and he chanted, regularly, "Devils, go away. Devils get lost. Devils, devils, devils."

He liked to draw and he swept his wrist across the sketch-book and wanted to do fingerpainting but could not find the paints. The telephone threatened him, and the Venetian blinds, and he thought he saw a water moccasin in the toilet.

He stopped for gas in Greenfield. At the entrance of the Shell station, a man was eating a submarine sandwich; the man wore a red flannel shirt and waders and was, Nicholas guessed, sixty-five. He was toothless and, while the attendant filled the tank and checked the oil, Nicholas watched the man eat. He licked the bread repeatedly and masticated it, jaw roiling, lips drawn down.

"We are marching to Cam-bod-i-a, Cam-bod-ia," Nicholas sang, "Cam-bod-i-a. We are marching through Cam-bod-i-a, Cam-bod-i-a, hurrah. Zap that Angkor Wat," he instructed himself, turning north on Route 22. "Zap them cong."

He was appalled, he had told Barbara, and would condone

assassination now. He dreamed of howitzers and biochemical warfare and the canisters exploding in Cossayuna Lake. "Just think," he told her, "of the Rocky Mountain Arsenal. How can you sleep with that thought?" He had propounded the domino theory, once. "In 1960," he said, "it made sense. And I'm still not sure they're consciously evil, those men. But they're lunatic."

These opinions too, he knew, were secondhand and easily purchased. Yet, lying in his bed, arms crossed, he labeled the devils as cabinet members and the heads of corporations and the joint chiefs of staff. He became incontinent and urinated, on the average, three times an hour. One afternoon, he tabulated his trips to the bathroom, and, from noon to five o'clock, he went there eighteen times. The water moccasin had, he saw, evacuated the toilet bowl. Legions of the crippled trotted on linoleum; his house was, he was certain, mined.

"Laos, Laos," he said to Barbara. "You have no sympathy."

"Of course I do," she said.

"Look what we're doing," he said. "My God, only look what we've done."

"What do you want me to see?" she asked.

"Napalm sunsets. Elephants that used to be people. Tanks. Laos, Laos, Laos," he accused her. "That's what I want you to see!"

He arrived at the farm in the late afternoon. He had forgotten the keys and skirted the house and entered through the bathroom window; he hurt his knee on the sill. He remembered bathing Michael, and shaving him without a razor blade, and the first time Michael needed a true shave. "Bodily collapse," he chanted, "bodily collapse. Nixon ordered Chinese food from the Imperial Palace, and he had it flown to San Clemente. Don't you think taxpayers pay?"

What he had loved in Jean, he knew, was her refusal. What

Barbara loved in him was, equally, distance; could there not be reciprocity? He opened doors. He braced the windows with wood, then hammered on the wood; he opened the windows and soaped them; he replaced storm windows with screens. He had, and this surprised him, no fear of the night nor of being alone. He opened black bean soup. He heated and stirred it and added too much salt. "Bodily collapse," he repeated to himself, "bodily collapse."

The spiral staircase needed polishing, he saw. He hunted for the stove black and a rag. He found the stove black but could not find a rag in the kitchen; he used, therefore, his handkerchief. On the third step, going up, he realized he was working in the wrong direction and that, even stretching, he could not reach the seventh step. He would sleep downstairs.

Nicholas unpacked the typewriter and placed it on the dining table and felt it totemic, at rest. He spelled "Key," then "THEN," then "Spiro T. Agnew eats the Hairy Bird." Love is an ease, a sinking, a generosity, he thought. He finished the soup and licked the bowl; he added "If Thine Eye Offend THEE" to the yellow sheet. Love is aspiration, he thought, and he was drained of aspiration; it is belief in the future, and he had no such belief. "Special things," he typed and used both index fingers, "are being squandered daily; consult *Das Kapital*." The gutter was without support, and a bird was nesting on its outer edge; he would check the roof for leakage, he decided, later, when the staircase dried. "Love is charity, expansion," he wrote, "and I can only contract."

Nicholas walked with a certain assurance through hotel lobbies and banks. When shopping, however, he found himself inert with the prospect of choice. He hunted seventeen minutes for Schweppes in the Greenwich A&P and, finding it, toppled the pyramid of cartons and was cut by the cascading glass. He slept, for the first days, till eleven-thirty each morning. He came to take pleasure, however, in early waking, and he set his alarm for six.

This became habitual and he rose at six, or earlier, to make himself coffee and two boiled eggs. He boiled the eggs five minutes and tapped them open with a spoon, never having learned to cut them properly. He used much salt and pepper and butter but drank his coffee black. He would wash the dishes meticulously, then shave, fingering his sideburns, and, every second day, he trimmed his nostril hair.

He had proposed to Barbara on August 3, 1953. He knew the date because he kept a journal at the time, and not because of engagement celebrations. They did not observe anniversaries, though he would have wished to, once. He had a parlor-arithmetic trick of deducing people's birthdays from the multiple of the numbers of their month and day. "Take your birthday, month and day, and add them together," he said. "Then multiply the whole thing by twenty and subtract the number of the month." By this system, August third was two hundred and twelve. From seventy-nine, for instance, he could figure January third. He subtracted the last digit from the nearest multiple of twenty, and determined the month; he then divided that multiple-sum by twenty, and subtracted the month, and determined the day.

Nicholas walked to the barn. He wore green rubber boots because it had rained heavily, and because the neighbor's tractors had churned mud. He opened the gate to the chicken pen; there was a dead chicken within, its carcass meshed with mud. Emblems of decay assailed him; the roof had sprung, the wire bellied out, the trough was upended, and a meal sack hosted rats.

Nicholas had the sense, at times, of nearly apprehended truth—that just around the next drink's corner, or one meadow farther than he felt he ought to walk in rain, one hundred push-ups more than he had ever steeled himself to make, reconciliation waited, naked, absolute. And this recognition would enfold him, would teach him calm and sanctity and ease. Sometimes, tying shoes, he recognized this feeling as the residue of faith. And he would be surprised by, beleaguered by faith. He fought surrender like weight. Yet he could see himself as an ancient, shawled, muttering man, the steps to the synagogue difficult, holding the banister rail.

He wore chinos with the belt behind, and a pair of sneakers; he went to a convention, once, in the Princeton Inn and felt elegiac for his clamorous, clambering youth. He had attended Columbia but had fancied ivy and fraternities and girls from Wellesley come to spend the weekend, skewered on the billiard table, and inordinate prowess with beer. He had held a lacrosse stick, once, in Riverside Park. He was hit on the cheekbone with the first toss and thought his cheekbone shattered, and stopped. He liked to row, however, and belonged to a health club and went there to row and to smoke a cigar while being massaged.

He had been friends with his sister's husband, Simon. Simon had a small company in the wig business, in which, he announced, he had left Nicholas stock. They drank Bloody Marys together, after exercise, and would go bowling together and share beer and Thursday poker and a sense of freedom; they watched stag movies once. Nicholas had also included Simon in his will, the gesture mattering more than the funds. Simon's stock, however, had suddenly multiplied, and the legacy had proved substantial. Simon was an avid hockey fan and admired Boom Boom Geoffrion, and his notion of success was a season's pass to see the Giants. He died of a massive occlusion as Alex Webster fumbled, going around left end. Nicholas's sister, Andrea, professed a love of the opera, but she neither went nor listened; she preferred

Darjeeling tea to coffee, and drank it everywhere. Simon died in 1963 and, one year later, Nicholas purchased the farm.

The farm had ninety-two acres and four fireplaces and several outbuildings. There was a horse shed and cow shed and chicken coop and a large barn; Nicholas kept no animals but would have liked a horse. He was not suicidal nor contemplative; he contemplated suicide. He would drink half a bottle of Scotch and swallow, he decided, barbiturates. He would leave this note, "Dear World: Rearrange the following words to form a well-known phrase or saying: OFF FUCK."

He had been, he knew, fraudulent at school and college; he felt inauthentic, also, at the farm. Acquired with Simon's leavings, it reeked of Dynel, Instant Afros, the panoply of wigs. He tallied every gesture of the previous three weeks and compiled these things: the wrecker's yellow snout upon him, Barbara's ankle bleeding where she had scratched the bite too hard, Eve bent, incompetent, over her steel-stringed guitar. "Don't tell me where you're going," she sang, " 'cause I ain't going to follow; don't tell me when you're leaving, 'cause I don't intend to mind."

Nicholas wished to remodel the kitchen. He envisioned housemaids with nothing on but aprons, and standing at the stove. Eve had been fanatical with horses; the two of them played rodeo, himself the bronco, her the cowboy, timing how long it would take her to tumble. He bucked and pitched and invited the twins in from next door to watch; Eve wept that her donkey didn't want a pin back there.

He bought a ladder-back chair for three dollars, and sanded the splinters off. The studio hut was airless and hot, and he liked sitting at the door, staring at the fields. The studio had been the milking shed. He had played with erector sets when a child and recollected his first built bridge; he had successfully traversed the bathtub, and he remembered the clean pride with which he spanned the taps. His father had been impressed. He had run the water without dislocating Nicholas's bridge; the bridge had remained there one week. Outside, a groundhog lay in sun; over the Hudson, clouds presaged rain. He saw himself refracted in the window; he waggled fingers from his ears and stuck out his tongue. He had thought himself a visionary, once.

Once, towns would coalesce in deserts and municipalities thrive beneath the sea. Once, his work would matter, and his buildings, numinous, would help. Outside, the barn cat yowled.

Nicholas purchased a ream of Eaton's Corrasable twenty-weight bond; he hefted the sheets and read the watermark. He pasted one of the sheets in the center of the single window of the hut; he used masking tape. He had studied calligraphy, once. He chose to type, however, because he did not wish to worry over ink or spacing or style. He used a Smith-Corona Classic 12. He would write a novel as an act of explication and an act of penance; he would expiate Michael, and Jean, and every failure embraced. He would re-create the past and resurrect it and enter into fantasy, not fact. Barbara, telephoning, asked him if he had to do this, really, and he answered, "I do. I really need to. I have to."

It was, in fact, necessity, not pleasure; Nicholas dreamed of his novel, its dying cadences, and dreamed that he was drowning, sucking sea.

Nicholas's first flight had been with a Kerry Blue terrier, in 1938, and the Kerry Blue terrier was ill, and that had made him airsick also. He had spent a week, once, with Barbara in Brewster, Maine, and recollected it as the high point of devotion. He thought that, somehow, had they not been married, joy beyond time might have persisted, would persist. Once, while staying at the Hotel Excelsior in Rome, he had slept with a German girl who turned out to be neither kindly nor cheap. "The lady with the long handbag," the porter, winking, said.

Barbara called. "How're you making it?" she asked.

"Fine," he said, "just fine."

"Did you open the shutters?" she asked. "What's the weather like?"

"Yes," he answered, "hot. What time is it?"

"Nine forty-five," she said. "I miss you very much."

"Yes."

"Did you have enough to eat, darling? What did you eat?"

"Black bean soup," he said, "yesterday, for lunch. I'm not very hungry," he said.

Moths fluttered, settling onto the fireplace wall.

"Are you all right?" she asked.

"How's Eve?" he asked.

"She's fine. She went to *Satyricon* last night. With Sandy. They liked it a lot."

"Maybe we should get tickets," he said.

"Yes. Was there much mail?" she asked.

"Three dunning letters from Macy's, a new telephone directory with a pastel well on top, and mountains."

"I paid the Macy's bill," she said.

"And fourteen packages of Enzyme-active Axion, or something very like, and a brochure for Ecolo-G, and one sample coffee," he said.

"Nicholas," Barbara said, "it's hot here, and they're threatening a brownout."

"Brownout, what a word. I don't mind an honest blackout," he said.

He pushed the rheostat and listened to the spotlight's soft hum, then pushed the rheostat again.

"Maybe we should come early," Barbara offered, "before it gets too hot. Or I could come up now. Eve could follow on the bus."

"There's nothing wrong," he said. "No ghosts about."

"You could come back."

"No," he said, "don't worry. Everything's fine."

"We could have some time alone," she said.

"Yes, I look forward to it. Very much," he concluded.

The people on the party line picked up the phone, then cradled it, heavily, twice. He hung up and tried to think of the Italian word for hanging up.

Nicholas named ten flowers. He named roses, dahlias, marigolds, black-eyed Susans, dandelions, daisies, narcissus, tulips, sunflowers and lilies. He named six animals. He named elephants, gibbons, anteaters, lions, cheetahs and a giraffe. He named eight cars: the Datsun, Oldsmobile, Cadillac, Dodge, Plymouth, Volkswagen, Mustang and Maserati; he found, at his upper field's rim, rusting tractor wheels and two Stutz lamps. He quartered the pencils on his desk, using his new knife, then cut off the erasers and sharpened the eight sides. He saw himself young, lucky, beloved; he discarded his boots. He ran his hand palm down along the table, hunting for splinters.

He had gone to grade school on Jerome Avenue. His backbone resonated to the sound of chalk on blackboard, and the eraser's sound. Betsy Lang in front of him had dark hair on her scalp and lighter hair where she tied it for a braid; twenty-two years later, he met her at the Fairmont newsstand, purchasing *Redbook*. "I'm married," she told him, "and I have three children. Brock, Bill and Janey; Janey's my favorite, of course. Bill was born with three fingers on each hand, but he still plays a wicked guitar."

"What does your husband do?" Nicholas asked.

"Nothing," she said. "We're divorced."

"Does that mean," Nicholas asked, "that he does nothing because you're divorced, or you're divorced because he does nothing?"

"She was only a colonel's daughter," Nicholas sang to himself, "but knew what Reggie meant." He drew the George Washington Bridge, and the Little Red Schoolhouse underneath it, and himself as a stick figure larger than the bridge. He had five days till Barbara arrived. "You must remember to open the shutters," he sang. "Go away from my shutters, beat it from my door, go away 'way from my shutters, and bother me no more." He had not shaved, would grow a beard, would learn to distinguish Allis-Chalmers equipment from John Deere. "We had hoped Morris could join us tonight." He capered for his imaginary audience—they wore red skirts, knees flared at him, and pink high-heeled shoes—"but, unfortunately, Morris was unable to be with us." He bowed and wheeled. "When I was first asked to speak here tonight, I thought it was too great an honor. But, on reflection, I think you all deserve it." He sat again, weary with performance, and trundled his chair to the desk. He wished for Eve's recorder; he wished that he truly could sing. Jean floated past and sucked the honey of his music vows. He told the following story:

"Once upon a time," he said, "in the little village sixteen miles southeast of Saratoga, bounded on the north by a pig farm and on the west by an enormous gravel pit, there lived a boy called Sam. Let's call him Sam," he said, "Sam's an acceptable name. And this boy had sixteen chickens and one rooster called Lawrence and one pig." He heard ringing in the house. He wondered, was that the phone? "They would beat on the gong," he continued, "for supper, and if Sam came late he rarely had his favorite dish. Which was and is and will always remain, for such is the province of fiction, ice cream. Which they served first in the house because anything you liked you always got first. Because everything gets worse after that. It is a great pleasure to be invited to speak here tonight before such a dense crowd. It is not difficult to see why you are all gathered here, it is impossible."

He pressed his eyes, and let the image of Michael escape. He thought, sometimes, when excitable, that he must have diabetes. Betsy Lang wore knickers and that was ridiculous, he thought, in the lobby of the Fairmont Hotel. A Mercedes revolved in the center, gleaming, and he wondered, if he leapt the guard-rail and started it, could he drive? "What about your wife?" she asked. He said, "Thank you for asking. She's very well." "I didn't know you got married," she said. "Is this the first time?"

Clouds banked above him. The roof was tarpaper, but he saw the sky through the wall's interstices; he also consulted the window and the door. "Nixon will be president forever and ever," he said. "Here's a campaign slogan: you can't lick our Dick."

He had preserved Jean's letters; he uncovered them. He selected aerograms from Rome and took them to the hut and decided she would be his hero's wife, and that they would be divorced. He initialed characters and advanced their initial one letter; Michael became N. and Jean was K. He would write in the first person and be his own antecedent; he would remodel the house. He would buy it as a boy and sell what Nicholas had bought; he imagined "I."

Nicholas inserted a sheet of Eaton's Corrasable twenty-weight bond in the typewriter carriage; he revolved the carriage until the paper fell out; he inserted the paper again. All his high flights grounded, he considered sanity and what he would eat for supper and whether he should drive to Saratoga or visit Michael's grave. His associates paraded past and assumed formation; he commenced to write.

III

JULY 1

March 23. Allright. This to be the record of the house. First recall how many alternative places obsessed you. The Vineyard swamp, the house in Nova Scotia by the snowdrift, by the sea, the Catlett place, the one hundred and fifty acres south of Granville. How often, indeed; the walks with D. through Pawlet, the place on Stratton Mountain; describe them each at length. All the alternative houses you've housed in, where, when: Wellfleet, Bolinas, Grasse, Hopewell Junction, Dubuque, Wetherby Gardens; name names. A foul day, full of ill omens, snow. Describe the broker, Tuttle, elsewhere; describe his hair. Max, I hear at the morning meal, dies, and Harrison, and Sidney dead of smoke, R. absolutely dispossessed. Tuesday therefore I visit, and put down a hundred-dollar binder for the week, return on Wednesday with K., Thursday with E., Friday with experts, the offer made that afternoon, a night of windstorms uprooting the willow, Saturday the bargain struck. A photograph proffered: four chimneys, two of them there for symmetry only, and fake, the slight kilt and seam off the house's right side; one open but narrow fireplace, one covered but sizable, I think. Or at least a Franklin stove-flue plausible. The tongue in groove boards. Ninety-two acres they call it, more or less. Newspapers in the attic berating Lincoln and papers from well before that war, and the freezer thrown in, and the barn hose looping, and the pond-network now insistent, and the ninety-foot drilled well with sweet water, chill, and a spring underneath the pond-bed. I've picked out the plausible studio site; there are fourteen new ewes spawning and one ancient, spavined horse. The cellar has potato rot but fourteen solid inches left per beam. I like the slate roof, the bomb shelter, the walls and the cleared fields full of sheep shit. The fact (as I keep repeating) one can live in it each of the seasons, and twenty years from now. You don't move power poles.

JULY 2

Well, what'll we call it? sez K. Buttonwood Farm, sez she. Tooneetsy poo, *n'est-ce-pas?* How about Ashcan Grove? Or Dunghill? Or Granvilla. Home Is Where the Hearth Is? Any number of plausible places: Dew Drop Inn. The Hallow. Cherchez la Farme. Myself, I hold for Farm and Content. This March 30, and Tuttle walked the lines, and mostly what has happened is that G., the owner, the almost previous owner, has said yes. (Or, as R. put it, sue him; sic on the A.C.L.U.) His wife wants the washer and dryer badly; welcome. We keep the refrigerator, stove, freezer, faucets, the sundry things attached.

O.E. at his family store in North Hoosick, forty-five perhaps, shell-shocked, takes out with shaking hands his 1622 copy of Plautus, brought to New York in 1682, ex libris Hunterlach, Geneva, and the whole lovingly preserved, kept in his safe and secured from dust; took two hundred man-hours, he boasts, to clean. He found it in a mill, mold-encrusted, swaddled with sheepskin, and that alone saved it from absolute rot; it's easier, he says, to refurbish stoves for use than standing. How many bereft men have manuscripts upstairs, old letters, say, and pore upon some treasure that they, shaking, undo; what else, what other houses, what? Catlett's farm had seventy-two acres: a barn, a pump house, well house, pond site or two. And the old man dying within. Property in Mendocino; derelict retaining walls. A list: those shown by P., six places D.— with his witted patience—showed, our log hovel, the unheated house in Dorset, a Granville house also smack in the center of town; my god, I've been at this for years. All the gnattering with friends; you pay half, so shall I. Mark this for the future if there's only anger left; I do feel cheerful now. Had hungered for a change of some sort; this, completely, it. A house decaying over time, then fixed up with masks as to wallpaper, the fireplaces stuffed, the floors covered with floors, kitchen roofed. Stage-set carpentry. All these things are rational but wrong. Full portraits of the lawyer, and his red setters and hat.

JULY 3

(A) Do I want a house at all, and (B) do I want this house? Advice unanimous as to the latter, no possible way to know of the former till tried. My analphabet writes. (*Darling, you crucify me. I don't want to*

*write this but must; I'll divorce you as soon as I can.
And screw my head off in the meantime; I do love you;
I did; I will; I can't.*) The house will hold my children's children, and the barn will last well past farming
days, skewed though it seem. Detritus gathering;
there's a breeder reactor projected in Easton; I'll grow
white and Scotch pine; the flooring is cherry and oak.
There are plastic beams available two dollars the foot,
inaccurately adzed. When you sandblast you have to
repaint; C. says I could do the whole house in ten days.
My father nearly lost his place to the Japanese Embassy, it also brick.

JULY 5

Enjoined by I.B.M. from using the initials, they re-
tarded the film's computer (subtracting one from
each initial) and baptized it H.A.L. Thus anthro
popometry. Whereas I proceed at random, sometimes
advancing and sometimes, for the sport of it, exact.
Ebullience at parties, the sudden landed gentry, showing the endless, dog-eared Polaroid. I have to figure
what the hell to do with K., myself quite clearly
gambling that the future augurs well. Three and a half
hours perhaps from New York, and, if they build a
Taconic extension, less. A little more from Boston.
A lot more from Montreal. East of Saratoga, two miles
beneath Lake Cossayuna, which I've yet to visit, must.
The bisector, approximately, of the diagonal between
Glens Falls and Arlington. Fifteen miles from Easton
where they talk of a breeder reactor, and nuclear
waste; myself in the new thick, therefore, of the land-
owner's fight. My mother's strange reaction: part the
implicit delight at a place to hang her aging head, part
fury and suspicion. That I'd deposit her in the old

people's home up the map. Part effulgence; please take all the furniture we own. Father rather more collected; choosing color schemes and Scandinavian stuffs; they've neither of them seen it yet, of course. Our first argument as to who would do which mural in the downstairs hall. T. says he's inherited integrity and can't be proud of it, just inherited integrity, that's all, it's like an extra thumb.

JULY 7

Chains were steel links, and one hundred measured sixty-six feet; still used as description for deeds. Back to lay some green onions and fence the garden plot; this May 16. The horse wheezes far too much, seems winded even if not; will clean the ash wood from the fence lines for the fire. A sense of coincidence, all of it negative, katabasis with éclat. K. should, must, will soon leave. The downstairs bathroom has one layer of paper plus paint. The little study has also one layer, and the plaster excellent. The ceiling throughout has two layers, I think, the paper in the living room two at least. (*So my love there's nothing to say but that I waltz around still on my Italian tenterhooks and love you very much and hope that you're all right today, tomorrow, forever. I wake many times in the night and always with your name, and when I think—as I frequently do now—we won't meet again, it turns me suicidal. You were my life, will be.*) What; sexual resentment turned to jealousy on the one hand, disdain on the other. Compounded by repeated infidelity, and the concomitant guilt. Does that explain it, this? Keep the silo as is, put a desk at the bottom, and Plexiglas to stall the snow. Or a plastic bubble top, and me in the height of it, a love seat suspended by pulleys, and the whole circular, or a winch system locking at top. Suggestions I wreck the within, make a spiral staircase, and do the kitchen on platforms, and turn the outside wall to the inside, and shift the bathroom sink so that it be plausible for the left-handed guests. Souvlaki sandwiches made by the waterfall, and a lamb, entire, skewered, and stilt-competition, and the mower and all of us drunk; plans, my darling, what of our plans?

JULY 9

From the papers. From a children's song by J. Yeames in the attic-floorboards; wasps nest there. "Little woman! see, she stands/ Face a-glow and dim-pled hands;/ Apron white be-fore her spread,/ Dust of flour on curl-y head./ Bus-y as the hum-ming bee,/ Grave and thought-ful 'midst her glee:/ Little wom-an! sweep-ing, scrubbing,/ Brushing, dust-ing, wax-ing, rub-bing,/ Broom and buck-et brave-ly wield-ing,/ Spot and stain be-fore her yield-ing."

From the district *School Journal for the State of New York/Albany*, September 1, 1841. Penmanship Anecdotes. "An English gentleman applied to the East India Company for an office for a friend of his in India, and succeeded in obtaining an appointment. His friend, after a while, wrote him a letter of thanks and signaled an intention to send him an equivalent. The Englishman could make nothing of the word but *elephant*, and being pleased with the idea of receiving such a noble animal, he was at the expense of erecting a suitable building for his accommodation. In a few weeks the equivalent came, which was nothing more nor less than a pot of sweetmeats."

A continued state of siege, the far hills bare, a hailstorm, the fields intractable for wind. Last night dinner with the Witts, Sam a mercenary, bumbling yet amenable man, not knowing for certain whether red wine goes in the icebox or no; this the first decision to be taken, how to resurrect the walls, paint over the paper or peel it. The conservation society will help with the pond, and teach me how to train the stream, and why not dam it and trail the whole about the milkshed; sons here return from Vietnam, blithering, or terrified of guns.

JULY 10

For sixty dollars I bought a deal of furniture, and the books given gratis, and the pitchforks for a dollar apiece, and the old stove for five. Three beds for fifteen, a set of tools I badly need, double saw, band saw, hacksaw, paints, two bureaus for ten, a snow fence for four, ladder for two, the fence tool for two. Contrapuntal throughout the sense of death and outrage and defeat; E. glimpsed in his doorway, weight lost, looking wan and shocked; the preacher and his wife both in the hospital, Max dying everywhere, and A. shooting himself each third night; men dead impossibly of Parkinson's, a stroke; a scythe and blades for a dollar, two snow shovels for the same; we dragged manure, pitching it into the barrow (this sold for twenty, I buy it for eight; a heavy-duty barrow) and then to the slate-patch I've selected for a garden, the garden hose for four.

JULY 11

P. was sitting in the third rank, on the left, of the Stamford local's second car. It was the 3:25, and he planned to exit at Columbus Avenue and he had hoped, without conviction, for a seat alone. Dapple mares cavorted, he thought, in the Bois de Boulogne. Picture his astonishment, therefore, when a lady opposite undid her handbag, wrangling with the clasps, and extricated therefrom a Dixie Derringer. Her bosom heaved suggestively, and with a sensual abandon her demeanor had belied. She beckoned to him, licked the pistol; he was reading "Peanuts" and loath to discontinue. . . .

Harrison kissed her hard on the lips.

O. attained to London and his majority in the selfsame month, that of October, 1592. He took lodgings near St. Paul's having the intention to apply himself to court and pursue to its conclusion the problem of his birth. He was cozened of his hat and plume and contracted the pox in a week. His faithful servant stirred the coals; they were as hell's hot scourge to O. "Did Thisbe," he inquired of the sutler, "fearfully o'ertrip. . . . ?"

Someone flung. . . .

Motherfucker, cop to this, you motherfucking dingbat. Put fire to your cakes. . . .

Key. THEN. Precious things. . . .

A tin can to time's tail; time's mooring slipped. . . .

JULY 12

April 30. We possess all issues of *The Cultivator* for 1885; Dr. Hay's Hair Health, a newspaper from 1888 recording the great blizzard and offering blizzard caps. Also, praise of Sanford's Liver Invigorator (this *The*

New York Weekly News for 1861) with Blood Puri-
fying Pills, with Spalding's Sure Cure Cephalic Pills,
and editorials damning the then-civil strife, and elegant
advertisements for God.

JULY 14

Independence Day. Bastille Day. (*Darling. I'm still
depressed by your letter of a week ago—where you
quoted purgatory. S'io credesse che mia risposta. . . .
It made me feel so sad, and not a little cruel. Do you
think I'm being cruel? I wish I could call you on the
phone and hear your voice and know you're there—
somewhere—on the end of something—with both feet
on this selfsame earth. As it is, I feel we're floating;
letters fly in and out; moods come and go like birds. I
only want to write you when my moods are solid, but
this life leaves me surprised. Because the changes are so
subtle and so quick. Better yet—I wish we could meet
right now. Downstairs. At the Trevi. There's so
much of this freedom I need. And so much I distrust.*)
When twenty-one I overturned a Citroen, convinced
of Mademoiselle DeFarge beneath, and that the paving
stones would turn to pillows, all manner of things be
revealed. And hung athwart a telephone pole, hunting
for C. Today a day of crystalline heat, and windless.
I think at this stage to whitewash the house, and add
shutters. One of the central skeins to weave is self-
reflexive here, and having to do with autobiography—
how this may flesh, with what sort of fabric; what's the
distinction, E. asks, between ravel and unravel; how
do we wind up?

(EDITOR'S NOTE: The following pagination refers to
the typescript of *In the Middle Distance*.)

EDITOR: p. 254, line 14: Change "she said" to "she would say"?

AUTHOR: All right, if you prefer. I do it on purpose, attempting to put the fantasy past probability's bounds, at this point. So that Nicholas is completely *within* his imaginings here.

EDITOR: p. 57, line 6: Our lady says that the last year Norman Thomas ran was 1932.

AUTHOR: p. 182, line 1: Punkt after "easily." New sentence, "That's easiest . . ."

JULY 15

June 15. J. is mad. Gone paranoiac, full of power games, won't speak of it, can't write of it. Try this. Ourselves on the Vineyard, a great final rush to record. The island, this old home, one day. A garrulous Bill Saunders turned pariah, his wife having had a hysterectomy, a bladder operation, cancer of the tongue, her mother having died of it, and her mother before, and the youngest son, six, contracted viral meningitis and couldn't keep his balance, standing up; here, says Bill, on this rock, ours the only family to get it, Jesus, so we kept him in a football helmet all winter and he could make it to the bathroom but had to crawl back; also Bill's boat sank because the bilge pump was shut by the owner, himself on a contract to stand by and service, and the engine hatches were open, and it did rain heavily, and the insurance covered it, but it cost eight thousand dollars to haul the boat back to Cape May; he refused, thereafter, to work on the engines, and only a wrench for the parts, and the owner wouldn't draw a private check so that it took all summer long for the insurance claim to be adjusted, and then, driving his family into Boston and the hospital, he lost two radial tires, or so he thought, and bought snow tires, but it turned out the transmission was faulty, and there wasn't that much snow about. He's standing at the window, flapping, wondering whether to jump (*how could you leave me, how?*), and the car was stolen, smack out from the garage. Together with a drill and all his tools, about eighteen hundred worth of equipment around, and they gave him a new car, but what the hell, I ask you, use is that. He found the car himself at a used car dealer in Milton, found his identifying marks. As follows. Three holes screwed beneath the dashboard where he placed the stereo, three scratches on the right rear door where once he'd eased off a rock, these repainted but visible still, two knee-dents in the roof, where he would lean to pack on a pillow, three drain holes in the rear so he could wash sand out with a hose, and a refitted belt on the left front light; the door, however, replaced, a light blue and the engine number inside to match (now in a Ford you have to take the windshield out, but that can be done in ten minutes, just wedge with a penknife and push, lie on your back and kick). This Saturday past, my love, I drove to the farm with B., via the Oasis Bar, the house completely empty now. B. recites Hopkins as we waddle burdened by junk to the garage, the floor boards excellent; then I mend the fence. "Hard work fascinates me," he says. "I could watch it for hours" (apostrophizing the cows as kittens, addressing the kitten as horse).

IV

On their second honeymoon, and when they had been married sixteen years, Nicholas and Barbara went to France. Michael was one year dead. They landed at Orly and checked into the Plaza Athénée—which Nicholas was told to use by Henry Letterman. Barbara used the bidet and then Nicholas washed his feet in the bidet and they went out to dinner by the Seine. The restaurant was small and fine and bustling with a German delegation to trade talks; Nicholas ordered champagne. The Germans were noisy and the proprietor, pouring Barbara champagne, said, "Madame, they shall pay for this. They must." Nicholas had terrine and *steak au poivre* and salad and cheese and *fraises des bois*. Barbara had *moules* and *truite au bleu* and salad and cheese and *framboises*. When the bill came, the champagne was not included. "I put it down for ces boches," the proprietor explained.

They loved the city, walking hills till Barbara had blisters, sitting for their portraits in the Tuileries. A man touched

Nicholas's arm. "Excuse me sir," he said, pronouncing it "saair." He wore a sleeveless sweater and serge pants. "You speak English, yes? This is right. The wind she is coming from isst." Nicholas confirmed that, yes, the wind was coming from the east, and they elaborated the other directions, wist, nairth, souse.

"I am night watchman," the man explained. "I am pensionnaire. I am night watchman Westminster bank, and, Saturday, Sunday, Bank du Canada." He was born in Moscow and imitated ("Zum, zum," he pressed his hands to ears) the bombing and had been a prisoner of war for five years. Each of his teeth had gold fillings. "I haf more in mouth"—he pointed, grinning—"than underneath mattress. Zum zum."

Nicholas wanted to go to Versailles, and to see the whores in the Place Pigalle. Barbara visited Givenchy and Guerlain and Chanel and bought shoes by Charles Jourdan. "They're worth it," she told him. "You'll see." She bought many postcards and aerograms and spent much time writing home, to their child, to friends. He was insulted by each letter sent.

"Live now. Here. In the present. For me." He complained, "Lord knows it's costing enough."

"But darling I do," she teased him. "They shine your shoes outside the door. They bring us breakfast in bed; they press your shirts. What more do you want, what more have you ever required?"

"Attention," he said, "isn't service."

"You can't pretend I shouldn't write," she said, "to Eve. You don't mean that."

"Sometimes I think of you as everything a man could want." He held her close, as he always did when unkind. "You know, a cook in the kitchen, lady in the living room, whore in the bed. And sometimes"—he embraced her—"you get it all wrong. Cook in the living room, whore in the kitchen, lady in bed."

"Don't be too generous," she said. "You needn't be. This honeymoon will only last another week."

"That's why I want you," he insisted, "to stop writing letters. We'll be home, dammit, before they arrive."

"OK." She snapped the pen in two and wiped her fingers on his shirt. "Now what?"

Yet they were, largely, happy. "If we didn't squabble we would be indifferent," she said. "We wouldn't be alive. I'm very glad to be here."

He sang her, as he had when courting, "Time After Time." He imagined himself Frank Sinatra, leaning from a passing train, singing to Laura on the platform or to shadows overhead. "I only know what I know," he sang, "the passing years will show," and she joined in the chorus and he was, absurdly, content. He finished with the introduction to "One for My Baby," and then they sang "We Kiss in a Shadow" by the bathroom sink.

"I'll buy you another shirt," she promised. "I've wanted to for days."

They stood at the Sacré Cocur, and he showed directions to her, mimicking the Russian. "Zat's wusst, zat's souse," he said, "zat's isst." He discoursed on city planning and the fact that monuments were nearly always military and on Louis Napoleon's reign.

"What's the Napoleonic code?" Barbara asked.

"What's mine is mine and what's yours is mine," he said, "roughly. But that's a different Napoleon, you know, the one with his hand on his chest."

"Picking at the pimples there," she said, "the way that you do. Marlon."

He ordered Perrier with each meal, and she promised to keep him stocked with Perrier at home.

They rented a car and drove to Versailles. There was a

traffic jam, and Nicholas kept pace with a Citroen carrying three japanese men in the back seat. They were asleep, wearing black suits, prickled with cameras, and the chauffeur, who was french, grimaced for Nicholas's sake. "*Ils ont trop bu,*" he mouthed, and motioned, hand as bottle, tilting his head back.

Versailles delighted Barbara. She said, "If I'd come here when I was six, I'd have known just what to do with it. This is the sort of place we always imagined we owned. 'Imagine you're a princess,' we'd say, 'imagine you own that fountain, those flowers, everything.'"

Chestnut leaves littered the ground; it was September's end. Chestnuts fell. They walked to the Grand Trianon and hunted for the Petit Trianon and passed it without recognition and found Marie Antoinette's fantasy village. Nicholas translated signs. "Rigorously interdicted," he read, "to walk on the lawns."

"Per lousing them," Barbara said. Her French was better than his.

They drove to Chartres also and a wedding took place in the cathedral; Barbara wept. "You've married the world's most sentimental person," she said. "You do know that." Insects slimed the windshield as they drove.

"Let me explain to you," she said, "about pathos. Remember that dwarf who runs the elevator at the hotel? The one who bobs us to our room. He's a stamp collector, and he asked me to be sure to send him stamps. He's partial to commemorative stamps. I won't. I know it already, and ten years from now, thinking about him, I'll still want to cry."

"So send him stamps," Nicholas said.

"But I don't know his name. I can't just address the envelope, 'Dwarf Elevator Operator. Plaza Athénée.'"

The road was stuffed with cars. He saw the limousine with the four japanese inside.

"I'll find his name out," Nicholas said.

"No, that would spoil it." Barbara put her hand in his. "Then I'd have nothing to feel pathetic about."

He thought her bathetic but charming, and himself the realist. The dwarf was not on duty; it was Saturday night, at eight.

"I want to care for you," Barbara told him, the next day, "when even this hill is too much. To climb. When you've got no hair on your head."

He tabulated women and knew himself defined by them, each diminution or growth signaled by some mate. "A ladies' man," he thought, "a fucking ladies' man." "I can count," he told her, "on the fingers of a single hand the months I've spent alone. In the last thirty years. On a single maimed hand."

"What is that supposed to mean?" she asked.

"I'd like some roasted chestnuts," he said. "Wouldn't you? They're all over the place on the ground."

"They're not edible," she said. "It's too early. What was that supposed to mean?"

"Nothing. Generosity, you know, was never my long suit. I wonder what happened to Iorgo. Or to Harry Burten. Or to any of the men I knew at Yale."

Waste assailed him, and the dream of days spent hunting in Ketchum, Idaho. They would eat elk steak nearly raw, or lay the deer that they shot in oak coals. He would go fly fishing, waders his only shoes, and moccasins. They would play poker and drink bourbon straight and not shave for days; the fire, guttering, would flame with the elk fat.

"From bed to bar and back again," he said. "The story of my life. It's because my mother died so young."

"That's not true," she said. "That's simply not the case."

"If I were to tell"—Nicholas considered his reflection in a papeterie window—"the story of my life, it would start and end with screwing. Getting screwed."

"Don't tell it then," she said.

He hurt her wittingly; he believed that pain was proof of love.

Men sold combs and the *International Herald Tribune* and watches; he watched the lace-boots fashionable there and thought of making love to Jean while she kept on her sweater and boots.

"I think of myself," he asserted, "as an ascetic person. Really."

"You think of yourself," Barbara said, "a great deal too much."

"I think about you too," he said. "I'm a fucking paragon."

Pain was flagellation; pain was proof of existence and of devotion and youth. He suffered Michael's memory, and Jean's, and suffered possibility; possibility, also, was pain. A man gyrated past, limping on his soles' sides. Nicholas said, "Would you like pistachios? Or *quelque chose à boire?*"

"It's not that I don't think you're ascetic," she said, "except you're mostly ascetic asleep."

The bear spoor reeked beneath him, and the pines were thick.

"You have the lowest opinion of me," he said, "of anyone I know."

"I'm entitled," she said. "I'm your wife."

Barbara's parents came from Germany; she was born on Filbert Street in San Francisco. "Nothing's been a hill to me," she told him as they courted, climbing, "since then."

Her father was a banker and retired in 1951. "One thing I'll say," he said, "for Wells Fargo. They do have a generous pension plan. Most generous indeed." Her mother was an active Zionist. Together they took trips to the Near East, then to the Middle East, then to the Far East, and then to Eastern Europe; returned, they would telephone Barbara and Nicholas and discuss the guide. "The cutest little redhead imaginable," her father would say. "You simply can't imagine."

Her mother, on the other phone, would say, "Oh, father, stop."

They bought an apartment in West Palm Beach and had a Ping-Pong table on the terrace and played Ping-Pong avidly; they lived there six months each year. On Easter vacations, Nicholas and Barbara and Michael and Eve went south. With Michael absent, Nicholas realized, he would be the youngest male at the seder, and would have to ask the questions; he refused, therefore, to attend the seder and had a turkey TV dinner instead. He thought this romantic and tough-minded, but the yams were bad.

Barbara was furious. "Tell me the difference," she said, "between passive and active joining. What would you be doing, really, that you haven't done before?"

"Why is this day," he mimicked, "different from all other days? I'll tell you why. Because little Nicholas has had enough." He ran his finger across his throat. "To here."

"That's unkind," she insisted. "That's flat out unkind."

"Better than this charade," he said. "A bunch of toothless brokers putting pickles up their nose. Getting drunk on Manischewitz. You killed our lord," he said, aping Hitler, "you jews."

"You want to watch the Dolphins and the Giants," she accused him. "That's all."

He turned the television off. "They're not playing tonight." Raquel Welch was slated for the Johnny Carson Show.

"The Whales, then, and the Pygmies. You want to jack off to the Salem ad. Shit."

"You're beautiful." He shook his head. "Do you know that? You're eloquent when angry. You're too beautiful for words."

49

"Don't use them then," she pleaded. "Just join us. Please."

He stared at himself in the set. Six months previous, they had considered visiting the Loire. In Paris he had ordered red wines, white wines, brandy, champagnes; he had relinquished Scotch. The Place de la Concorde was clean, and the Louvre, and they were sandblasting monuments. "Some face-lift," he had said. "You can sand faces too," she told him. "If you had the smallpox, say, and want to get smooth skin."

Flower beds at Versailles had been shaped into the king's insignia; the trees were perfect cones. He had envisioned marriage as salvation once. He had courted Barbara with impatience, wanting to propose as soon as possible. Shopping for her ring, he thought of Jean's jade bracelet; obtaining the license, he thought the whole a masque. The blood test results were delayed in the mail; he concluded that meant syphilis and that he would be absolved. "It's like entering the priesthood," he told friends, "or castration. In reverse. Any sort of change."

Yet he had loved and needed her and thought the marriage sensible and loved her wit and strength. She had been submissive to his early dominance—delighted, as her mother told him, with the catch. She brought him coffee with walnut extract and made excellent salads and was a joyous lover, cackling in bed. She had attended Skidmore College and her parents had a country house in the Napa valley, then. The first summer (he had asked her to marry in August, and they wed at August's end) they took the California Zephyr west together, so that he could meet her parents. They stayed in their compartment for hours, and she whispered, "Do it" to the rhythm of the rails.

He liked her family. They had a tennis court and introduced him to the Lewisohns and said, "Maybe you could build us some buildings out here."

"That's not for me to decide," Nicholas said, "but the clients. That's their decision. I'd certainly, though, like to try."

Barbara had a younger sister, Anne. In hindsight or when maudlin, Nicholas knew her death-marked: one of those maidens, he thought, whom Death takes for His own. She had an inner stillness, dancing, that he wondered at. She was twenty-four when she was killed in Maine in 1956; she fell asleep while driving and drove into a tree. A single piece of glass, the doctor said, pierced her skull and brain; the face remained intact. Nicholas had a friend who worked for the obituary section of the *Chicago Sun-Times*; he had a form for lesser deaths and would check the appropriate space: after a long illness, after a short illness, suddenly. The front half of the car was, Barbara observed, a David Smith. "I'm empty." She wept. "I'm empty. There's nothing left. We're all of us empty."

"Remember," Nicholas said, "her in her shack with Peter. Asking for a reading list. Or sleeping on our floor. Campaigning for Philip Wofford. Convinced he'd change the world."

"The world won't change," Barbara said. "Screw the world."

All around him vastation, he thought, and emptiness, and Anne erased. "There's no kind of comfort," he said; "take comfort anyhow."

Barbara sobbed without sound, her cheeks refracting light. She put dark glasses on and glistened and he had no way to help and loved her very much. Anne had long brown hair, and a stutter when excited, and skin that seemed opalescent; she had smoked two packs of cigarettes per day. The tree had been a large pine tree that folded back upon the car, its branches splintering; they picked pine needles from Anne's ears. Sap caked the hood. She had attended Stanford and been the single white in a production of *All God's Chillun Got Wings;* she had offered her parents' home for the cast party, and her parents, for that evening, dismissed the colored maid. Anne spoke of joining a kibbutz and had been, Barbara said, too fragile to survive. Nicholas considered growth the consolidation of loss.

"What was she doing," he asked, "in Maine?"

"Distributing leaflets. Following moose. Who knows?" Barbara said. "What does it matter where, when? It matters *that.*"

(Anne had asserted, "I'd shoot Roy Cohn. Or Schine. Or that drunken senator. I'd shoot them if I could shoot."

"Why don't you learn?" Nicholas asked. He lit her cigarette. He wondered if she slept with black men at Stanford, and if she would sleep with him. Peter, her boyfriend, was a pacifist and carpenter and the son of a vice-president of Ford. "What do you know about Lewis Mumford," Peter asked, "or any of the planned communities?"

Nicholas offered them Scotch or wine or tea; they accepted tea. "Not a whole hell of a lot," he admitted, and Anne shifted weight. It was 1953, the first time they had met.

Barbara, eight years older than her sister, was solicitous. "What's this elder generation," she grinned, "coming to?"

"No, seriously," Anne inquired, "what do you think?"

"I think," said Nicholas, and toasted them, "you're filthy pinko fascist commie faggot jews. Whom I refuse to incriminate. Who should learn, if you mean it, to shoot. Chin-chin."

He clinked the two wine glasses and offered one to Barbara; they drank.

"My father," Peter said, "believes that stuff."

"My father," Nicholas said, "believes the opposite. And we're still watching McCarthy and Welch, still inviting you to lunch. Still mucking around with Japan."

52

"Don't mind him," Barbara said, "he's argumentative today." She offered deviled eggs.

"I'm the devil's advocate," said Nicholas. "I eat liberals up. Fee-fie-fo, yum-yum."

"Peter joined the *Advocate*," Anne said, "and quit."

"Sure," Peter said, "all of us fancy boys renouncing. Easy stuff." He was modest and, Nicholas decided, likable; he had been expunged from Harvard's records for gluing pennies to the keyholes of Memorial Hall. He used epoxy glue.)

Anne had been traveling, the police determined, forty miles per hour when she crashed. They found her in the morning; she had been, police deduced, at least six hours dead.

At Chartres, Barbara said, "We've lost each other somehow, darling, we've lost touch. Does this happen, do you think, to every marriage; is it the change of love's life?"

He was in love with her, he said, but no longer felt the need to iterate it endlessly; they sent postcards of the west stained-glass window to friends. "Romance," he said, "is not the sort of thing you live with. You marry what you need."

He commenced a regimen of sit-ups, and did one hundred and fifty the first time to prove to himself he still could. The next afternoon he thought his appendix had burst, girdling his stomach with pain, and he called the American Embassy to find a recommended doctor. The secretary asked if he had once had a hernia, and Nicholas remembered the sit-ups and hung up embarrassed, asserting it was only muscle strain. "You'll kill yourself," said Barbara. "You're not that young or strong."

Eve was content at school. She wrote about field hockey and a girl from Milton and, at long last, making sense of multiplication; she urged them to be happy, being away.

"Scream, compromise, screw," said Barbara. "That's how we've been for sixteen years."

"Some dialectic," he said.

(In Paris, after snails for lunch, he had the following dream. His assistant, Sergei Vergun, went shopping with him at Barney's. They each selected tapered pants that flared at the ankles, and had stripes. Nicholas entered his dressing room and tried the pants on and did knee bends to see if they stretched, and was well pleased with the fit. He called to the next dressing room to see how Sergei was doing and received no answer and chinned on the partition to see. He saw Sergei, crumpled, on the floor, neck slit. Next Nicholas was running, razor in hand, motionless, down Seventh Avenue to ward off attackers and to summon help. Help came, and was Henry Letterman and Jean; Jean anointed his bruises with oil. "Tell me where it hurts," she urged him, and he pointed.

"Here."

She pressed him there, hard, doubling pain. "I just wanted to make certain," she said, " 'dis mus' be de place.' "

Robert Kennedy was killed, as Martin Luther King had been, and Malcolm X before him, and John Kennedy. "A litany of chickens," Barbara intoned, in his dream, "returning to the roost. Let's leave this country, darling, just us two."

"What about Eve?" he inquired. "What about Michael; what about papaito and Jean?"

"They're better off alone," she said, "or left alone." She spoke with fluency. "Michael can shave and wants to wear striped pants and is in heaven consorting with prigs. And would have been in S.D.S., I think.")

He woke, the light still bright, and read Barbara's note; she was at the pedicurist's, she wrote, and would meet him at six. He envisioned Tolstoy, beard about him like a shawl, completing his last pilgrimage to Astapovo. Approximating godliness, at the railway station, Nicholas would pay all bills—the pedicurist, the Plaza Athénée, the rented Renault. Then, with his traveler's checks inside his sock and using them only when needful or in order to comfort the poor, Nicholas would wheel himself to some northern harbor, Barfleur. How would he end, he wondered, on the farm or in the office, in the Funny Farm? He emptied his bladder, as liberation's gesture, into the sink; he considered bellpulls and wondered, were he to hang from them, would the bell ring constantly or would the cord snap free? The notion of a novel, something full of air and ease, came to him then; he would write a best-selling book. He would be reviewed in *Look* and *Life* and the *Saturday Review* and would have his picture on the cover of *Paris Match*. Fifteen taxi drivers told him, "Listen. I've lived such a life. You want to see my poems, hey you ought to hear the story of my life. Just once. My man. Just once. To blow your mind."

He had believed that a man should travel with no more than a pack, or with packages a bicycle could hold. He came to think this illusionary and that man should have a car. He had accreted cars and houses and children and was an amalgam of his objects now. "Don't judge a book by its cover," Barbara said, "but that's a pretty good lead."

"Hostages to fortune," he complained. "You can't imagine the taxes. Or the insurance policy. Or what I have to earn so that Eve can study with a bunch of snots. One thing's certain," he said. "Any man who marries her will have to do it for love."

"So don't pay your taxes," Barbara said, "at least not that sixty percent."

Nicholas and Barbara had attended the third night of *The Most Happy Fella*. He sang her, in imitation of Robert Weede imitating an Italian, "I'm a da mos' happy fella, in a da whole Napa valley, da mos' happy man, 'assa me."

Barbara's father had a portrait of his father, with a dress

sword and helmet, painted in the Franco-Prussian war. "He thought that Bismarck was the nuts," her father said. "We all of us did."

"And Kaiser Billy in the First World War?" asked Nicholas.

"By that time," her father said, "we had moved here."

"Have you been to Germany since?" asked Nicholas.

"Since when?"

"Since Hitler's war?"

"You're joking. Certainly not. I used to live on the Alster and canoe to school."

(Barbara whistled "If I Loved You" and they drank chartreuse and contemplated, her head on his upper arm, the future with assurance; she would make him happy, she said, and babies when he wanted and be good for him. They met as campaign workers for Adlai Stevenson in 1952; and they thought that he might win. They worked for him again in 1956 and knew he had no chance. In 1960, Nicholas worked hard for Kennedy and they stayed up all night with friends, switching channels, drinking champagne and keeping track of totals on a ʿdemographic map. "That's the end of Nixon," Nicholas exulted, at six. "*Ciao, ciao, bambina*. Bye. And all his bully boys."

His friends sang, "Give my love to Checkers," and Nicholas walked home with his wife and coupled with her and did not go to the office and deserved, he decided, the sleep.)

He wanted to join Marcel Breuer and Associates. He had lunch with Breuer and was tongue-tied at first, then garrulous. He had a notion of minimal form, he asserted, that would nonetheless prove maximal. "All we'd have to do," he said, "is to convert computers into space."

"What does that mean?" Breuer asked.

They ate Hungarian food. Breuer asked for extra paprika. He combed his hair forward and wore a wide tie.

"That space has changed completely since the space age," Nicholas said. "That we've got to utilize the atom as our building block. That computers change man's habitat more completely than the wheel."

He was not offered the job. "I went to the wrong person," he told Barbara. "That's Bauhaus shit still. Passé."

Yet he was disappointed and resolved not to drink at lunch and spoke warmly, later, of his friendship with Breuer. "Me and Marcel," he would say and hold two fingers up and press them together and wink, "peas in a pod. Like that."

He built bookshelves for the apartment and dadoed the joints. He installed indirect lighting and two spotlights for the zuñi bowls and for the Ekoi head. The head was covered with antelope skin but he called it human skin, attempting to shock guests. He sensed, obliquely, decline, and the chance his heights were foothills and was not reconciled. He attempted to remember, one Thursday, what he had done the ten previous Thursdays, and there was neither distinction nor growth. "Standing still," he complained to Barbara, "is the same as going backwards in this work."

She hunched her shoulders when walking; her left breast was larger than the right. She had slightly bowed legs and black hair that she wore à la Audrey Hepburn; he wanted her to grow it, but she said, "Buy me a wig. Or get Simon to give you one, presuming his are any good. And while you're at it," she said, "inquire about a toupée."

They read of forest fires in the L'Estérel. "Humanity," he told her, "that's what you ain't got."

"Look who's talking," she said, "Mister Generosity. Mister Political Involvement. How much of our income goes to alms?"

"Taxes," he said. "Fifty-five hundred a year."

"That's arms," she said. "I mean charity."

She fenced for exercise, and he envisioned her lunging, legs bowed, the point unbuttoned, at his heart. "Your notion of love," he said, "is parry, beat and thrust."

"Who made it that way?" she asked. "It takes two. How did this happen anyway and how can we ever stop?"

(Eve, their second child, united them; it was an easy pregnancy and birth. "These hips helped," she smiled at Nicholas; he twisted the hospital sheets. "The doctor said I was terrific. Darling. How are you?")

Barbara had studied anthropology and archaeology, and had received a Fulbright to study pre-columbian structures in Guatemala. She was to join a dig sponsored by the Musée de l'Homme; she had studied French. She understood the problems of the architect, she said, in terms of historical perspective; there was always opposition between the private and the public building needs. Nicholas imagined her at excavations, khaki shorts rolled up, twice rolled, legs brown, leaning on a pick. She would wear bandanas and her breasts would sweat and the natives would admire her, offering mangoes and pulque. He asked her to marry him, and she forsook the year in Guatemala, writing to the director of the dig, in French, that personal considerations intervened. "*Mais regrets les plus sincères,*" she wrote, "*mais je serais épouse.*"

Later, without bitterness, she reminded Nicholas that he had ended her career, that she had been effectively finished because their marriage began. "You can't renounce a Fulbright," she said, "just like that. And not feel a little bit bad. But I did it consciously, darling, and would do it again. The mayans got along without me and still can."

He felt himself, therefore, doubly responsible and urged her to continue work. "At least take night classes," he said.

"Where, at the New School?" she said. "The Sociology of Pyramids, or: What a Steep Step Implies? No," she insisted, "it's finished, and I won't complain."

For the first years, in their seeming stability, they were a magnet for friends. All his single or unhappy or divorcing friends would visit and treat them as a unit and complain; "You two don't know how lucky you are."

"We worked for it," said Nicholas. "We worked."

Barbara's master's thesis had dealt with the cenote at Chichén. She discussed the implications of human sacrifice as building block, and how the rain god still received manna from drownings; workmen, she told Nicholas, refused to dredge that well. "The last body they pulled up," she said, "was three years old. Not a baby, not three years old that way, but three years drowned."

Holy structures, she maintained, always had some human loss attached. She asked Nicholas about tunnels and bridges and high buildings where construction workers died. "What kind of value," she asked him, "what variety of myth pertained? Even the gold spike," she said, "on the transcontinental railroad, or the champagne bottle broken over ships—even that applies."

"Applies to what?" Nicholas cracked eggs and tried to do it one-handed; they had seen Audrey Hepburn as Sabrina the previous night.

"Applies to my thesis, dummy." She kissed him. "You're not listening."

"I'm listening," said Nicholas. "Applies to what?"

"The notion of sacrifice in building; how buildings become holy."

Nicholas lowered the flame.

"The secret in an omelette," he said, "is to burn the eggs just slightly in the first instant, then to cook them slowly; that's the way you get crust."

"How much parsley?" Barbara asked, aggrieved.

"A few sprigs. Cut them up fine. Continue," he said.

"Continue what?"

"I'm listening," he said. "Sacrifice in building; how buildings become holy; go on."

She chopped thyme and dill and would not continue and he asked her what she thought of William Holden anyway.

(Pity is a passion, he thought, also; pity welds one far more firmly than does admiration; pity is the central link in every marriage chain. Nor can it be contravened, he thought, nor disavowed. He had made her, he decided—neurasthenic, brittle, nagging, fat—in his image and therefore had to worship and was responsible.)

Barbara was an excellent mother and described herself as lioness with cubs. She sang lullabies each night and strewed candy underneath a neighborhood rock and, taking Eve and Michael for a walk, would take them to the magic candy rock. She was overprotective, Nicholas thought, and he said, "The way to swim is throw the kids in water."

She answered, "You don't believe that. You can't."

"I do," he said. "That's what my sainted father did with me."

"Bull-shit," she said, "bull-shit fantasy."

"*Dans la présence des enfants,*" he said, "don't swear."

"That didn't happen," she said.

Nicholas lied, "Sure. When I was a kid my father put me on top of the refrigerator. I was scared of heights and I said, 'Daddy, daddy, let me down.' He said, 'Sure, kid, jump.' And I said, 'Will you catch me?' and he said, 'Of course.' So I jumped and he stepped aside and I fell splat on the kitchen floor and he said, 'There, that'll learn you; don't ever trust anybody on this bitch of an earth.' "

Persuaded by his rhetoric, he mimed the act of falling; Barbara was appalled. She woke him once and asked, "Did I dream it or did you say you loved me?" He lied, "Yes, I woke you to say that," and she fell asleep. She slept twined to him, smiling, breathing heavily.

Eve was beset by fears. Three years younger, she needed night-lights longer, and liked baby-sitters less. Nicholas and Barbara went to Martha's Vineyard for a weekend, alone. "Let the woman have a rest," the seven-year-old Michael counseled his sister. "She'll come back."

They stayed in Edgartown, with friends. It was October, and the island barren; the single open restaurant was in Oak Bluffs. They drove to Chappaquiddick and tried to swim; Nicholas swam, on principle, but Barbara remained huddled, wearing sweaters, on the beach. When Kennedy made Chappaquiddick famous, seven years later, they feigned familiarity with the dirt road and bridge. "I've been there," Nicholas said. "Only an authentic drunk could lose his way."

He remembered wind and sandpipers and the shock of immersion and a kind of purple gorse. He could not remember the ferry nor if the island were inhabited nor the dirt road or any sort of bridge.

Barbara made resolutions to diet. He shared and broke them and enjoyed food greatly; she made, he said, the world's best Bloody Marys. She used V-8 juice and lemon and Worcestershire sauce and quantities of vodka and Tabasco and herbs; sometimes she froze the herbs in ice cubes, and they would melt slowly, changing the drink's flavor over time.

Over time he labeled each of the deadly sins in Barbara. "But you've got all of the cardinal virtues besides," he said; "you're the entire universe."

"Sloth and gluttony," she said. "What else?"

"Oh, a lot of lust." He teased her. "A great deal of concupiscence. Yes."

"You never let me say," she said, "anything about the way I want to decorate. Maybe this isn't my taste?"

He produced Marimekko curtains and D/R pillows and he bought, with a designer's discount, six Breuer chairs. They had a refectory table and prints of a Picasso show and she framed, elaborately, an oil she did of the Edgartown harbor, showing masts. He papered the bedroom walls and ceiling with the same floral design and reproduced the pattern for the bedspread and pillows; it was a black sunflower, with the black embossed.

"I call that vulgar," she said. "You didn't even ask. It may be fashionable as all hell, but I think it's vulgar." He had had the room repapered for her as a birthday present, and as a surprise. "That's your generosity," she said, "all consideration on the surface and, underneath, egocentric and selfish as hell. Next year why don't you buy me a jockstrap? Or maybe a man's suitcase? Or talcum powder? You know, something I really can use."

He found her sexy when profane, and said so; she beat at him with open fists, as a prelude to love. "Then there's envy, avarice, greed," he said and forced her legs apart. "What else? I've left something out."

"Faith, hope, charity," she said, receiving him. "Thank you, darling, for this room. It's beautiful."

They fell back on the bed. He rumpled the cover and pillows and watched the fabric crease and wondered if dry cleaning would be best.

They considered a third child. "I could have a baseball team of Michaels," he said, "or a bowling squad. We could go on television; Nick's tenpins."

The susurrus of the water had remained with him, and the boats beating gently, lines fast, and Michael's glad cry when they came back, Sunday night: "Eve thought you were dead."

Nicholas stood in the hall, bags at his feet, his children wreathed to him, encircling, and was the circle's center, he felt, and circumference.

"Your mother and I," he told them, stooping, "are very glad to be back." They lit the dining table's candelabra, and he told the story starting, "It was a dark and stormy night. . . ."

V

JULY 18

A complementary problem. The study of autobiography in some sense ratifying this. The authen-
tification, via data, of life that's nonexistent, word made
flesh. Or, notes toward a supreme nonfiction. And,
perhaps, the lie can be compulsive (with farmers,
women, critics), and perhaps it can be conscious. But
the central and ravening paradox (how we each forge
truth) should certainly apply. Andy rolls earwax with
thumbs. This, from *The Cultivator* for July, 1860.
"I have used some guano and superphosphate of lime
the past two seasons. In 1853, superphosphate was of no
perceptible benefit to my carrots. It was sown in the
drill with the seed, on moist ground."

JULY 19

*(Last year the strange sense of loss that I simply
couldn't repress. And then I guess we were actually*

looking for different life styles and trying to force those jagged edges together. I don't even want to think about the farm. I feel sometimes as if it were the only real home I've had since early childhood. The peace and solace there. This past year I've been happier, perhaps, than ever—surrounded as we always were by such landscapes, faces. But I also felt, and the irrationality of such feelings ain't of any consequence, that I was being compelled to lead a life I hadn't particularly chosen. Everything happened so easily and naturally. I wish I could articulate what has been past describing all this time. That none of this, nothing was intentional. That it derived from disillusion, pain, rather than from cunning and deceit. And that I have suffered for you as well as you for me. I have given up a great deal, you see. And I realize it. You are not even the only one I miss. But perhaps you know all about that too.)

Also. "Truths of this kind seem to be very generally forgotten by some of those who have occasion to keep their horses in the stable throughout the whole year."

JULY 20

Fiction, as I never tire telling my class in fiction is a series of strategies for truth. Autobiography, as I never tire telling my class in autobiography, is a selection of truths mounted to adumbrate fiction. Prove that I, to paraphrase that class, those statements, lie. March 21. H. considered himself an adept of dumps. He had always been intrigued with steam shovels, tractors, the winch, beam, banana peel crushed. Fascinated by buckets, he spent his childhood hauling slops; on beaches he dug castles and owned, you said, the world's biggest sandbox; he preferred to dig above the watermark. Watching the walls slide and tumble, H. knew himself an engineer, content. (H. broke his arm when six years old by falling on a garbage heap behind his uncle's hedge. He had jumped from the maple's first fork, fell athwart his elbow and was comforted by chocolate and had a cast for weeks. Q. paneled his fraternity lounge with a wall of empty cans. He had jumped from the maple's first fork, and landed there with Betsy Jackson, skirt athwart his elbow, and she was a comfort for weeks.) Scrap this.

JULY 21

This July 7 and many things, *chela*, many things. A kind of release in destruction, the first day back, with Alex; we took hammers and hatchets and had us a high old time, tearing at the downstairs chimney till it stood revealed. This a radical error, though needful, as the whole had been bricked to contain a furnace flue. We nonetheless wielded a twelve-pound sledge, and though I slapped bricks, tentative, Alex hauled back and cracked three through (himself six-foot-six, two hundred and forty pounds, and not proprietor), therefore reached ceramic brick and the furnace detritus of years. All of this plausible mayhap, but wacky, and then with one blunt hatchet and one axe and three hammers and two vise grips, what did we do but reveal the upstairs chimney also, this crashing down upon us in a plaster-rain, myself thinking the dust manna of sorts, and primed the pump, the next day with D. E. took down the master bedroom's cover, that of plasterboard, and chipped at the side walls till unable to hold the hammer and hatchet, then ripped up the little back room's floor, this with wedges, and difficult, the linoleum glued to plywood, that nailed securely into linoleum which sits on the random-width pine, now revealed. That small room (its red diamond paper, windows to the north and west, access to the bathroom, single radiator) once was three, floor markings show, nor could the total space have been more than five hundred cubic feet per room, and that with ten-foot ceilings, hedged against heat loss. With each layer revealed, the house seems more its stately self, exorcising at last previous ghosts (curious, the first time we made love on the downstairs trundle bed I was haunted by the daughters, how many spread here, where, when): let's work backwards; I'll buy free-floating fireplaces for the upstairs bedrooms; what of the attic turnbuckles; are they structural? Arrived with a trailer full of furniture, cannot take the Taconic, drove the Thruway therefore and Northway to Saratoga, and Exit 14 to Route 29, then east to Cossayuna, into the hills beneath Cossayuna; what to call it; The Bucolic Plague, the Funny Farm. We ate, and then I said it seems not a bad thing to eat—since one establishes oneself in a house not necessarily by the first bath or fuck but meal, and then Richard said yes if you can fuck while eating in the bathtub that's really it, that's really ownership, and speaking of squatter's rights, there's also some of that.

JULY 22

M. believed, devoutly, and in her first confessions confessed she had stolen one grape. The father confessor pursed lips. Is that all, my child, he queried, is that truly all? You mean, I take it, a cluster. No, father, she implored him, I took one single grape. She registered, however, that he was used to larger sins; she sinned accordingly. By fifteen she would purchase her confessional certificate from friends. . . .

Seventeen stories begun. Am happy with dust sheets,

only, space. Assembled the beds, and I hung the javanese masks; had chicken and corn and raspberries gathered from the shed field. Have taken blinds off all the windows; found, hunting for the dump, a flooded quarry; swam.

JULY 24

Today June 1, and, curiously, both of my timepieces stopped. Continued to raze the rear trees; cut two pine; having worked with an axe for twenty minutes I came in here to type. And scarcely can, the fingers of my right hand tremble, little finger curled so that it cannot stretch, the typing hand gone weak with strength. Notes. Riddle Road runs through to Cossayuna Lake. The bowl for slopping hogs. These are Norfolk latches on the door. Cut the oxymoron: weak with strength. Spiders multiply in the bath; a daddy longlegs straddles this page. They only started to saw beams in 1830 here; any plumber could do rough work and wield the adze better than this. We admire, therefore, evidenced incompetence on beams. Or they knew the beams would be covered, would have laughed at exposure, our effort-filled display of shoddy workmanship. The allergy, as Mills calls them, are starting to swarm in the pond. There used to be malaria if you portaged through the tamarack swamp, rather than up to Champlain. The two-mile trek more dangerous than this elseway ten. I've built the sawhorse too wide and high, can't get my back in it yet. Lines drawn: the telephone pole, the remnants of the dry stone wall, then 270 degrees across the hill's head.

JULY 25

R. and I took down the whole of the fireplace wall,

two inches of plaster per brick; have three further vats filled, and ripped off a bookcase to boot. Flashing's shot around the kitchen chimney; I attempt to clean the bricks with a mason's chisel. Need a plastic pail and wire brush and muriatic acid; a bird nests in the furnace flue. I remember standing outside the house on White Chapel Road, watching the heat go out for thirty feet, calculating cost. The joists of the house are fantastic, and the central beams, but in the bedroom there are set-ins, and two feet apart, and nothing much. Drove here alone last night, in a rage with K., who slapped me driving to the Larsons' party. I left her therefore there and, had I been less sleepy or New York less far, would have fashioned, altogether, escape.

(EDITOR'S NOTE: The following pagination refers to the typescript of *In the Middle Distance*.)

AUTHOR: Would "ball" as slang expression for fornicatrix major, etc., esq., have been plausible for Nicholas in 1951? Line 1. He should wash his mouth with soap.

EDITOR: p. 180: It may very well be that "ball" wasn't current in 1951, but I suspect balling itself was (being only nine at the time and having lost my plum—girls have cherries, boys, plums—only the year previous—to a chambermaid employed on my parents' estate, but in the stable, it was, the rain pelting down and I out there to tend to Pablum, our champion roan, to keep him steady amidst the lightning and the thunder, and as I bent to take in my hand some hay for food and comfort, who should I uncover but the naked chambermaid, Yika, whose affair with Pablum we had all known of for several months but whose affections for me—remember, I was not a thin boy and just nine and not very talkative for fear of my double chin being noticed—were until that moment hidden, to say the least, though, to my credit, I hope, I appeared to accept her advances nonchalantly enough to pass as experienced and gave up my plum with no little pleasure, pleasure for me, certainly, and for Yika too, I have no doubt, if one can judge by the way her cries of "Ball me! Ball me!" soon—but not too soon, for I was a steady boy—dwindled into gasps of affection and, soon, tears), and if balling itself was, and if Yika, in fact, knew and used the term (though I like to think that I inspired its first entrance into language), then I see no reason why—I shall try to say this modestly—we can't let my personal experience stand as universal and allow into your book, "ball."

AUTHOR: p. 86, line 10: Slip the word "to" in after the comma. "You, to put us in . . ."

EDITOR: p. 67, line 18: The movie, with old Audrey as Sabrina, came out in 1954. So can this stand?

JULY 27

Have been steaming for one week. Hallucinate the steamer, and the perfect strip. Four layers of wallpaper throughout, interlocked and metaphoric; the tomato plant, then deer delicately prancing in front of the hunter, then families entire sledding to church, the bells red. Then strawberry plants. Have worked, at the minimum, thirteen hours per day with the steamer, the bubble and pucker of paper my only novel, news. Bought and transported a butcher block. Have taken down the living room ceiling, which was difficult, the

Sheetrock splintering and filled with nails, and painted the bathroom and kitchen two times. Using three cans of semigloss latex base, white. Plaster was made with buttermilk in the eighteenth century, and now no modern paint will adhere; buttermilk and whitewash, though, works. A plan to gut the center of the house entirely, and build a walkway within. The Millses got five hundred eighty-two bales from the near field, and two hundred thirty-five from the rear. They used to call Mills shear-pin Jim; he's been running tractors since twelve, could shear one hundred pins a day when starting. Pretty near. Elaborated on the notion of autobiography, the maculate conception—or, in the beginning was World. Will paint the studio next, and the guest bedroom; the Celotex ceiling I'd assumed was white was pink.

JULY 29

Why do men ruin themselves? B. asks. By committing suicide or theft or treason. For a hole. That's all it is, he wails, that's all it fucking is. The summer half done, and I'm rending the downstairs entirely, have taken down the non-bearing walls, the ceilings, up to the secondary floor. Fourteen truckloads to the dump. And all the steaming done; seven yellow guerdons in the dining room's insignia. Walked corn rows, hallucinating bayonets and the enemy ahead. It has rained one full week now, and strangely I cannot remember which room had which kind of wall. Sanded furniture back; glued the pump together and tied it with a windlass. Took out the upstairs closet with Alex, thereby transforming it to a second studio, and this was complicated demolition, *i.e.* economical. He takes out nails, I, screws. Think of this nation, somehow, as settling to its fill; three thousand miles of sewage dug to the frost line, or lower, Route 66 spread over Schlitz.

JULY 31

These are the things that she writes. (Will write? Has written?) *I wish, oh how I wish, I could tell you, could call. That I, for all my distance and discovery here, feel a great surging longing for you. And it grows rather than abates. I reread two of your letters just now—from mid-April—and stared at the photographs and, for the first time since I've been here, really wept. How are the lawyers, are you? Disbelieve me if you will, but I love you very much.* (Meantime I pack her things and store them, folding the dresses precisely, looping the letters with string, separating cutlery and books.) *I've dreamt several times of return, the enormous relief we would feel, but something in me refuses to accept it. And I wait for your decision; should we try again? You know those telescopes; smash a quarter in and get a scenic view for sixty seconds—that's how I feel. Come all this distance in order to stare at you, to put us in perspective—and then the image goes blank.* (Last night, and for the first time, the house felt moribund, as if some rancid ghost were loose. I unscrewed the banister head and simply ripped the banister away, its spokes giving easily.) *But I want to know right now what your plans are, and where they do or might include me. I sense you holding distance with pride and anger* (Meantime, I precisely pack six cartons with her photographs, earrings, iron, robes)*—and yet I feel no pride and only a shifting panoply of emotions—the color range from love to loss. All is not lost yet. Hardly. And you must trust me that much. Darling, darling,*

darling, I don't want to be lost and you must know that, darling. (I've run out of string; the fifth carton folds into itself and is an adequate container. But the sixth ought to be tied.)

AUGUST 1

July 26. Need a tractor to do the mowing. Will dredge the pond, am welted with nettles, and leeches; the pond mostly shelfing and ledge-encrusted, and cows should not wander near it because they foot mud within. The silo has no top because it can't be taxed that way. *(But we must give each other time to know. No, distance doesn't frighten me at all. I hate space, desolate and bizarre, that absence brings, but I also love these colors in its wake.)* She must have been reading imagists, petals on the wet-backed golden bough. Forming her style on some acceptable model at last. And who bought for her, or for whom did she select, the jerkin she wore for *The Rome Daily American;* I don't recognize the handbag, nor the scarf. *(The clarity and brilliance with which I sometimes see our life now. All of it clear and good. Darling, let's not be too proud. Your distance can only serve to leave me at sea. And neither of us needs that. I truly believe we're coming out all right.)* This is ridiculous, and wrenching; why juggle time so, what kind of poultice in that? Why reread, or reproduce this jetsam; it floats here, that's all. A note in a bottle. Unstoppered. *(The letters simply stuffing gaps time leaves. Like the chinking in our cabin, darling, do you remember? I don't know. I don't know. Feel as if I haven't heard from you in years. And I hate it. Don't think we can afford to cut each other off, to leave it to those bloodsucking briefs. Our papers. Nor can I believe that's what you're doing.*) Having filled the suitcases, one a battered straw trunk without handles, one an army surplus trunk, two blue plastic, one imitation leather, three duffel bags of varying sizes, the largest forty-eight inches in length and two feet in diameter, I closed but did not lock the closet door. Were it to have been locked, and myself absent at her return, and the key not immediately evident—in which case why bother with the locking—there might have been some sort of trouble. Removing. Her effects. (*But I want to know. Want to know what happens. Want to tell you that I love you. Still. Want to say I'm all right, darling. Good night.*)

Problems with Montgomery Ward. They can't or won't produce the stove; all I ask is to pay them, and they act as if it's an insult. Delivery troubles, months in the ordering, nonsense, nonsense, nonsense. This a natural basin. That horse trader won't sell your horse until two in the morning; you'd better be there, says Mills, the whole time, else he'll cut and run on price. The old Tucker gravestones are laid flat on a hill behind the house, left there by the previous owner, who didn't wish to consider mortality so. Walked past electric wire and then barbed wire and then sheep wire—into the marsh. Poked about among the ceiling beams—time to renovate.

VI

Nicholas made, of his son, expectation's vehicle, and he attempted to program success. "The kid should have advantages," he said, "not like me. He won't have to lick any boots or pull any bootstraps, not him." Barbara mocked his image of paternity as retribution, and of his own past as hard. "Fieldston must have been some orphanage," she said. "How loud could you beat on your soup bowl with that silver spoon?"

"It wasn't a soup bowl," Nicholas said. "It was a slop bowl. And that's not what I mean."

"What do you mean?" she asked.

"We fired three cooks. They were called dietitians, I think. Everything I want to do, or wanted to do and couldn't, I want him to do."

"Oh christ," she said, "you can't be serious."

"No," he said, "just trying that hat on for size."

Yet some part of him did funnel disappointment, and channel

it to Michael—as if capitulation could be hedged, and the bet on failure, and age undercut. "One gets a kind of immortality from kids," he said. "One gets a second chance."

He did a quick soft-shoe. "Stop clowning," she said. "That's banal."

"I won't deny it," Nicholas said. "It's banal."

He had, for one week, this recurrent dream. He dreamed his daughter, Eve, wore a leotard in the pool, and the points of her breasts were as lilies, and she commenced to sing. She sang the "Ode to Joy," and dried herself by walking, and Michael, his only son, followed. They walked together, he playing the french horn and flute and harmonica, down the Northway and Thruway and were in New York. Executives noted her and joined in the chorus, and a brakeman for the IRT was the baritone. By noon of that day the entire subway system was converted: men with briefcases and women with satchels sang the "Ode to Joy."

Nicholas stormed Wall Street at the second movement's start, and he was irascible with those who merely clapped. "*Schöner Götterfunken*," he would instruct them. "*Sanfterl Flügel weilt.*" They made pincer movements in the boroughs and took Staten Island by the reprise. The Tombs were liberated; police locked hands with blacks. All of New York was redeemed.

Michael liked swimming and rowing but was not competitive and liked the side stroke best. He learned to read early but was, Nicholas discovered, faking; he memorized the passages and would declaim them, pretending to study the words. He took piano lessons and faked music for the maid. "This is modern stuff," he said, and ran his elbow down the board and back. He knew, by the third grade, the capitals of all the fifty states, and the state flowers, and nearly all the mottoes; he could not remember Idaho's, or Alabama's, or Missouri's motto, and he pretended to forget New York's. *"Excelsior,"* Nicholas offered, and Michael said, "Anybody knows that much. I knew it all along."

Eve and he had to make their beds before they would get breakfast, and Michael wore space-suit pajamas and, sometimes, his Red Sox cap. He had pollen fever every spring. Nicholas hoped he would ski and study karate and physics; Michael watched The Mickey Mouse Club with interest, and Captain Kangaroo. "Mickey Mouse," he sang, "Mickey Mouse; forever let us hold our banner high. . . ." He was, they discovered, left-handed and his letters slanted steeply; later, he would learn to write with his left hand.

Nicholas loved Michael very much, and was impatient that he grow, and helped him with his coin collection. Nicholas cut slots out in cardboard, and they taped the coins in. Michael started with two nickels, taping the buffalo face up on the first, and the Indian on the second. He amassed quarters and half-penny pieces, and a half-a-crown. He acquired kurus and lire, and his favorite was an Italian *Gettone Telefonico*: he taped this with the intaglioed telephone facing up. He was less concerned with value than design, nor did he collect paper money; Michael had dark brown hair and a snub nose that seemed Irish, and fine teeth.

"The dentist said," he said, "that I could brush my teeth with Coca-Cola if I wanted to."

"That was a joke. And you'd get cavities."

"He said," said Michael, "I wouldn't. I haven't had one ever. And I could go ahead and eat all the candy I want."

He circled, warily; he peeled the Nestlé's wrapper off and grinned. They had a clear, level space in the backyard of Pinebrook Boulevard; Nicholas considered boundary markers, and lime.

"Sure, and you could eat a football too," he said. "If you

wanted to. Did he say what would happen then? The dentist."

"What?"

"You mean he didn't tell you?"

"What?"

"No kind of warning at all? What sort of dentist is this? What would happen"—Nicholas advanced—"if you swallowed the whole thing?"

"Laces too?"

"Laces too."

"It's too big," Michael said.

"Not for a boy who only eats candy; pretty soon you'll be big as a blimp."

"What's a blimp?"

"A Zeppelin." Nicholas continued to stalk him. "A balloon. A dirigible. A big balloon. A lead balloon like the football in your stomach."

"It isn't," Michael said.

"It is. And know what I'd do then?"

"What?" Michael regarded his shirt.

"I'd pick you up," said Nicholas, swooping, and did, "and tuck you under my arm, like this, and run for forty yards."

He executed maneuvers in the garden, feinting, his left arm a straight arm, swiping air. Michael bellowed and pummeled at him, vised by his right elbow, light; then Nicholas attempted to teach him how to punt. Michael ate his seventh Nestlé's Crunch.

"Take your shoes off," Barbara said; they went inside, shoeless, for lunch. "Those were my azaleas," Barbara said.

They went, in 1964, with Michael nine, to a summer resort in Maine. The horseflies were numerous and the nights wet; Nicholas attempted to locate constellations and could not. The lake was cold and its bottom full of cans, and the badminton net flapped in tatters; they remained three weeks. The cabins were genuine log cabins and there was an extensive entertainment program; they raised a screen by the lake and projected silent movies every night. Nicholas would watch Garfield and Novarro and the multitude of moths in the projector's beam; Barbara liked daiquiris and they would drink daiquiris and play canasta or hearts.

Their waitress was named Kathy, and she attended Bennett College and wanted to be a physical therapist. "For the handicapped," she said. "You just can't do enough for them, I think. Look at that Kennedy girl, for instance; look what they've done for her."

She was blonde and high-breasted and became good friends with Michael; she flirted with him over lunch. "You're going to look like your daddy," she said. "You're going to be a beautiful man. Wow, we can hardly wait."

"Who can?" Michael asked.

"The waitresses," she said. "We think you're a beautiful boy."

Nicholas had come to sense estrangement, and to harass his son. "You don't honor me," he said, "and this includes you, Eve. It says Honor Thy Father and Mother. Notice who comes first. Bring me my slippers and paper and pipe; I deserve affectionate respect."

He was only half joking; he felt the family in league and against him. They cackled in the bath about him, he was sure. "What's so funny?" he demanded. "What did I do now?"

"Nothing, dad," Michael would say, "except only look at your socks."

Nicholas was color-blind and wore socks with patterns so as to distinguish them, but he still made mistakes. He pulled up his pants and registered the diamond insignia and could not tell which sock was gray and which blue. He pulled off his shoes and asked, "Well, which is which?"

"They're both blue," Michael said, and exploded with delight. Nicholas ducked him, then, and he came up spluttering. "Hey, that water's soapy," he said.

There was also a lifeguard and water-skiing instructor named Bob Lipton. He played chess with Barbara and other guests and had the deeply tanned face and chest and the white back of a man who always positioned himself facing the sun. Kathy took the children into her room and let them handle her cosmetics, and Michael came to supper smelling of Chanel. Kathy and Bob Lipton were lovers, Nicholas assumed, but Kathy told him no. "He's happily married," she said, "I think. Just like you must be."

They drove to Kennebunkport and Brunswick and to Campobello, once. Nicholas felt reverential, and he pointed out the rocking chairs and writing implements and chamber pots. "This explains your middle name," Barbara said to Michael. Michael's middle name was Franklin; friends, teasing, called him "Frankie"; Eve touched the photographs.

When the children were asleep, or out, Nicholas and Barbara made love; they made love, one evening, on the raft. Nicholas ate lobster whenever it was offered, and a seaplane brought lobsters to the hotel. Michael liked to watch it land and come scudding through the lake. He grew adept at badminton and shuffleboard and he would lie on Kathy's bed, rumpling her pillow and sheets. She talked to him, Nicholas knew, of physical therapy's role. "There's two ways to live your life," she said, "just two ways, as far as I see. For yourself or for others." Michael asked, "What about God?"

He was restive-seeming and watched Bob Lipton's triceps when Bob Lipton moved a pawn. Nicholas went trolling with him after trout. Michael's lines were tangled, and he was impatient with the reel, but he caught a four-pound trout, and

Nicholas clubbed it against the boat's bow. They had the cook broil it for supper, and Michael gave Kathy a piece. "This is as good as *truite au bleu*," Barbara said, "or *truite meunière*."

Michael thought that Henry Aaron was the greatest active baseball player, and possibly the greatest living, and that he had a bad deal playing for Milwaukee. "You'll see," he said, "he'll be playing long after Mantle or Mays. And he maybe will overtake Ruth. He'll have the second-most homers; you'll see."

"He's just slow and steady," Nicholas said. "That never won no race."

The restaurant had lanterns with electric candles.

"For dessert," Kathy announced, "we have the usual, plus pecan pie. And we've got that nice dutch cheese tonight."

"Say the ice creams," Eve said. "Say them as fast as you can."

"Vanilla-chocolate-coffee-mocha-pistachio-strawberry-lime-and-orange sherbet," Kathy said. She rested her hip on Nicholas's elbow. Michael said, "Kathy was born in Milwaukee. She knows."

"Knows what?" Barbara ordered the fruit bowl, and a slice of Gouda.

"About the newspapers there, and how Henry Aaron must be getting a bad deal."

Nicholas ordered only coffee. "Got to keep that belly back," he said. When the fruit bowl came, however, he selected grapes.

He thought of Breuer's buildings, and the notion of the monolith; he pictured an electric blue concrete. The concrete would be such bright blue that even he could tell. Kathy, rotating, departed, and Eve said, "She showed me her mother's photograph."

They all stood when Barbara left the table for the ladies' room, and when she returned. She attempted to make Michael wipe his mouth before he drank. "It costs nothing," she would say, "to be polite." She beat Bob Lipton twice at chess, using the four-knights opening, and then a Ruy Lopez defense. Nicholas met Kathy by the badminton court, and she put her hand on his penis, and he said, "You don't understand. I'm tryin for fidelity. Just once."

She said, "But it's so lonely here." And he answered, "Not for me. Not us."

She said, rubbing him, "I believe in free and honest love. If you want to ball, let's ball." "I'm sorry," he answered and withdrew, unexcited, renouncing, "I don't."

Nicholas lay on the sand. He tried Balkan Sobranie tobacco and felt no need to read and was, purposively, patient with the children. Eve buried Michael in sand. Barbara wore sun goggles and was, he decided, abstract. He would watch her shucking peas or in the bathtub or straightening her slip and be familiar with the gesture and not know why she made it; the sand had been hauled from the coast. He liked the smell of pine sap and did thirty seconds of leg-raisers and then rested for thirty, then raised both legs again. His favorite wood-paneling was teak.

Michael pulled at his feet. "Hey, let's play shuffleboard," he said. "I'm bored. Just sitting here is boring."

"Wouldn't you rather fish?" Nicholas asked. "After yesterday. I could get that boat."

"No." Michael insisted. "Let's play shuffleboard." They did, and Michael won by seven points; it rained. Nicholas considered withholding his telephone tax as a protest against our Far-Eastern involvement, and whether there would be a draft by 1976; he studied Michael's hair. They played Monopoly, and Michael won, and Nicholas considered claiming he had lost on purpose; "Pride of accomplishment," he said to Barbara. "That's what I want him to have."

Michael went to grade school in the New Rochelle public system; he attended Fieldston in the seventh grade. When they moved to Boston he attended Boston Latin, but he wanted to attend, instead, the Commonwealth School. Nicholas and Barbara inquired as to the Commonwealth School, and thought it might make sense. They were wary, however, of the changes Michael had already made, and they thought another might prove too unsettling. They urged him, therefore, to remain at Boston Latin for one year. He was twelve and wanted a blazer and followed Jim Lonberg's career with avidity; he wore a big red button saying "YAZ." He had a Schwinn racing bike and, though three years older, did remain friendly with Eve. He was sizable and, with time, his nose enlarged, and his teeth had to be straightened but they did remain intact.

Nicholas purchased a Lionel train set for Michael's eighth birthday. He bought a diesel engine and a steam engine and a lumber car and coal car and milk car and helped make papier-mâché mountains and had two transformers. "You can call it second childhood," he told Barbara, "but there's something wonderful in this kind of control. You know. A world that's six by fourteen feet. A universe that's bounded by a Ping-Pong table. Nice."

"Why not enlarge it?" she mocked him. "You could put a piece of plywood on the couch."

"What's wrong," he asked, "what's the matter; what's so very bad about enjoyment? *Goce la vida*, my love."

Michael made exhibitions of cowboys, and had owned a fleet of trucks. He had a sense of probity that mocked his father's easy scheming; he wanted to learn horseback riding and learn to ride bareback. When ten he had collapsed with what the doctor labeled "athlete's heart." Michael had not been good at sports, and he took pride in the title; he missed, however, one semester of school and lay, recuperating from rheumatic fever, on his back for the whole spring. He swallowed one teaspoonful of raspberry-flavored penicillin every day, and Nicholas carried him to the bathroom, since he had been forbidden to walk. Even Barbara could carry him, and she wept at night that he was only bone. He had been plump, and his belly had furled when he sat.

Nicholas returned from work each night with a new puzzle, or Hardy Boys book. He bore them up to Michael's room as offerings. He would stand there in his raincoat, briefcase at his feet, tentative, intent. Michael would turn on his pillow to grin, asking how the office was, and how was the trip home. A suitor to his son, and reeking of health-sweat and lunch, Nicholas opened the briefcase and said, "Guess what I found coming back?"

"What?"

"Guess."

"I can't."

"You can."

"I can't. You tell me, daddy, what?"

"The Taj Mahal. The rest of Nefertiti."

"What's that?"

"The best part, dummy. Don't they teach you anything in school?"

"We only did the Greeks," Michael allowed. "This spring I would have done the Punic Wars."

"The Taj Mahal's a building in India, and I've never seen it either, and it's certainly too big to carry home."

"So what did you bring me?"

"Trouble. A kiss."

Nicholas leaned over his son, and they rubbed cheeks. Nicholas said, as he always did, fingering his bristles and then

Michael's chin, "My, my, you've shaved well." His son's curls were cauterized, distinct.

"I know," Michael said, "quite a bit about the Greeks. Who was Alcibiades?" he asked.

Nicholas shed his raincoat and opened the briefcase and produced an autographed baseball with the entire Dodger roster of 1954. He told Michael of Campanella and Jackie Robinson and Snider and Furillo and Pee Wee Reese, of Preacher Roe's spitball and what Branch Rickey accomplished; Michael traced the seams.

"This must be expensive," he said.

"Expensive. Why it could buy the Taj Mahal. Supposing that you wanted it. Or the rest of Nefertiti, come to that."

"Who's Nefertiti?" Michael asked. "How much did this cost?"

Nicholas bought ten Hardy Boys books at a time, and had them gift-wrapped, and selected one—on returning, and if he had nothing else—from the hall closet. He had paid five dollars for the baseball, in Anthony's Sports Shoppe.

"This is a relic," he said, "this is a holy thing. You can touch it because you're my son, and I'm fond of you this evening, and you seem to have been an acceptable patient today. See how many of those names you know; see how many you can read."

Michael was patient, and contemplative, and lost weight all that summer. He was, the doctors assured them, on the road to recovery; even in the third month, they said all that he needed was time. They carried him outside to let him lie in the hammock; Nicholas bought a standing hammock so that he could lie in sun, but Michael preferred the shade. He would lie, strung between two japanese maples, rocking ceaselessly, reading the Hardy Boys stories, or Chip Hilton stories, or Jules Verne. Nicholas bought him a dog. It was an Irish setter and they named him Pharaoh, and Michael roused some-what; he would stroke and scratch Pharaoh, who was a silent puppy, and jingle a plastic bone with balls on it. They played fetch with a tennis ball, and Pharaoh learned to fetch.

Nicholas returned from work with a Doggie Dooley; it was an imitation fire hydrant, with chemical briquettes that sani-tized droppings. It had a galvanized shovel for lifting and a year's supply of chemical briquettes. "This is your backyard conversation piece," the advertisement proclaimed.

"We could use this," Nicholas said, "to ensure a parking space. Just drop it off before we park and pick it up on arrival. And leave a load of Pharaoh by the A&P."

The doctor said that Michael could travel by July, and that he needed distraction. "He lies there like a corpse," Nicholas complained, "he's making love to death." The family—and Pharaoh—drove to Aspen; Michael could go horseback riding, Nicholas promised, bareback. The drive there took two weeks, and they had planned to stay for two, but Michael turned pale in the mountains and was short of breath. They spanned the continental divide, therefore, and turned south. Each morning, at every motel, Nicholas ordered cream for Michael's cereal, and pancakes and maple syrup; Michael pre-ferred french toast. He did put on weight, however, and, as they traveled in a convertible, lost his pallor also. "Daddy," he would ask, "is the top open if it's up, or closed if it's down, or closed if it's up and open if it's down?"

They discussed this gravely, and Nicholas attempted further riddles. "If Moses is the son of Pharaoh's daughter," he would say, "then Moses is the daughter of Pharaoh's son." This puzzled Michael and Eve, and Nicholas explained the use of the possessive apostrophe; each time that they spoke his name, Pharaoh's ears would flap.

86

"Pick a number," Michael said, "any number. From one to one hundred. And don't tell me what it is."

"Can it be fractions?" Nicholas asked.

"Yes, it can be anything. It doesn't bother me. Except it'll be hard for you that way. It's better to take something simple."

Eve knew the trick, she said. Nicholas picked four. He imagined the number that Pier Luigi Nervi would pick. He changed his selection to eight.

"Now double it," said Michael; "now add twelve. Now divide the whole thing by two, and subtract the number you had in the first place."

Nicholas turned his windshield spray on, in order to clean off the bugs.

"Your answer's six," Michael said.

"The answer's always six," Eve asserted. "It would work for any number. It would have to be six."

"OK," Michael said, "let's try it again."

Nicholas picked six.

"Pick a number, any number, and don't tell me what it is. Triple it; add, let's say, twenty-seven; divide the whole thing by three, and subtract the number you had in the first place. Your answer," Michael concluded, "is nine."

He settled back, triumphant, and would not explain the trick to Eve. She had excellent eyes and could read the Burma Shave signs long before he could. She wore her hair in bangs, and long, and would be taking Enovid, Nicholas thought, in four years.

He tried to circumvent Chicago, and they spent the night in Joliet. When they had settled in the motel, Nicholas went swimming; the water was lit from beneath and heavily chlorined and his legs seemed green. He showered and asked Barbara what she would like to drink; she said, "Gin and tonic," and he drove to a liquor store to purchase gin. While there, he attempted to telephone Jean; first the line was busy and then he got no answer and then Hal Burling answered the phone. Nicholas had telephoned person to person, and Hal Burling told the operator, "Mrs. Burling's not at home."

"Is there another number where we might reach her?" the operator asked. "When do you expect her back?"

She received no answer, and Nicholas gathered his change, and then Hal Burling said, "Operator, please don't ask me questions like that." His voice was pleasant, without edge, and his manner polite. "Now that's an invasion of privacy, don't you see? Those are questions I'm not required to answer; I could plead the fifth amendment, operator, dig? It's a kind of wiretap. I could have you arrested, if I chose, or placed under surveillance. What is this, operator, some kind of third degree?"

Nicholas returned to the motel, and Michael was asleep with Pharaoh, and he made drinks for his wife and let his daughter taste the drink and regretted the absence of lemon. They rocked for some time in plastic rockers, and Eve announced that she could smell the stockyards and also went in to sleep. "I'll see you in the morning," she said. "When do you want to get up?"

"Let's leave at nine," said Nicholas. "Let's get an early start."

They sat and drank in silence, and he pictured Jean battered by her husband's belly, or tacking in Lake Michigan; the sign across the highway read "Impeach Earl Warren. Now!" His wife was excellent with fires and cooked *moules marinières* and was immaculate. She had many fears and a nervous competence and she controlled fear for the children's sake. When he swore, or clowned, or quarreled, she said, "What kind of example is that?" She was terrified of insects and driving at night and cellars; she uncrossed her legs and stretched, and he felt the gin muster lust.

A sign across the highway nictated and was erased; they went inside.

"Why don't you want to go to Chicago?" she asked. "Why not? For heaven's sakes, we spent three days in Omaha."

"Because Michael needed to," he said.

Michael recovered and studied the guitar and wore rimless glasses while reading; Nicholas instructed him in heat and ventilation and the geodesic dome. They went on a beach picnic at night, and Michael took his guitar. He took lessons in the classical guitar but preferred folk music; he attempted to adapt Villa-Lobos as blues. He was not an accomplished musician but had a soft, high voice; his voice cracked when he was twelve. They gathered driftwood and stones to guard the fire, and Eve and Eve's friends swam. Nicholas popped a champagne cork and Michael missed the catch; Barbara cooked *moules marinières.*

Nicholas went swimming after supper, and his wife stood in front of the fire and watched him; her legs appeared enormous and her torso framed with flame. He was happy and drunken and Michael practiced the changes for "Delia," then played "Barbara Allen" and "When the Saints Go Marchin' In."

"You remind me," said Nicholas, as Barbara gave him a towel, "of lime. Now why should you do that?" He toweled himself. "You remind me of a lime."

"Is that a compliment?" she asked.

"I think so; I like lime. You remind me of a lime."

Nicholas liked to tell stories, and Michael followed him intently. When Michael was a child, Nicholas told a story every night. He told the story of the snail who walked to the Atlantic from Cooperstown, New York; he told the story of the turtle who dove for treasure in the South Pacific, and built an island out of billiard balls he found. The billiard balls were hollow, and had fish inside, and every color was a color nobody ever had seen.

Michael's favorite hero was an Indian called Lope. Lope was friends with wolves and used to sleep on cactus so he wouldn't sleep too well. Lope could build a cabin out of buffalo fur and a tree, and he could split an apple's seed with a bow and arrow from five hundred yards. But he never used his strength unwisely, and he had a fondness for corn liquor and was close friends with President Grant. Michael said, "That makes him dead," and Nicholas agreed.

"But he comes back to life each time you think of him," he said. "He's grateful if you do. He once harpooned a whale with his toothpick and nursed the whale and tamed it. They became excellent friends, also, and he used the whale to go sailing; he had a whale canoe."

"How could they get down streams?" Michael asked. "The whale would be too big."

"Not if he stood on his tail. And, in the littlest streams, Lope would pick the whale up and carry him pickaback; it worked out pretty well."

Lope learned to talk horse-talk and Latin and built the first Ferrari racing car. He built it out of tumbleweed and snakeskins and a bicycle; he could hit a baseball from Idaho to Texas, if the wind was right. "That means south," said Michael, "that means to the bottom of the map."

Michael died in August, when he was thirteen, at camp. He had gone hiking with a junior counselor and four boys and two girls. It was an overnight hike, and not dangerous or difficult, eleven miles round trip. They had taken steaks and popcorn and wet-sheets and Michael took his guitar. It rained, and Michael played "Comin' Round the Mountain When She Comes."

He was on the chorus and exhorting them to join when lightning struck a maple tree. A branch hit Michael and killed him, the junior counselor reported, instantly; he felt no pain, the junior counselor said, not even shock or surprise. Nicholas received the call at eight in the morning, and he wakened Barbara and they drove to the camp; it was a four-hour drive.

Barbara was blank; he had given her a sedative with coffee. She lay athwart the seat, weeping, saying, "But this is absurd. That's crazy; it must be a joke. Let's turn around. Let's turn around. Let's negotiate a split U-turn the way they do in driving manuals; remember; you correct."

He played the radio but every song seemed mockery, nor could he listen to the news. "Then there's a Trooper's U-Turn," Barbara said, "but I think it's illegal; you back the car around." He rehearsed estrangement, and anger at the counselor, and the last time Michael had been home.

"Do you want some coffee?" Nicholas asked.

"Yes," she had answered, "and bananas. And I'll make some bacon if you like."

"I wonder," Nicholas said, "whether we could put in some sort of fan. You know, a ceiling outlet to take that smell away."

They shared a love of kippered herring, and Barbara could not bear the smell. The ate it, therefore, with the kitchen door shut and the windows open and washed the dishes carefully and took the garbage out. Barbara would come down hours later and stand in the pantry and sniff; they felt like conspirators but she would always catch them nonetheless.

"I'm never very hungry," Michael said, "before I take a trip."

He had done a project on the mafia for school and sported

a fedora with a wide brim. "They call the men from Italy," he told his father, "wide hats. They're the ones who run the show, and they wear this kind of hat."

Michael's body had been prepared, and the camp had provided a coffin. "Free of charge," the camp director said. Nicholas considered lawsuits and what they might accomplish and opening the coffin to take Michael in his arms one final time. It was raining, and the camp director had extremely hairy arms; the hair on his forearms was bleached. His shirt had two missing buttons, and he wore a yellow undershirt. Barbara said, "Darling. Which of these alternatives do you consider feasible? We could buy a luggage rack and tote the coffin home. Or take Michael out of the box and wrap him in a blanket, providing, of course, that they do have blankets here. We've got sufficient space, I think, on the rear seat. But this coffin won't fit in the trunk; he was a growing boy, you know, he's not little any longer. And it is raining, after all. Though the rain might stop. I wouldn't want to test the workmanship up there. Of the box, I mean."

Nicholas quieted her, and the camp music instructor, with his two bugle pupils, played "Taps." The entire camp was ranged around the flagpole; there were seven- to fifteen-year-olds, and then assistant counselors, then junior counselors, then counselors. "Which is the wood-working group?" Barbara asked. "I'd like to praise them. Which?"

"Grief comes later to me," Nicholas thought. "Later. I'll be inconsolable next week."

He thought of a horse farm he had visited in Carbondale, Colorado, and thought of the timberline there. Is the timberline, he wondered, merely a function of height, or does it have to do with climate also; how could Mount Olympus, he wondered, have a snow-tipped peak? One girl at the last row's edge was not wearing a brassiere, and the rain had

92

accented her nipples, and he gauged the angle of her breast's decline. The loss would be perpetual, he thought, and the absence cumulative, and the sorrow of it, later, would be absolute; Barbara looked, he thought, like a Greek mask. He remembered Michael's indrawn, soundless cry when an infant, the mouth stretched to its outer limit, and grief in abeyance, eyes shut. Sometimes Nicholas proved fast enough to tickle or distract his son, and the wailing had dissolved. He thought about the tack he fitted on his horse in Carbondale, and the design of the halter, and the bit's soft spume. He was too old for further sons, he thought. Eve was visiting in Westport, and they had been unable to reach her by phone. The music counselor played the Villa-Lobos piece that Michael had transposed; he played Michael's guitar. The camp director gave them Michael's duffel bag, intact, and his tennis racket, and a refund for the five weeks missed. Grief would come, Nicholas thought, and fury, and the sense of waste, later, when he was alone. Barbara dropped her head and rested her hand on his elbow, and he whispered, "Darling, I do love you. Very much."

He had no love left, he decided, nor any charity.

VII

AUGUST 2

Raining still, the wet incessant; melons rot. The hens roost in trees. The downstairs beams soaked, and the cellar cacophonous with frogs; the cat's two kittens have not as yet opened their eyes. Slate stacked behind the garage. The downstairs toilet leaks. Robert, making movies, is responsible for this. Robert: making movies is responsible for this. Killed a bat with a broom, found a way to release three others. Night. There are certain sorts of distance one simply cannot bridge, a kind of severance apology can't heal. Trust, that difficult thing to make, is easy to break, and irrevocably. Rub a galvanized pipe with vinegar and leave it outside to take the galvanizing off. Or muriatic acid, if used with care, and the incinerator. I'm a sanctimonious, talkative clown, and full of self-pity that masquerades as pride. Robert, for the title, all my thanks.

AUGUST 3

An italian delicatessen, a hellish trip to Albany, with the
gamut imposed by Montgomery Ward, that I run from
one warehouse to the next, the salesmen incompetent,
"suspicioning" how to fix the thing, finding missing
parts. Still, the strange, tentative way of handling
tools; all these are questions of authority. Have just
bought twenty-foot two-by-fours, and shall attempt to
build the scaffolding. "Little bit of everything in this
mason line," says Frank, who has cut down his trees
and will bring me a couple of cords. Slung on the
back of that orange Ford truck. I need a metaphor,
some sort of tale to tell. How the tomato plants found
plaster at their back. Full of fits and starts, mirroring
this wacky way: not the austere chronicle planned.
At the Oasis Bar, at six last night, they were signing,
with a magic marker, some crippled woman's left leg's
cast. Accurate use of the possessive apostrophe. At
least. And the man on my right drank beer till stupe-
fied; the bartender, subtracting from his heap of change
(this whole piled high, in quarters, so that the customer
need not keep count) regularly refilled. Her letters
set me howling and do not diminish pain. Avoid the
inaccurate parallel construction; don't use contractions
in critical prose.

AUGUST 4

Have gone through the basement walls with Frank and
hammer and chisel and laid down the base and this
morning we're starting the cinderblock chimney; lay-
ing it is relatively easy, keeping it level, less so. Have
to keep the whole thing plumb, that little water bubble
bouncing left, right, down, up, interminable adjust-
ments. We lay three blocks, eight by twelve, then de-

posit (and for the first rank we've laid, also, a steel supporting rod) a ceramic-tile flue inside. And a clean-out door cut in. And have ordered twenty-seven furnace flues and received thirty-three. And had to rotate the whole thing, with a crowbar, two degrees or so. O. (though proud of his antecedents, disguises, or, more properly, aggrandizes them, making the comfortable wealthy, the recent the old, and is that also possibly why, returning to his birthplace, he could not recognize the house, chose almost as if by instinct—and that inaccurate—the largest on the street; being accustomed, therefore, to the twitter of exaggeration, flabby, he nonetheless sucks in his stomach and, when touched, or touching, does so with force) shakes hands.

AUGUST 6

Sweating pride. This the first sentence typed at my new, constructed desk. Coffee cup in one hand and last night's rancid wine in the other; two slabs of birch flush doors, one six-foot-six and one six-foot-eight, their widths being one-foot-six and two-foot-two respectively, making the desk top, at ninety degrees; a pipe rack built into the support (he will give up smoking, has). And adjustable shelves. A loud coughing noise, this dawn, not a fox. The support beams to the kitchen chimney rotted through.

(EDITOR'S NOTE: The following pagination refers to the typescript of *In the Middle Distance*.)

EDITOR: p. 131, line 5: "Michael was nine" (actually, "just turned nine"—p. 156, line 7). Just checking to make sure this is correct. Nicholas is at this point forty, which puts this about eight years prior to time present, or 1955, which means he might more likely be eight (or even seven) than nine, though I'm not at all sure my calculations are right.

AUTHOR: Nicholas is not quite forty yet. And it's the summer of his turning age, and when he buys the farm. Which is, I believe, 1964, one year after Simon dies. Argal Michael is just turned nine. The real problem here is that I didn't imagine I'd get the book done this quickly, and computed it all for publication in 1972. What to do? Shoot for immortality, or make it eight, and have Simon, p. 19, die in '62. Let's do it that way, & hope the whole comes out right.

Disregard. Make him forty-one.

EDITOR: p. 167: Where is end parenthesis that begins in line 9 ("She was . . ." ?

AUTHOR: Substitute, p. 6, line 18, "every night"; for "incessantly"; Moderation above, before all.

AUGUST 8

Rows of brick two across, two astraddle, I laid my first one, and that a kind of virginity taken also. Rear left row, second from the back and side; again the plumb line central. Have connected the furnace piping and fixed it with sheet metal screws. Sanded chairs. An eloquent defense of apartheid by S. M., and that most strange indeed. Masai live on a mixture of cow's milk, bull's blood and urine as preservative, he said; congenital syphilitics; if human beings ate, he said, what those people ate they'd be dead in a week. Kikuyu threw down machine guns when faced with Masai waving spears. And the slowest of them beat all existing track records. The flooring, tongue in groove, will lever up, or should, with some efficiency. Built a sawhorse from some of the lumber lying about; the trouble with so strong a memory is that all seems déjà vu. (*We shouldn't write such letters. Just anecdotes of family and friends. Stay on the light side. I don't want to seem gloomy and I don't want you to. Since this is finally an exercise in levity and expansion. Isn't it? Darling. Where do love and freedom meet? Something I don't yet know. But I know the love is there. For you. More later. . . .*)

AUGUST 11

Today, all day, I cleaned and split brick. Variations on a title: CBCompany, or Kisco, or Kensico, embossed initials on the hearth. Have repointed the fireplace wall and shored the mold. Will make the dampers and insert them sometime next week. The upstairs stoves are bolted and mortared in place. With a slight final down-kilt so that the wood sap, the green soot, Frank calls it, won't come coursing back. I spent the shut of a morning attempting to burn paint off brick with a propane torch, succeeded merely in making it blister, and black. Frank recollects, twenty years since, a painter spilt paint all over the kitchen roof tiles—and that, for fifteen years at least, the stain, though scrubbed, signified his shift to third going downhill, second up. There was a bucket and winch where we grow, next to the outhouse and pump, the garden now. A horse barn in the ruined foundation to the northwest; a corncrib also; you could drive to the cellar, as he remembers it, long before cars. (*As you can no doubt tell I'm sad that you don't deign to write. My behavior may not be made to order for your specification, but it's honest and necessary, as I've said.*

And I refuse to let this wrench us asunder, that's
childish. I read, this morning, of a man in Nottingham
who married the same dame three times. All I do know
is that you travel here with me, and that I love you
and think of you and want to know what has hap-
pened. We are too close not to give that much; don't
you think? Don't I deserve that much?)

AUGUST 12

Regeneration, you said, is a thing of the spirit; not so,
it is of the flesh. I think of Ari spitting blood, his
lungs in his teeth, and have little patience with the
doctrines of composure. Meek and mild. Fruitfulness,
you said, is an inner state; not so, it is an orchard
spangled with clothing and food. Them that's got
shall get; them that's not must, consequently, take.

AUGUST 13

August 13. Frank dislikes a sloppy job and thinks
the old way of doing things sloppy. No way of tying
wall ties to the brick, for instance. And the header row
built every which way. On a hundred-thousand-dollar
house, he says, and shakes with disgust, he saw wall-
boards so rotten they'd been taken from a barn. What
kind of paneling is that? he asks, cows have rubbed it
thin. And lives in a trailer. Can't help but make the
soldier row buckle and curve, since I got only irregular
ones; all of this distresses him, and the fact that the
wall is not totally clean. With some of the lime cling-
ing still. He prefers to work with cinderblock; it
makes a neater job. Tried to drill for studs with an
electric drill and blunted it merely by going through
brick. The upstairs study, therefore, had its plaster laid

directly on. Have the borrow of a jeep, and winch. Frank has a tattoo with a snake that curls around the American flag, spitting "Mom." *(Parrotfish. The pyramids. The little boy who loved horses but later women and was the hero of the Mary O'Hara books I read when a child—My Friend Flicka, Thunderhead— used to have a special word for such joy-times. He called them "kernels of life" and used to store them up to barricade against want. I wonder how many kernels we get, and if they're all as lovely as these last weeks have been. Presumptious to predict more, but I can feel them in my wise left knee.)*

Let us, he continued, continue. Accustomed to precipitous places as, from earliest childhood, was P. (the first view of his father being foreshortened from shoulders, and the first sense of manhood generated in a hayloft, two bales above, and three to the left, of his cousin copulating with the neighbor, Luke, though then he called it wrestling and swung, to encourage her, whistling, from eaves) he nonetheless held breath. Nor Notre Dame's gargoyles, wherefrom he emerged, a globule on some pocked stone tongue, nor Uxmal's pyramidal height, or the melting southern face of Allaline in avalanche season had heretofore alarmed him as did she.

Nonsense. I read the life of Burton and have ripped out the ceilings and floors. The pleasures of imagination and a swollen purse. The first of these twinned outposts, the building of a book. Nonsense. The house a shell.

AUGUST 14

The loves and sorrows of Harry Atlas. (From the mountains of Kentucky, gimp-legged, a painter, forty-six, once perhaps looked like Pan, therefore is enamored

of goats, and takes Massimo, his present goat, everywhere, took his predecessor to Palm Beach where,
wearing only beads, she cavorted down the beach and
got into the society page, this vexing Harry somewhat,
as his own, the owner's name, was omitted; taken up,
no doubt, by some wealthy pederast once and plopped
in Taormina like a plum.) Tentatively titled: Memoirs
of a Nelly Queen as Filtered Through a Fourth-Rate
Novelist in Drag. "I was born of a wealthy family,
being a second cousin relation to William Adamson,
and my grandfather died a wealthy man, with a mansion in Bowling Green. But his children squandered
the inheritance, and, particularly, my father was not a
very nice man, and mother died when I was two. In
1929 we started eating only slops; for years then I
had malnutrition, god bless them, look at my leg. And
can eat only grapes, and nuts, and am just mad for
citrus fruit, was hungry once in Biloxi. Since the
sailors were coming all over the wharf, and I'd had
nothing to eat but a dozen of them. Well. I was sent
when I was five from a foster home into the Kentucky
hills and stayed there till I was fifteen. My foster
family raised tobacco, and corn, and the stench that
first December I'll never get out of my nostrils. We'd
kill a hog a month to feed the twenty-eight people
living in this house. And have gravy from the pig's
drippings for weeks, and I near to died from the boils,
which is why I don't eat pork. So I had sissified ways,
and wished to paint, but they tore my graven images
up, and poems, and my first sex was with Elmer; we
pulled each other off by the creek. At eleven, just like
that. I used to watch Ray and Ruth fucking underneath the porch, and my little thing was also in evidence. I run home to ask, Mommy, what does screwing signify?; Ray and Ruth go up and down just

like your rocking chair. And Ruth's dingle is all sucked in. When I was fifteen, then, and it was September, since I can still smell the leaves, yes, it must have been September, I bought new shoes on credit and hid them in an elm-crook by the well. I was bound and determined, you do understand, to be an artist then. I reached up and took them come nighttime and walked with pride down the dirt road, twenty-five miles, terrified of cars (the first was my first, do you see). And it appeared to be the Beast of the Apocalypse come to gobble me up for having trespassed, lights and the engine roaring, and, under the barbed wire Mrs. Atlas's little boy was hunkering to weeds. After the third such time I recollected automobiles and that those lamps were not angelic. Oh, not at all. Later, I learned to hitch and also what truckdrivers wanted, and I was making it, exactly, to California and through the deep south often. Always being bought my hotel room or a meal, because of a certain, they call it, panache. Made my first set of connections, you see, in the lunch counter at bus stations—who hasn't been fucked on a Greyhound? But then at a Cincinnati businessman's club, where you encounter the right sort of people, but I'm getting ahead of myself, and found my uncle in London, Kentucky, and told him that I figured I would go to Cleveland, Ohio, or Cincinnati perhaps. But since mother hadn't written—I called her mother, also, of course—they telephoned back, and the next morning (twelve miles from the phone to the house, sixty in all) my parents arrived, and with much weeping and gnashing of teeth. Back I went with the promise the next time I'd only need to announce it and go. I remember these things. If you want the story of my life you'll have to ask permission. I remember this. Not having asked the woman at the first farm I passed, I anyway got biscuits and blueberry jam. I can still taste the things freely given and without the coarse necessity to beg, though the mountain people understand my greenback language now, indeed. I wrote the social worker that my parents tried to poison me. And she arrived quickly all right. So she found it was a lie, and I suppose it was, but what's truth; really in a way they'd tried to poison me, and I went back to dayschool with her. She also understands my greenback language now. And stole sheets and women's clothing from the people from Cincinnati six fields down, and I hid them in the school-loft, the school being on the property. It was my duty to stoke up the morning stove; I got no sort of sentence but only just a reprimand. This was later repeated by a night in the Louisville jail, and a more serious larceny I can't even recollect. But the social worker, Mrs. Fipps, she was, stalked out with little Harry underneath her arm, saying I'm still underage, and my lavender ways were the town talk, really. The mountain boys all wore lipstick and curlers but none of them took notice, it not being a sex-thing but an act of decoration; nevertheless I persisted, and I did wear lipstick in the motel the first night. She was bringing me back to London, you see. And I didn't know how to wash my hands or go to the bathroom, though the washstand and the toilet were in a corner, and she'd pointed them out. Stories get a little hazy now, the Life at Home and As a Broad. I was in a reformatory twelve miles from town, attending art school and unable to master technique. I was living with my brother and sister, who later sent me west, over the river to Indiana, saying, Harry, that way's California, here's fifty cents, follow the sun, don't turn around. What else. My travel years. Arrested again, going out of Biloxi; I was just getting into costume since we'd not got a ride there for hours, and I was becoming Ann Sothern, but they'd seen me cross tobacco fields, and I guess they thought I must have been a spy, it being World War II. The police tell us, we just want to get you fellas or whatever you are out of town. After dark. So that you're not arrested again, or hung. And we sit in a cell, I was with Mickey then, and the police say, only there's one thing you have to do for us. In return. Promise. And we promise. I'm terrified of murder or a serious indictment now, can scarcely get it up. But I'm ordered to go down on Mickey, and he has his turn on me, and the police roar at us, delighted, taking photographs. We're driven out of town by the local FBI director, who picks up sailors on the way and stages quite an operation in his house. Mansion, I should say. Masturbating on the balcony. And on the way to Birmingham next morning, he arrests a Salvation Army lady who was passing out leaflets to sailors. For Soliciting. With VD. He hated women that much, you see. Well, when I arrived at L.A., and it would take too long to tell, I filled my arms with calla lilies, put on my fright wig, made a mouth and tried to get into Finocchio's. Dressed to the stocking's teeth, you might say. And upset the man who was running it since he asked who is this Harry Atlas, and he threw me out for being underage. But I stood at the door anyhow, offering a lily to each person leaving, and my name was, you understand, made. It's really the sweetness that counts, the chance, as our dear Saviour said, to turn the other cheek. What else? When the cowboys came shooting at me in my first picture (I'd never seen a screen before) I ran. Boils from that food for a week. Now I have seven houses, three in Lexington, two in the hills, two that are farms, one in Key West, and one business in Lexington. Now I know more famous people than I'd care to name; the whole world's gay now, really, or will be. Only way to solve the population problem, really. Having been arrested in Washington D.C.—and isn't that a funny name—for corrupting the morals of a minor (who turned out to be thirteen though his groin was certainly older), I was locked up. For three months, prior to court, and knew I'd get at least a year. So I was taken, after three fits in front of the doctor, to St. Elizabeth's. And my next room's neighbor was Ezra Pound, who howled to himself as he wrote. Those animal noises, you understand, fending off the ruckus of the hospital. Mr. Pound, what is an image? I asked. And he'd tell me, patiently, this is an image, Harry, this is a symbol as such."

VIII

Nicholas wielded a scythe. He had found it in the barn, rusting, wedged behind wire, and he sharpened it and oiled it and swiped at thistles, bending them. His wife was in Mount Desert Island with the children for three days; they had gone to look at boarding schools. Michael was nine and Eve six, and Barbara had no intention of sending them to boarding school, but she wished to be prepared. They would stay with Barbara's friends, the Becks. Mrs. Beck was an albino and had attended Skidmore with Nicholas's wife.

He was hot and lonely, and he propped the scythe against the porch and made himself a gin and tonic and called, person to person, for Jean. She was not surprised to hear from him, she said, and had been planning a trip to New York.

"I'll be at O'Hare by two o'clock," she said. "I'll take that two o'clock flight. I can stay till Tuesday. Will that give you time?"

"Yes," he said, "I'll drive down the Thruway. That's fine."

He called his wife and said that he had to go to New York, but would be back by Wednesday to meet them. "I miss you very much," he said. "It rained last night. I miss you all very much."

Nicholas thought himself a ruin of a man, with his torso crumbled turrets, flesh girdling the body like walls. When squatting, his legs hurt; he diagnosed the onset of phlebitis and scratched at his scalp without interference, and his left bicep seemed slack. He would be forty-one on August twenty-seventh and had, his doctor told him, an excellent physique; still he should go easy on the Scotch. He had profuse body hair.

He had been born, the second of two children, with his father forty-four; his father, eighty-five, had been born in Spain. Still brittle and an anarchist, the old man mourned Asturias, and he berated his son. "You have a corn god," he said, "a corn god made of money, and he's in the supermarket. May this nation rot."

He did not need a cane but rarely left his apartment on the Concourse; he watched Walter Cronkite with devotion and wore detachable collars and had not remarried, though his wife was thirty-two years dead. He ate cottage cheese and shrimp and raisins with gusto; he drank quantities of Pabst. He had lost his left ear when a policeman slashed at him, from a horse and using a weighted club, in 1932. He had refused a plastic ear, and the stump was brown. He wrote letters frequently, and one awaited Nicholas; Nicholas read:

> Dear son. As usual I sleep better in the day time, and I enjoy writing in the calm of the night when I feel rested. Yesterday and today were fine days in New York City and I try to walk a little and then sit in the park for a couple of hours. Enjoying the sun rays and the sight of familiar faces which I have come to regard

as part of my family—although I share no bread with them and I do not share their opinions or way of life either. I felt bad to leave as Tuesday last when you called you said you may visit "mañana" and as I never put much faith in "mañana" nor do I hold anyone responsible for what "mañana" will bring, I stay out as usual and was back home at 5 pm when I began to expect again.

Summer is going and you perhaps are commencing to feel it and are anxious to keep moving to see what other older societies have to show for the right to survival in a world of goats who fear god but have no respect for his commandments when it comes to grab the land and all that grows on it too. And as other mortals do they go right back into the same earth to then feed those that are waiting to be fed, and perpetuate the destruction of all they think they keep for ever. Do not mind all this.

Peru. French Indo-China. Not the same faces but all comes to the same end. It is the poor everywhere that get the worst in war or peace. "Mañana" says Hoover in 1930. "Mañana," they promise today. But as rich as we are, so was England once and France and Egypt and the poor Chinese stopped us and so every little man and little country in the world will. One Fidel done a lot. There may be many more flowers growing. What will all the flowers be doing mañana?

Although I do not say it as well as you do, you know I like and miss you and expect a call. Received a letter from Andrea today. She is OK and tells me nothing of what she promised to tell me: OK.

Nicholas could not remember the last drinkless day and had written his election board for an absentee ballot; he had the notion of departure and did, this one time, want to vote. He had known a Kennedy cousin, and had done volunteer fund-raising in 1960; he had amassed, in four nights' work, eight hundred thirteen dollars and eighty-five cents. "Not bad," his wife acknowledged. "Maybe you should solicit for us."

They had bought the farm with Simon's legacy and from an advertisement he saw in the *Saturday Review*. Barbara had encouraged him and was enthusiastic; he had been dissatisfied with life in New Rochelle. Closure had been two weeks previous. He had asked Jean to marry him, thirteen years before, and she had refused; she was working for *Variety* and wanted a career. It was noon and 84 degrees; he showered and drove to New York.

Jean had trouble with her knees and was overweight and thought of herself as an actress manqué; she played occasional parts in revivals and knew the Second City coterie. She still loved Nicholas, she said, and she was electric to him still. They had met three times in New York, once, by accident, in Boston, and once in New Orleans. They shared, he knew, nostalgia and disdain; they coupled clumsily, in the Sheraton or Sherry-Netherland. He had ordered pâté and champagne for their first reunion; he had not remembered that she disliked pâté. She had had, since her marriage, a series of affairs. "I was always looking for you," she said, "or for someone like you. In the end."

She wore a hairpiece, and he unpinned it carefully; he finished the pâté and wanted to lick the pot rim. He rubbed her back and neck and said, "Tell me about your kids. Tim and Dan. Timmy and Dan. Which one is older?" he asked.

They had written infrequently, exchanging photographs of children and news of houses and health. She lived in Chicago and was married to Hal Burling; he described himself as "in fragrances" and was a vice-president in charge of sales; he made, before taxes and with fringe benefits included, forty-two thousand, five hundred dollars a year. Jean had two sons and a three-story house on Pine Grove Avenue and was, she wrote him, not content. Working with the Second City made some difference, she wrote, and so did the chance to salvage dunes in Indiana, and they liked Ravinia and kept a boat on the lake. Hal said "cuming aboot" when he tacked and swore by Whiskey Sour Mix, and they sent their children to the Francis Parker School.

He reached La Guardia with time to spare, because of the time lapse from Chicago to New York, and he made a reservation at the Sherry-Netherland. She kept cats in Chicago, and a parakeet. She brought a sizable suitcase, and he remembered anger at the time she took to pack. They had argued, often, as to clothes and Lenin and the nature of fidelity; Jean thought herself a legatee of the I.W.W. She smoked a ladies' pipe. Hal Burling hated cigarettes, and she had chain-smoked Gauloises, and this was a compromise. She had tried, repeatedly, to give up cigarette smoking, but she called it an addiction and could not resist.

"In Soviet usage," Nicholas said, "the noun for compromise is invariably associated with the adjective for putrid."

He loved the physical bravado in her, and the energy. She had walked in rains that wilted him, and through thick bush-clusters that tore. She liked the snow and skiing and was adept with animals; she called him "city boy." She had persuaded him to rent a farm in Peterboro and then had left him there. "Yes, Miss Mayflower," he said. "Yes, Miss D.A.R."

She had no fear of heights nor of the Atlantic in April and was, he had asserted, bred to insouciance.

"Society," he said, "has made it clear. You're guaranteed. They'll take your signature from Cedar Rapids to Chicago, and no questions asked. That's what we call inflation or insurance or just upper middle class."

Jean wore a dirndl, and he found that funny, and her hair had darkened. "If you fall you do so on a trampoline," he had said. She had planned the trip, she said, to visit with her mother.

"Let's do that right away," she kissed him. "Let's drive on out there now. Then I can call Hal tomorrow and tell him that I've done it and we'll have the whole time clear."

Her mother had Parkinson's, badly, but was under supervision and had registered improvement; she had regained the use of her left hand. They drove to the nursing home in Forest Hills, and he wheeled Jean's mother down the gravel walks. Jean walked in front of him, discussing the weather and children and the boat; her mother had a patent leather handbag and pink heels. Nicholas attempted to distinguish spruce from pine and thought about the chance that love might outlast lust. He was not tempted by the secretaries in his office, nor the student-teachers in his daughter's school; he had not had affairs. It was, he knew, his own youth he pursued in her, not someone's surrogate, and he was weary, largely, of the memory of youth.

Grateful that the Sherry-Netherland did not have mirrors by the bed, he buried his face in her breasts. It was absurd— he lathered them—and they had grown flaccid and he shut his eyes and licked.

"Darling," she said, "darling, Nicky, I've missed you so much."

She had called him Nicholas before. He thought of the farm and the setter he wanted and the blue mexican tile he had installed. He had lined the kitchen counter and the upstairs bedroom walls. He thought of his wife's dressing table and the horsehair pillow she preferred, and he anticipated cocoa with his daughter Eve on thursday morning at ten. She would have quartered oranges and he had to fix the washer on the sink; he pictured the slow leak. It had discolored the enamel and diminished the hot water pressure; Eve would feed her dolls the orange peel. All was ordered, accurate; he would wash the car. He had a one-step cleaner wax and chamois and a brush for chrome. He had eighteen thousand miles on the car and not a single scratch. Michael, not grumbling, would help.

Jean moved beneath him, muttered, "Love" and he scratched his ankle with his instep; he had a spider's bite. This ridiculous matron, his darling, this collection of pustules—would he sacrifice, he asked himself, all he had fashioned for this? Jean repeated, "Love" and she rolled her eyes back so that he could only see the whites. He wondered if she practiced and what she saw there, in the socket's arch.

His dog stalked flies, and snapped, and missed; he envisioned the presence of God. No rationale he offered could explain such leaves; his eyes itched from the goldenrod; he sneezed. He watched a hawk wheel, plummet after sparrows, miss and fight to regain height, the sparrows scattering. Nicholas knew no theology, and knew, of the Koran, only this phrase—that dead warriors disport with "maidens with swelling breasts the same age as themselves."

Jean was amiable when he woke; she told him of a cider vat they had installed, on Pine Grove Avenue, as an auxiliary tub.

"Mayor Daley *is* a pig," she said. "That's an expression we have. You know, you look at that man and you do understand the expression. Hal hates to drive through the South Side; he wants to join the Tavern Club. Good God."

Nicholas had been to Chicago and had been invited to the Tavern Club for dinner and had thought it a pleasant place, with a remarkable view.

"And he'll grow up to be president," Jean said. "Of the Tavern Club, I mean. And the whole thing is impossible."

"What thing?" he asked.

"Fragrances," she answered, "that cider vat. Our life."

"Don't be melodramatic." Nicholas considered a shower. "You're being melodramatic." He indicated her breasts. "You're the American Dream."

They went to El Morocco at midnight and Nicholas felt dapper and attempted to participate in several versions of the twist. They drank Singapore Slings and ate prosciutto and melon and he wished he were not prone to sweat and that he were thirty pounds lighter; she dipped her napkin in water and touched his ears, nose, neck. Jean read poetry with fervor and knew the editorial staff of *Poetry* magazine. She knew Williams, Service, Duncan, Creeley, and intimated that she slept with Ferlinghetti once. He had remembered her prideful, and unwilling to be pushed, and her great need had been for independence, once. Now she was the rancid leavings, merely, of that hope; she drank three glasses quickly and was drunk.

"Why it is," she asked him, "you waited; what did you wait for, really? When I said no that time. In Trastevere. I work with the S.C.L.C. Hal hates my doing that."

The maître d'hôtel offered a rose; Jean giggled and accepted it. "He wouldn't have waited," she said.

He had never loved the strength in her as now he loved this weakness; self-pity transmuted to pity and Nicholas was moved. It was July twenty-eighth, and the city on a "pollution alert." Echoes bleated in his brain of all he had professed to her, and all he had hoped to accomplish; he paid and they walked west and he fashioned cardboard kites from a discarded packing case. They passed the Seagram Building, and his own failed structures splintered, or were at best maquettes.

"That isn't where the action is," he defended himself, "that's not it at all. I just can't get excited by a solitary building—even if it's Mies or Le Corbu. After all, Marseilles is still a dying town. With a housing shortage." His father flung a crushed Pabst can at mice, and missed. "The stakes are higher now."

He reshaped the kite as glider and sailed it at a traffic light. "You've got to play for keeps. It's that way with environment; just play for keeps or don't play."

"Can you still do the split?" Jean asked.

"What?"

"The split, you know, the split. All those tumbling tricks. The way you stood on your elbow that time. Full lotus or whatever. You know, those acrobat tricks."

He was attempting to fashion a blimp; he looked up to find her weeping and was, again, engulfed. Why did, he asked himself, compassion supersede respect, and why should it prove so much the more powerful? He kissed her, several times; he dropped the cardboard blimp.

Jean blubbered; her eyeliner ran. "Remember how we danced? And when we rowed the Boston Whaler all the way through that lagoon? Because you cut the engine, refusing to pollute it? Hal is an excellent sailor, you know. He wants a catamaran. I want you."

"My darling," he said, "just don't cry."

"I'm not really crying," she cried, "or only out of happiness. That great blue heron, those terns. I want your next thirty years. You've got that many; I want them."

Park Avenue was clear. It had rained, then stopped, and the avenue was washed; he looked north at the mirrored lights and watched the green lights shift.

"Let's drive," he said, "to the farm."

"Surely," she said, "anywhere out of this world. *N'importe où*. What farm?"

"Mine. The pig farm built and operated by H. F. Rensselaer in the late eighteenth century. Home. Home of the eighteen gables. With its series of slop bowls for toilets and its skeletal pigs in the closet and a garden full of thistles and turnips and owl-nests in the flue." He felt venturesome. "My wife," he said, "and children are away." He heard the red lights hum. "You are, were, will be my wife. I'll leave that farm for you, perhaps. I want you to see it tonight."

"Darling," she said. "Darling, darling, are you certain? Aren't you tired?"

"Yes. Yes, I'm certain."

They left their bags at the hotel and went directly to the garage; Nicholas took down the top and took off his tie and it was, the radio announced, 73 degrees. He turned east and got on the East Side Drive at Sixty-third Street and took the bridge to the Deegan and was on the New York State Thruway and settled back to drive. It was three fifteen, and he shared the passing lane with trucks. Jean fell asleep near Harriman, and he turned the volume down and smoked a cigar, sobering. He had bought the farm with his wife and she was raveled in it past the chance of disengagement; he would be, he knew, the one to quit. He considered Europe and the West Coast and the Caribbean and whether to request divorce or, simply, separate. The firm had asked him to work in Lima; he resisted it, he had told them, for the children's sake. Jean wakened south of Albany and he wondered if the children had not been excuse and whether he could bear Peru and why a thirty-five-year-old woman in the Social Register should wear a knee-length dress. She woke, glazed, saw him without recognition, then surfaced and was beautiful and undid his zipper and put her mouth on him. "Hey, Jack, keep your eyes on the road," she said, "just keep in the middle lane; this is breakfast." He reached a climax at the turn for the Northway and paid the toll erect; they turned again at Saratoga, and he drove through dawn-sun, a rising dew and Schuylerville; the stopped for gas and to watch cows and they reached the farm at six forty-eight.

"My god," she said, "it's lovely, oh my god."

"Not much, but we do call it home."

He was enormously proud of the whole, and flourished her through the front door; a pair of purple tights hung from the staircase rail. The house was of red brick with four fireplaces and random-width oak floors; it had been restored with care and had, in the front windows, eighteen original panes. There were Norfolk latches on the door, and a marble entrance step. Jean stood in the center hall and stretched.

"Show me the kitchen; I'll make some coffee. You look exhausted, love."

"Ain't gwine to see the nether side o'sixty," he intoned. "Tell in me bones there's a rainstorm coming from up to Savannah. Kitchen's back yon by the pots."

She put water on to boil, and he registered the leak again.

"The packing's shot," he said. "I've got to fix the packing on the sink."

"Hal believes," said Jean, "that J. Edgar Hoover is God. And that whoever murdered Kennedy—though he wouldn't say this—wasn't all that wrong."

Nicholas selected his favorite tin cup; it was blue, and chipped.

"And that Mao Tse-tung," Jean said, "is in league with the martians and Arthur Miller, and that perfume helps."

Nicholas imagined the apocalypse and was, obscurely, relieved. Were this country to collapse, his own might not be noticed; how to extend, he wondered, his four-week vacation to six?

"Will you really leave them?" Jean asked.

"Who?"

"Them. Your wife, your daughter, your son. This." Jean waved her hand at the wall.

"I bought it, I can sell it." He twisted the hot water tap.

"Yes, but them."

"The real estate market goes up. That's one thing you can count on, even if it's hard to find a buyer. Short of a full-scale depression, this land does nothing but appreciate. It's the only investment I have."

"You're not answering."

"Answering. Answering what?"

"I asked," said Jean, "whether you do want to leave."

"What's in it for me?" he asked. "What's your per annum take? Out of that trust fund, me-love."

"Three thousand eight hundred dollars after taxes," she said, "not enough. I'm no heiress and you're forty-one and this isn't all that funny and you ought to answer me."

Nicholas turned the stove off. The gas puckered and popped; beads of water coalesced on the pot's rim.

"Forty," he said. "I don't know. I'm just not certain. Yet."

He walked to her, unbuttoning his shirt. He took her by the hand and led her to the downstairs bedroom and turned the radio on.

"What's your opinion," he asked, "and what's the prognosis?"

He pushed her to the bed, and knelt, and lifted off her shoes.

"What's the diagnosis, nurse, and what would you recommend? Whatever shall we do? I've got an idea," he said.

He fell upon her then, and she resisted him. "This is the guest room," he said. "*Mi casa su casa*. Welcome. Welcome, my darling, to Rome."

In the back of his brain, a puppet was having hysterics; his daughter came, and cheered, wearing her purple tights. There was nothing, he announced, he would not foul nor could.

Jean was sour and yielding and manipulated him and he was not romantic but was purposeful. He would take her to Lima, soon, and they would grow incompetent, toothless together, rocking on some hacienda's front porch.

"I drink rum anyway," he articulated, and she said, "I love you very much."

He made love with alarm, and then abandon, and then a slow surrendering he would not know again. He heard sheep and they walked to the pond and lay beneath a willow tree and he gathered blueberries and Queen Anne's Lace for her. He thought of mayans hauling ice to some stone temple in the Yucatan. They used a block and tackle system and, by the time the ice was elevated to the pyramid's top stone, it had melted utterly, was air. Nicholas guided the tow-line and had the Coca-Cola concession and ordered Coca-Colas for every workman there; they called him "*Tuan*" and "*papaito*" and he was content. His hammock was in a malarial swamp and his daughter had mosquito netting and they slept as though in shrouds; the men rode bicycles and hunted jaguar and the women wore mosquito netting on their breasts. Michael was reconciled, and they offered up, in consequence, a suckling pig. Nicholas could broad jump farther than any of the mayans, a slight people, could. The winch sliced ice and twined to itself and he did accept the job in Lima and was glad.

When, after an hour, they finished, he went to the kitchen for coffee and undertook to measure out six spoons. He did this with precision, standing naked, having set the water back to boil. At the fourth spoon measured, he noticed the sun; it illuminated the rim of the pot, and the grounds were of exactly that umber he had used as poster paint when six. Though color-blind with blues and greens, he could distinguish brown. Nicholas knew, and knew absolutely, he would never be that happy, in that way, again. His work was going well; he still could profess a political conscience; he sucked in, and could, his stomach; he had made successful love, and had achieved three orgasms since dawn; he was surrounded by possessions and they pleased him mightily; he felt the instant stretch. It encompassed past, present and the future with no diminution at all. He heard Iago's drinking song on the radio; he finished with the coffee, then fitted the rim on the can, then replaced it on the shelf. Jean was humming Puccini, and he noticed that; she offered him a cigarette, and said, "You look well enough pleased."

"I am," he said, "I am," and declined the cigarette and kissed her on the ear.

"As punch," she said. "Me too."

"It isn't all that easy," Nicholas said. "Give me time."

"I know, I know," she said, "I really do. And I don't mind playing games. It's just we have to know the rules, that's all."

"So you do think of this as a game?"

"I didn't say that. And don't. And it isn't a whole lot of fun. I prefer tennis, or suicide, or bridge."

"It's a game we're used to playing," he said, "with each other, anyhow. I sometimes wonder what would happen if we took it seriously. All of this," he lifted his head to the room, saluting the far wall, "might be illusion, really, and ourselves the only truth."

"Is that a fact," she mocked him, "is that an actual fact? Red and yellow are real, blue an illusion shared by all mankind. Except the color-blind: disprove."

"I could find you four-leaf clovers if we went outside," he said.

"Yes."

"Shall we go for a walk, then?"

"Yes."

He reached for his shirt.

"Soon. I'd prefer it a whole lot," she said, "if this were not a game."

"I'll get the coffee," Nicholas said. "It must be ready now."

"You know," she said, "I'll be a little maudlin now. Think of it. We've shared how many thousand cups of coffee, ten? And I'll bet you can't remember if I like it with or without milk, and how many spoons of sugar."

"You prefer cream," he said, "and salt."

"It doesn't matter," Jean answered. "Milk. Because I can't remember yours."

"Which doesn't matter either," and he returned to the bed. "That's the point; you're not the sort of habit I can make or break."

"Darling," she said, "Nicholas. It's as if you're the current I've been swimming against all my life. I know I'm being maudlin but that's just the way I feel. You can't finish love just like that."

He switched the radio off.

"I want so much," Jean said, "to let myself drift with you instead, just once, just now. Or like a fish with your hook in me, swimming away, playing out."

He smelled the coffee, moved for it again.

"I'm all played out," she said, "I simply don't want games."

He had been married at the Mark Hopkins and, for a wedding trip, had stayed in St. John for three weeks. They had gone scuba diving, stayed at Caneel Bay, and rented a jeep. He bounced along mule-tracks and negotiated beaches and dreamed of Jean consistently; she had been very ill in his dream. He had visited the hospital, and she did not speak to him, and another man sat at the bed's base, though elongated, stroking her feet. The room was white, and cool, and when he opened eyes to see his wife beside him he was not relieved.

"I love this place," he said. "I'll miss it very much."

"Yes."

"We're not young," he said. "I'm bald, I'm fat."

"We would be poor. What sort of a place is Peru?"

"We'd miss them very much."

"Not really," Jean said. "What is this, a *catalogue raisonné?* A series of reasons to stop. Half of them aren't true, the other half don't matter, and you're being sentimental too. It makes you look monkish, that spot."

"Some monk."

"Okay, let's go for that walk."

"Sometimes I do have the feeling," he said, "that these are, each of them, only roles assumed. That I could be on a street corner in Madras next week, with a cowl and begging bowl, and that would still be Nicholas but bear no relation to this."

They removed and drank the coffee, went out of the kitchen and up.

"How much of this land do you own?" Jean asked.

"Fur as the eye can see. And got me air rights three mile up," he said. "I's gwine ter take a shotgun to them fences, wait and see. The only good neighbor," he drawled, "the oniest good neighbor ain't been born."

They climbed the hill, attempting to distinguish timothy from weed, and which was once alfalfa; the walk, snaking around the barn to the hill's crest, took eleven minutes. He balanced, precariously, on a wall that might shelter snakes; she noted a woodpecker, and one dead elm. His studio had been a hay and milk shed once, and the wood maintained a sweet, rubbed, rotting smell. It had been converted, sometime since, into a semi-insulated stall. Nicholas had neither running water nor electricity there, but a long pine plank for desk, and army surplus cot, and a photograph of Everest, and books. The door hitched to with rope. The floor was poured concrete, four inches thick at the front of the hut and one inch thick at the rear, to accommodate the hill. Nicholas kept pencils on his drawing board, and a compass and straight-edge. He had one bentwood chair, and pillow, and a sleeping bag unrolled upon the cot. He imagined snowstorms and himself surviving on melted snow and splinters, from which he extracted the juice. From the southwest window he could see the Hudson Valley; his pencils were each blunt.

Nicholas had been designing pre-fab units, and he had completed five hundred units in Franconia. He had a passion for bridges and wanted to build one before he retired; he dreamed of spanning the Amazon, or Ganges, or the Nile. He read *The New York Times* with care, and he played poker, without fail, on Thursday night. His children resembled their mother and were, he sometimes complained, non-paying guests in his house. He contributed liberally to the S.C.L.C. He disliked mosquitoes and had an acute allergenic response to duck-eggs; he broke out in fever and hives and, once, lost consciousness. He had eaten mayonnaise specially prepared with duck eggs and might, the doctors told him, but for the Isuprel he carried, not have lived. He did not fear mortality but had a fear of maiming, or decline; he loved Jean very much.

"How long have you lived here?" she asked.

"I used to travel in the summer. You know. Just two weeks."

"But it really does seem home."

"It really is," he said. "I knew that the very first day."

"How is your father?" she asked.

"Endless." Nicholas grinned. "Interminable. Fine. He'll be glad I saw you and would want to send regards."

"Yes. Are all those teeth still his? I remember how proud

he used to be of that; 'No silver fillings,' he would say, 'nothing the lightning would want.' "

" 'Compuesta, no hay mujer fea,' " Nicholas intoned. "Made up, no woman is ugly. He called you a fine piece of ass. I believe the phrase was 'figure of a woman,' but it comes out to the same."

His father led the charge, howling "Venceremos." Nicholas was hot and surveyed his domain and was the enemy; should the setter, he wondered, be English or Irish. He knew it should be male.

Jean brushed burrs and pleaded with him: "Listen. You're not listening. I have to have some sort of hope that you mean this. Please."

He wondered if indifference could also be reprisal, and how much of this was retribution merely. He had written poetry when an adolescent, but lost it, and was not tempted to continue; he had misplaced his chemistry books also, and at the time that mattered more. For three years he took chemistry and physics and biology and kept a series of notebooks with telephone numbers and box scores and cartoon doodles. He liked "Little Orphan Annie" and copied the sketch style. He was attentive to his family and cared and provided for them and knew his love reciprocal—yet they remained discrete. Something in a woman's sense of occupation had baffled him always, and would. He knew the space Jean filled but not its boundary; she might shuck, he thought, the habit of him like skin.

"I was born," he answered, "two blocks from the Concourse. Catty-corner to the Nedicks there. My mother did believe in paper bags."

"And mine in sphagnum moss instead of Tampax; listen, you're not listening. I don't want to lose you, love."

Spiders had masked a groundhog's hole; the mesh was wet

beneath the long grass, and opaque. He laid two sticks across it gently, and it held. Nicholas told his joke that ended, "I like apples too. Let's fuck."

He was weary, having had no sleep that night, and it was nearly Monday afternoon, and he very much wanted to swim. He had an army-surplus raft and inflated it by mouth; they floated down the Battenkill, warding off rocks with his paddle, making a slow progress, noting trout. They swam above the tissue mill; the river was not deep, but fast. He balanced the raft on a rock and swam against the current; he wanted to avoid the white sludge-slicks downstream.

Jean wore his wife's bathing suit, and it was a little tight, and neither mentioned that. He made her keep her knees up so they would not crack on rocks. Leaves eddied past and, when he found the current, kept at his paddle's side; he stayed abreast of one piece of planking marked SCHLITZ. They shipped water badly and he watched his stomach bulge and watched the welts on her back.

"This is a survival raft," he said.

"Some survivors. The halt and the blind. Hal has a better boat."

"Yes, and will be president of the Tavern Club. And you go to Ravinia, of course."

"Of course."

"You have season tickets, probably, and probably a box. Mayor Daley must be pleased with that."

"You have a wife," she turned to him.

"And children."

"And no real intention of leaving. I have a husband," Jean said, "who has a box at Ravinia, and a better boat than this."

"And sons." He studied her back.

"And sons."

"Watch for that log," he cautioned. "Starboard and sharply, mate."

He fended them off; the log bowed, straightened, and he asked, "How much farther do you want to go? We'll have to walk back to the car."

"How about that bridge," she said. "Why don't we stop under there?"

He recollected saying once, as parody, "I'm not as young as I was," or "in my great old age."

He steered them to the bank and nosed along it, hunting for purchase; the ferns were high, and bushes thick, and the mud substantial. He held to the bridge pilings; the near birds exploded, complaining, and kingfishers hurtled past. Michael had brown hair and a scurrying quickness at tag and had just turned nine. Mr. Beck had promised, Barbara said, to play tennis with him twice. They had traveled half a mile at most, and Nicholas could smell the tissue mill. Bees swarmed about the stump above them, and he was not happy nor redeemed.

"Know what this raft is called?" he asked. "George, that's what I call it. George Raft."

He would drive her, he was certain, to New York or Albany —if he could persuade her that the bus from Albany made sense. He would promise, he was certain, to decide within the week. He would not do so, weary of partings, weary of decisions that were contravened by need, sick of the illusion he had mustered as security that what he needed mattered, and would be truly manifest in action and in speech, and would be consequential. "If the great wall be not in the hearts of the people," he recited, "how long, though built, may it stand?" They would meet again, perhaps, in Taos on the twenty-third, and contrive a kind of lust out of nostalgia, habit, secrecy and the sense of shared escape, that furtive assault on the future which could only burlesque the past. His paddle caught on weeds; he would sleep and be all right by Wednesday and would write his father that the fight was being fought. Shame beleaguered him, then, and he pulled the raft up to the shore and unplugged the air-plugs and commenced to deflate it by pushing; he would drive her to the city, after all. He would collect his bag and maintain decorum and maybe, he decided, copulate one last time at the Sherry-Netherland. He would have to pay for the room nonetheless, then drive her to the airport and return; he stepped on the raft to force air out more quickly, and handed her the paddles and rolled the raft in on itself.

IX

AUGUST 15

Breakdowns. When I held her, she sitting in the corner, making those animal noises, hearing people only as animals. You were an elephant, maybe, or something gentled, lamb-like, but I was her giraffe. Who spoke straight through the neck. With those murder-dreams. And I taught her how to walk again and how to go to the toilet and how to stand and even, after four days, how to dance. We shuffled back and forth across that living room, must have logged one hundred miles one week. She didn't sleep for any of it, then took to sleeping eighteen hours per day. (Render this dramatically?) Her strong sense of being a bird. Able to fly when we danced; building a nest out of chairs, pillows, clothes. And a little bit of wine would calm her and chanting, Devils, go away devils, and sometimes it would help to rock. And all she ate was macaroni, this without the cutlery. And she wept incessantly, but was dry by the third day. *(Please don't ever write me another letter like that! Ever! Never! My hands are shaking so it's hard for me to write this. Hard anyway. Listen. I do not have any other man. Listen, I'm in limbo here. And if you ever write me another letter like the one I just received I'll go crazy. It's that simple. It's not an easy thing but I know it's useful, even necessary, and that we won't destroy everything of ourselves. Am I asking too much? Two weeks in another town? Will we really lose each other; do you really think that? Do you believe that? Do you really think love drifts away, snap and it's over. Snap snap snap. Shit. Shit. Don't ever write me like that again. We'll get over this molehill mountain. Really. You've frightened me badly; forgive.)* So then we'd hum to ourselves and I taught her how to breathe and soon she could touch me again, not easily but without flinching, so that we'd hold hands and dance across the living room, gravely—I put the phonograph on automatic repeat, and we played "Down in the Valley" over and over again. What is this book but record: the motion circular, the pattern spiral, and therefore the needle transcribes a straight line. She'd sleep with gloves on, and she asked me to tie her hands down. She didn't sleep; she lay there, dribbling spittle, staring at the rabbit shapes I made on walls. Once I achieved an antelope, and she applauded and maintained the applause for three minutes. I repaired the television set and she watched that with fixity and went for a walk with me after the third week.

AUGUST 16

The church the Germans bombed. The man at the hotel desk having learned English in Liverpool, and that overriding his Italian accent. The third gray day; the amphitheater pinched by houses; where are we now, in Taormina, eating *dentice*, the toothed fish, says Giuseppe, accent on the ultimate, very, how do you say in this language, sweet. *Mein gott* but I am old, says he, adjusting the tilt of his hat. He once brought bread to D.H. Lawrence and the Signora Lawrence offered chocolates, and his grandfather went with the writer up Etna for five days. Today a long walk to Castelmola and an abandoned Saracen castle and a picnic and balancing acts while I speared wine with cacti; Americans, said Giuseppe, are an excellent people when sleeping.

AUGUST 17

Gertrude Esmond. Owns the Casa Esmond and a garden behind with ducks and goats and a pool built to reflect Mount Etna. But the Italians strung electric lights between, so now she gets a mirror image of the electric power pole. Inherited the whole in 1948 and came to Taormina to dispose of the estate and has not left, with the exception of Augusts, since. Passed two previous years in the States. With two hundred dollars only, and labored in forty-six of the then forty-eight states. Cats range about me, starving, and this locale not yet fleshed out, and within the next weeks I could leave. The Casa Esmond occupied three times—by Germans who were very correct, since the Sicilians were. Only one officer put a single bullet through one picture while drunk. And apologized. By the Italians (who left it disarrayed but clean) and by the English (who left it neat but filthy). Prior to each occupation, and at night, the "little people" (as she called them, but with no trace of condescension) took each of the treasures and hid them. Priceless, lovely things. Rugs, icons, chairs. Apologizing for the broken vase, and for the fact that her uncle's car had been burned. Having attempted to drive it into the peasant's hut for safety. She Harry's legatee; I signed his last will and testament at noon. Four houses provided for Gertrude, love and kisses to the world. (*And I think of this bitter weather and the farm wrapped in silence and the lack of life. Darling I love you and I don't know what to say. I cannot this moment return, and what of the legal process, and I'm beating on my brains for the final answer. It will come. Don't think that severance is endless, please, do not think that.*)

AUGUST 18

She took to drawing, to assuring me we would inherit vast sums from her foster uncle; she played the violin. She displayed her pastel-stains with care. She laid her right wrist on the pad and flapped it, exchanging the pastel when worn, and moving from the top left hand corner of the page. She neither reached nor tried for circularity—she would angle along with the page-edge— and, by the fifth crayon, would quit. She tacked the sheets to the mantel, then crumpled and burned them; on the fifth day, I emptied the fireplace ash. (*Sometimes I think I should set myself out on an island and gnaw my own heart and mind until the pain draws an answer as bites draw blood. But that would be unreal— and this, for all the tinsel and foil of it—is real. Perhaps I should counsel you to continue, to implement divorce. I too wish we had the same balance, the same acceptance, needs. And in many ways we did. We do. But this—this floating aloneness of mine—call it desertion, if you like—is very necessary and sad. Whatever the*

consequences. Let's not consider consequences. We're
survivors, you said, we survive.) The only art which
permits of more brazen and persistent lying than politics
is fiction. Is maturity the art of making snap judgments
or of not making them? This endless protestation, love,
it's a word we should cancel. I shall leave for Istanbul
and maybe Teheran. Gathering myself for charity and
comfort, who have very little to spare. Does "misery
loves company" mean that of other misery—or of the
joyous, that it may corrupt?

AUGUST 19

Further penmanship anecdotes. September 1, 1841.
"A clergyman in Massachusetts, more than a century
ago, addressed a letter to the General Court on some
subject of interest that was under discussion. The clerk
read the letter, in which there was this remarkable
sentence; 'I address you not as magistrates but as *Indian
devils.*' The clerk hesitated, and looked carefully and
said, 'Yes, he addressed you as *Indian devils.*' The
wrath of the honorable body was aroused, they passed
a vote of censure, and wrote to the reverend gentleman for an explanation; from which it appeared, that
he did not address them as magistrates, but as
individuals."

What else to report. The year uneventful, concluded, huge quantities of snow. I stained the floors
for Thanksgiving, myself twitching till dawn on them,
rubbing rags, elbows, knees. The silo a citadel of sorts,
the barn full with machines, and the hay long since
eaten, the chickens flatted with frost. Breast cancer is
an exceedingly rare disease in men. I'm growing weary
of data, do wish for stories to tell. Of men with
machine guns hanging from cliffs and nubile ladies

naked on the top. So, what sort of pattern; the house building up as the life topples down, the man imprisoned in plaster, the woman in wood. (*Here azaleas are pink and full all along the streets. I do dream sometimes in my knobby bed of those sweet mornings on the farm. Of my herbs and animals. And I always tell myself I'll have it soon again.*) L. said that, since her stepfather's death, her novel shall have to be rewritten —a kind of desperate effort to keep art one step behind. Shadowing life. And, as with Zeno's paradox, that halving doubles time through space; no sooner does it occur than the transubstantiation. From butterfly to chrysalid and back. This an interesting notion, the last line careening helplessly off into art. They lived happily ever after, they did not live happily ever after; they live, they did not. (*Darling we're too young to get tied up in knots. Improvisation is terrifying and sometimes disastrous, I know. But right now seems an exercise in sanity. I miss you very much.*)

AUGUST 20

Saratoga. The Washington Spa (with the Roosevelt shut for the winter, this November). Used to be upwards, said the masseur, of five thousand customers a day, even in off-season, now less than three, even at the season's height, and Diamond Jim Brady used to give ten bucks away for the hanging of his coat (so that I fish a second quarter out, and will take plastic ducks and boats back for the bath), that swirling mineral whirl, and oil, the only non-sulphur bath, he says, east of the Rockies, and the hot sheets, sleep, rattan furniture, tiled floor, a washstand and screen and sizable sink, the tub has three taps, with pull-cords for the attendants and grips for the dying, handholds on each

wall, and corpses stretched on new-made beds throughout. I have to leave, I have to go, I have to travel,
start. Though there's a weariness that comes of competence, and this the only time I've known or noticed
it—except perhaps when playing chess or Ping-Pong
with opponents I knew no challenge, the desperate
attempt to keep attention up. The furnace draw is
down to one which means the points need cleaning. Or
a dead owl in the pipe. There's a house in Washington
County, said the spider to the fly. Where we could
cover the second-best bed, be happy, you and I.

AUGUST 21

Yesterday a long, dispassionate fantasy as to attendance
at my funeral. The arrogance of the auto-didact, myself experiencing need for the sheer, mere interest in it.
Have disregarded the chance to join the cost-sharing
program for the pond; the house does distance itself.
And I ain't got no money no mo'. Called Henry Letterman. Asked for and received an extension and a lunch,
not in that order. Went to New York and the Museum
of Natural History and stood beneath the blue styro-
foam whale. Passed the exhibits of Alaska brown bear
and the musk-ox and a girl was dancing for her boy in
front of the moose. Jim insists, and not without justice,
that I'll have hell's own time telling the world of self,
that confession comes difficult now. Question: how
directly are these guises disguises, do they mean to
penetrate guard? Answer: I don't as yet know. With
the concomitant that it's much easier to write of
people when they're gone. Laid insulation down in the
attic; it makes a difference; I did some final spackling
in shirt-sleeves. The attic full of wasps. How can the
little, live things possibly survive this snow; what sort
of tracks were those around the elm?

(EDITOR'S NOTE: The following pagination refers to the typescript of *In the Middle Distance*.)

EDITOR: p. 54, line 9: Despite Patty's urgings to the contrary concerning not only my health but my exalted position in business and culture and life in general, I do eat turkey TV dinners and know very well that *my* brand (Swanson—the best, by the way, at least in the moderate price range) never have and hopefully never will contained (contain) yams. I question whether others do either (though it wouldn't surprise me—the Morton people, for instance, turn out the most execrable products). However, if you're writing here out of personal experience, then, by all means, leave the yams in. If you're just guessing, though, why not change "the yams were bad" to, maybe, "the sauce was sour."

AUTHOR: Hullo, Patty. Yes yr position is exalted; no I hain't never et no Thanksgiving preprepared Turkey. Come next november from Springfield to Greenwich. Springfield to Eagleville. Springfield to Cossayuna. Substitute "sauce" for "yams." "The sauce was bad."

EDITOR: p. 101, line 20: Question the presents of Hardy Boy books in 1965.

AUTHOR: Great literature undies. Stet. P. 148, line 6: add "and" after present, "past, present and the future. . ."

AUGUST 22

This January 17 and flying time and luncheon on the hopper and what else to report; the car installed sans battery, the five books read, locks locked. Loneliness

perhaps the rarest thing tasted since June. What sort of
sentence is that? (She was, of course, endlessly, cor-
ruscatingly beautiful. The necessary attribute of every
heroine. Illustrations follow. Perhaps the most beautiful woman he had ever seen. Not perhaps. Certainly.
Each of the formulaics apply; men turned in streets to
stare, crowds gathered where she sat. Generations read
of her, immortalized in prose. I wear the shirt she
bought me now; shopping for it, merely, she would
have been offered a discount, accosted by the clerk.
Those eyes, into which she measured yearly three
bottles of Visine. Framed with mascara (the color
changing with her dress but principally blue and
green), eye shadow, liner, enormous eyes. Fill in the
rest. I suppose what mattered, though, was a certain
sense of bearing, herself a careless container. Pitcher
hurtling at the well. Abandon-cum-restraint, some-
such. That heedless, wavering ease.) *(Oh my darling,*
New Year's Eve is morose without you; I've sworn
never to attempt it again; the price is too high. If we'd
been together we could have simply toasted each other
in bed—but this solitary celebration is miserable, as am
I without you. The joint was dry and lonely last
night, as am I without you. Refrain. The real pleasure
of the evening was my discovery of yr letter of the
28th, which had been misplaced. Someday I'll be in
charge of New Year's Eve again. We'll have an endless
champagne fountain and everyone we care for will
appear with bells on—no solitaries allowed. It will be
quite a fete; sometimes I think that you've become my
sanity. Perhaps we'll talk again today; I cannot wait.
I danced relentlessly but stayed away from the gray-
templed gents surrounding. Darling. Without you I
am lost.) Perhaps we should learn to write letters to
people in the next room, or a telephone away. Then

they would not deal so dully with distance, or take separation as text. He wakened with her eyes on him, and legs.

AUGUST 23

K. comes in to scream that I must take the purple pants. Because it's like getting my hair cut I don't care what she likes. It doesn't matter, she bellows, not to you. This will be a flight taken together, fingers curled back into fist. Let's attempt escape; where will we land first. In Rome. (He taped this brochure to the bathroom mirror, and stopped shaving. He copied the brochure. "The old building Galta Tower had stood in 6. century, 528 A.C. by Regio Sycaena, when the emperor Justinianus reigned the most beautiful city IS-TANBUL which is best-riding both Europe and Asia. The historian Theophanes in relating the attacks of the Islamic armies and fleet on Byzantium in 717 used the name Kastellion Ton Galatou for this tower. The armies of the 4. Crusode conquered this fortress called Tor de Galathas by Geoffrey de Villehardouin on 1203. . . . On 17 century the first Turkish flier Hezarfen Ahmet Celebi flew from the Galata Tower and landed in Üsküdar Dogancilar with the hand-Made wings attached to his arms. The tower is more than 140 mt. tall the weight height of the tower is 61 mt. . . . Till the 3th floor the tower is a Geneoese building from here to up was rebuild during the Turkish reign. That Galata Tower with his pointed cap and massive body's miniatures is just like the Jeroma Maurand's engraving, we proff that in the books named MENZIL-NAME and HÜNARNAME.") How long, J. asks, would those embossed wood doors last in the air of New York?

AUGUST 24

(Darling. This is too strange. I receive your letter, yesterday, dated the eighteenth.) I'm glad you found an apartment, liked the Coast. The croupier saying he didn't notice you bet your last pile on the black. *Hello to Annabelle. The name of the restaurant is, was La Colombe d'Or.* (Am left with this ash-taste, a rusting set of suitcase keys, and the inability to say "Love" with conviction. Something of a present. But nothing of a future.)

AUGUST 25

I thumb these old love letters, pressing on them to relocate pain; none of it rings true. The whole was a charade, and we were far too wordy for the gestures to come clear. This agglomerate of verbiage, being's insistent drone. All of this opaque and webbed with time; I can't remember Annabelle (Jennifer, J?) or any restaurant.

X

It had proved difficult, even with his agent's aid, even first class, to find a plane to Rome; the flights were booked days in advance. He settled for a flight that was four hours delayed and went via Madrid; the alternative flight was to Shannon. He would have had to change in London, and then, again, in Milan. Nicholas had walked, swinging his suitcase, the final mile to Idlewild; when he commenced to count, he passed two hundred and thirty-six cars. It was July third, 1952, would be the fourth in Rome, and he planned to say to Jean, "Happy Independence Day."

He sat next to a pediatrician who had just been to Denver and who praised it, saying, "A man could live there, I tell you. A man could breathe that stuff." Nicholas ordered three splits of Moët et Chandon, telling the stewardess, "We ought to celebrate. Release." She did not answer, and he toasted her. "Release." The flight proved uneventful; he tried to sleep and thought of Jean and smoked a cigar; his seatmate was displeased.

Jean loved baths with bath salts; she sent a mexican seed necklace to her cousin in Dubuque. She instructed her cousin not to open the package till Christmas and, when her cousin did so, worms escaped; Jean had sent the package north in June. "That girl," she said, "wipes the kitchen counter off with alcohol each night; Jesus, but she was upset. The maggots must have hatched."

Jean did fear fire, and was nervous when she smelled smoke, but she had few other fears and overcame them easily. Her eyes itched near cats.

Friends from Fieldston called him Nicky; at work, sometimes, he introduced himself as Niccolo; Jean had called him Nicholas throughout. He had an intermittent elegance and trouble with his teeth and studied *Architectural Forum* with care. He disliked his dentist and sweated profusely in the chair, but he wanted his teeth salvaged and the dentist was quite good. He had not seen Jean for six months and had, he thought, eradicated need. She telephoned, inviting him to Rome. "You can't just cut me off," she said, "like this. You can't just cut me off."

"Listen," Nicholas said, and calculated the time differential, and cost. "No one person ever leaves another. It's always reciprocal, see."

He wore a shirt she gave him, and a cufflink set, and tie. He thought of her knee and the scar there from surgery; he could have stared for decades at that waddling grace. In the early morning he requested an electric shaver from the stewardess; when he returned from the bathroom, she said, "You look so fresh."

Jean met him at the airport and he was, as always, taken by surprise; no amount of preparation seemed to still the shock. She was brown and enormous-eyed and a little drunk with waiting; he cradled her in his right arm; she led him to the car. She had learned Italian in the interim, and wore less makeup than he recollected, and thong sandals and a leather skirt.

"Happy Independence Day," he said.

Jean had bought a secondhand Fiat, and they drove to Ostia Antica, and then, slowly, getting lost, to her apartment in Trastevere. Three years previous, he had taught her to drive.

"You're not sad you came?" she asked.

"No. You've always been," he answered, "beauty incarnate for me. And I'm in the presence of beauty and that makes me very glad."

Nicholas was twenty-seven and had attended architecture school at Yale and was, when moved, theatrical.

"I love you very much," he said, "and can't be sad I came."

She had white wine waiting and took off his clothes with precision, fingering the tie. He wore a beige linen suit. They both had lost a deal of weight and were reticent about desire, and his suitcase was full of her things. He returned a camera and journal and traveling iron; he unwrapped bottles of perfume, and books.

"If they'd opened the bag up at customs," he laughed, "that would have been some scene. Architect travels disguised."

Nicholas had won citations that spring, and he stressed success. He had proposed to her, one year previous, and she had refused. They agreed a separation would clarify choice; secretive, he had withdrawn, yet it was an act of will. She loved him, she announced, and would forever, and would marry no one else, but she had to learn of independence first.

"It's a time-thing," she said, and they clicked glasses gravely. "To the past, the present."

He added, "And the future?" making that a question; he put his hand on her neck.

"*Salud, pesetas y amor.*"

"That's spanish," he said. "This is Rome."

"Yes, but we used to say it there. In Guanajuato, remember."

"*Salud y pesetas.*"

They drank. He remembered the road full of caves, a sudden rainstorm, pulque.

"You've been so wonderful," she said. "Your letters were so wonderful. And it's been harder than you think, hard to think of you. In all of our places, alone. Or, worse, with other people. Christ, but I've missed you so much."

Jean was twenty-three and worked for *Variety* and had secured an interview with Claude Rains that week. She came from Cedar Rapids where her father had been mayor, and his uncle before him; her parents were divorced. Her blouse had fourteen buttons; he undid them, numbering.

"I was terrified," she said. "There was a lump in my breast."

They kissed again; the church across the square sounded the hour. She said, "It does that all night. Welcome, my darling, to Rome."

Jean considered therapy and political involvement; her mother had supported Henry Wallace once. Her mother admired black men and had once met Jackie Robinson and thought him wonderful. Jean called Nicholas "careerist lackey" and he reminded her that she had attended Smith. She owned designer dresses and three gowns by Dior, but preferred flea-market clothes, or his. She played the accordion, badly, but he liked to listen to her practice, and she could silk-screen.

He put his hand inside her, fingering a diaphragm and felt, as she commenced to move, absolute betrayal. When did she insert it last, he wondered, and with whom? "You're shameless," he said, roused, "wearing that to the airport. I thought I'd come here to talk."

He did, and told her he loved her, and she, in twenty

minutes, achieved an orgasm. Strangely, the sex had not altered; he had expected either release or constraint. She was ease incarnate when dancing, or on a horse, or boat. She moved, however, as though by prescription in bed, and with each gesture mimed. They had lived together three years. They had traveled to the Caribbean, Norway, Nova Scotia and, twice, to Mexico.

"Fidelity." She toweled him. "It's in the orgasm now."

He cast about her body like a bloodhound sniffing spoor, hunting for his trail, and traces, and the time elapsed.

"It's laughable to think," he said, "there might be some way to apportion need. So that you could be, as you so prettily put it, both available to me and others."

He felt revelatory, eloquent, and he studied Chartres framed on the far wall.

"You can't know," he said, "how much I hoped for your call, how many times I dreamed of it. And rushed to the phone for those first weeks, assuming it still you." He considered doing penance, and the buttress system, and return. "Forgive; I've known for a long time this would happen; it's graceless to rail at it now."

They made repeated love that afternoon and showered and walked to the Tiber; it was opalescent, and he thought he saw a swan. Nicholas felt weary past sleeping, and a little drunk, and a breach seemed blasted in his resolve for control. The habits of endearment, broken by distance that spring, rushed redoubled back; her fingers were as tendrils to his arm.

"This is a love story," she said, "like a bad movie, or book."

Her bedroom had stained beams and a tile floor and faced directly west. That late afternoon, he closed the shutters, and the window; men gyrated beneath. They lay, eating cheese and tomatoes with olive oil and basil; in his arms, she wept. The room was a cocoon.

142

"Oh, darling, what can I tell you that you don't already know? I am lonely here, sometimes, and there is a bit of panic in this newfound strength. But I can't yet give anybody else my life. If I could at all, it would be yours forever; darling, can you see that?"

He could, and could not accept it; he had wanted to be intimate, raveled past distinguishing which ear or foot was which. He wanted to be yoked, to introduce a woman as "My wife." Promiscuous by circumstance, he had exalted fidelity, the notion of entities paired. He thought himself neither generous nor handsome, but did have a capacity for faith. He thought of New York, sometimes, as his private wilderness, and the women as temptation to belief. Nicholas stretched. He had lost virginity when sixteen, on the beach. He cultivated lust as the sham simulacrum of love; he exercised twice weekly at the New York A.C.

"You're looking very fit," she said, and put her mouth on him, "very, very fit."

He had to return in three days. They drove along the Appia Antica, and to Frascati, past women selling fruit. They circled statues, aqueducts, and decided not to see the catacombs. She showed him stars' villas and said, "I'll do a story there soon."

Jean had real skills and no dominant ability; Nicholas had one. All that he saw composed itself in space; structure held no mystery, made sense. In a concert hall he concentrated on acoustics, at the theater on sight-lines. He could lay brick and understood stress and could draw parallelepipeds in section; he wanted to build cities in the sea.

That night they had dinner with friends, and it was a festive meal, full of wine and humor and the sense of loss obliterated, all possibility pledged. Later he bought brandies at the Tre Scalini and, grinning at the fountain, said, "I've an announcement to make. Jean and I are getting married after all."

They cheered and toasted him and he added, "To other people. In the fall."

She put her hand on his thigh and, to ease them, said, "We've got to laugh, you see. Otherwise we lie back and bawl."

"Or ball," he said. "A convenient prospect, wouldn't you say? *Auguri*."

He slept fitfully and woke with bells for the dawn mass; she breathed with a low snuffling, turned away. He raised on his right elbow, bending above her, breathing in unison; he admired the line of her nose. It was his insistence, he decided, that had ordained refusal, and she would continue to withdraw. Of the fourteen women with whom he had been unfaithful to her, twelve had proved more gratifying, nor would he have asked her to wed him had he not known she would decline. Nicholas memorized license plates and telephone numbers without trouble, and he did keep count.

He had taken two weeks off and moved from New York to the farm. It was in Peterboro, a place he had rented one year since. They had shared it—for weekends and his summer vacation—six months. They replastered the downstairs and he painted it white, considering the bearing walls and which, were he the owner, he might remove. They dammed a brook and swam in the pond that it formed. Jean wanted to raise horses and he had promised her two; they tried organic gardening, and her baked loaves would not rise.

They used his office credit card to call friends all over the country and to wish them well. Nicholas felt, at night, sometimes, attempting to place Betelgeuse, that he could live contentedly with her in some henhouse. They foraged for mushrooms and envisioned a wine cellar and possible lake site; they spent days naked, drinking tea, and he felt regenerate, replete. He had a dog he greatly loved that died eating a beaver; the beaver had been poisoned and his dog died in great pain. Jean cooked with pleasure and attention; in Rome, she told him, she had been unable to cook. She had urged him—he was city-raised and -bred—to rent the farm. Nicholas built shelves and borrowed a chain saw and cleared some near deadwood; later, he would write her they had just been playing house.

"But we were serious," she said. "I mean it, I did mean to stay."

He had found her in the bathroom, wailing, "I've got more complexes than you can name. I'm fat and frightened and will probably regret you for the whole rest of my life. Just a kid from Cedar Rapids who's fucked up."

Often he caught that caged look in her, and the sense of boundaries despised. He did not wish to act as warden nor think of thirty rented acres as constraint. She was too young, she said, to feel her world so organized, even if the system pleased. She worked first as a stringer for *Variety* and then on staff. She was recognized at Sardi's, and this made her proud. The first months they met, she had described her other lovers with scorn; she said, "He makes pee-pee for love." Later, Nicholas would wonder how he fared in her catalog, and with what sort of charity she might describe him next. "You'll replace the sex," he said. "You'll supplant that easily, that's easiest." He stroked her knee. Yet she had been utterly faithful once his, and gave him no occasion for rage; he was jealous, nonetheless, and coveted life on the farm. He was ravened by suspicion that she might be unfaithful; they made love, often, in the barn, and he said to her, "You make masturbation obsolete."

Her two rooms served as sanctuary; he could not brook the Colosseum, or the Piazza di Spagna, or the Quirinale. The city teemed; men gestured obscenely; he found it hard to breathe. His second night, they drove to dinner by the sea. He ate the shrimp heads entirely, and she told him of a hepatitis scare in

Siracusa. She wore her hair up, and amethyst earrings he had given her, and he loved her very much and said so; she rested her foot in his groin.

She had taught him how to ski, and he related stories of Stowe that spring. They ordered strawberries and cheese and he took a bottle of brandy to the shore; they passed a railroad siding and a wayside chapel, and the sand was black. They both shucked shoes and Jean took off her stockings and they skirted the tide line. They swam, and he dried her by rubbing, and they copulated on his shirt, and he wondered why the sex had not been adequate before.

Elegiac, he told her of cello suites, coffee in his vacant house, and all he had hoped for erased. He listened to Dvorak frequently, and Bach, and Perry Como. When angry, in New York that spring, he had named her fat, failed, childish, and had indeed mustered contempt.

"That's nostalgia," she said. "That's a lie. You wouldn't really want me back. If I said yes now, you'd say no."

"Try me."

"Yes."

"Yes."

"No."

"You're right, of course," Nicholas said. "I came over here just to confirm. That you're impossible. That this is nonsense. That we love others, do already, and will live a long and happy life."

Maudlin with the need to claim rejection, he upended the bottle, then spat. That spring he had been argumentative, and violent twice, and frequently drunk. Yet he had felt in contact with some central part of himself, some sort of honesty long since lost. The nearest he could come to claiming need was counterfeit; he felt his suit there fraudulent, and was relieved she knew.

146

(Nicholas's sister, Andrea, was thirty-four years old. " 'I'm dirty,' said the immigrant," said Nicholas, " 'and my wife is dirty-two.' " Andrea's fiancé, Thomas, had been a violinist. He had been an excellent violinist and played with the NBC Orchestra and had volunteered for the Navy Band. He had soft blond hair and a beer belly and fingers that Nicholas admired very much. Thomas manicured them and ate gelatin for his nails; he filed his left nails down and let his right nails grow. "The top musicians all around here volunteered," he comforted Andrea. "They'll take good care of us." He had a special uniform without insignia and lyres for his buttons, signifying musician first class.

In order to perform as part of the band, however, Thomas had to learn a wind instrument. The bulk of his work was with the United States Navy String Quartet and the United States Navy Orchestra, but he also had to march in parades. For this he learned the oboe, though he was not good at it and sounded, he told Nicholas, like Donald Duck.

Nights, Thomas sat guard duty in the sail house. A room full of french cane was on his floor, and he whittled at cane ceaselessly, attempting to whittle an oboe reed. By eight o'clock in the morning, he would have a pile of shavings at his feet and, with luck, one acceptable reed. "Musicians all over the country," he told Andrea, "are crying for the stuff. And it's a government offense to sneak it out." He came to visit, often, sleeping on the floor of a troop train.

At one performance, the solo oboist was ill, and Thomas had to play two solo bars. He blew each note inaccurately and had no tone at all; after the performance, the conductor said, "Turn in your reeds."

"At this rate," Thomas wrote, "I'll end the war musician second class."

"The outfit is pretty comical," he wrote. "We were at some

147

general's funeral and the Marine color guard was too. We had to wait about three hours for the thing to start, and of course the Marine color guard stood at attention, and of course we sat around tying our shoes or tuning our instruments or playing cards. You know. And then some general of the Navy came up for review and let out a bellow, E-flat, you could hear all the way to the White House. So we've been confined to barracks for two weeks, and I can't come this weekend, and I miss you very much." Nicholas read to "Lover, when I think of you," and he wanted to turn the page and continue, but Andrea took the letter back.

Thomas was killed in the chartered band bus, driving to Fort Wayne. Thomas's parents called Andrea to commiserate. "He was killed in action," they said. "You mustn't forget that part of it. It was his kind of action, do you see?"

"No, I don't see," Andrea said, "I don't see."

"He would have had a great career," they said.

"They had his past," she told Nicholas later, "and I would have had his future. All of his babies," she said.

Andrea went to Mexico and solaced herself with rum and learned how to water-ski. She married Simon one year later, in 1942, and moved to Central Park West and was content.)

"The problem," Nicholas declaimed, "is this. Narcissus did know quantities about the beauty gig. You danced with me, beauty, as if on parade; you courted me for cameras; fuck off."

"Darling," she said, "darling, darling, let's not spoil it now."

"It's this parody," he said, "of a sex goddess. What kind of number is that? What isn't left to spoil? Just tell me what you want, exactly what charade."

She gestured, vaguely, at his shirt. She picked up his belt and tinkered with the buckle.

"Decency," she said.

148

And the sense of role assumed made them seem suddenly comic; they grinned, drank, and he sang "Come All Ye Fair and Tender Ladies."

"That's my theme song," he finished, "in a minor key. Hey, come on up and see my itchings; how ya fixed for blades?"

"Funny," Jean said, churning sand, "I'm not angry, or jealous; funny. Funny strange, I mean, not funny ha-ha. It mostly makes me sad. To think of you hating yourself, hurting yourself that way all spring. Not to mention them. The ladies, I mean, that you hurt."

"There ain't," he drawled, and was in Texas, "no itch, lady, you don't scratch. Pussel-gutted Calamity Jane."

He had loved, in her, unassailable distance, and attempted to obliterate it, failed. The songs he found himself choosing to sing each heralded departure, each denied reprieve.

" 'Two bordering, protective solitudes,' " she said. "That's Rilke. Also love."

"Listen, let's get back. They'll think we've run out on the check. I had hoped to grow together but we grew apart."

He built a wall, then flatted it with palms.

Jean liked making leek quiche, and they had a freezer, and once a month Jean had baked quantities of quiche. His apartment in New York was at Eighty-fourth Street and Riverside Drive. It was fitted with barred windows and a police lock, and the police lock jammed twice. He purchased shutters for the windows, and he refinished the floors. Jean was a careless housekeeper but had what she described as "cleaning fits." He would find her polishing the candlesticks or, once, at seven, with the hall floor half waxed. "Don't come in," she swore at him, "you'll muck it all up; don't." He threw the *New York Post* at her and jumped.

They went to Cedar Rapids for their final New Year's Eve. The mayor was distrustful, and Nicholas wore his Savile Row suit; he lied, claiming friendship with Frank Lloyd Wright and Harold Stassen and did know Grover Cleveland Alexander's lifetime E.R.A. He remembered Paul Waner well, and that also helped. They were given hats and horns and champagne in clear plastic disposable cups; at one, the mayor brought out snowshoes, and they lumbered through the garden, over snow. Nicholas attempted not to break the crust, and there was a full moon, and Jean challenged him to click heels. She was to leave in two weeks. He tried, and failed, and fell, and pulled her down with him; they lay, transcribing snow angels, and he pulled his paper horn out and unfurled it at the moon.

Rome was hot, and tourist-filled, and he wanted to buy her a necklace but did not. "Ancient Tuscan proverb," Nicholas declaimed. "He who rake the Trevi fountain in July own a Fiat in August. I'm going to buy," he told her, "a jeep soon. I've got the contract for a factory in Panama; come."

Jean admired Jennifer and called her a gypsy and said, "That's how I mean to live. Just picking up and going to London and looking for work. Not any kind of nine-to-five job, you do understand. I'll never forget you," she said. "I will always love you, you see."

"Then marry me, dumb-ass."

"And if I took a husband, it would certainly be you."

"Then marry me, dumb-ass."

She did not answer, and he entered her and stayed on his knees in the bed, and, for the third time, this time in earnest, proposed. She came and did not answer and he deflated, sweating, determining to leave. His chest hair had shed on her breast.

They ate a final supper, and Nicholas talked of parents, plans, and how he had let the farm's lease lapse. Her eyes were redrimmed, her nails unclean, and he felt like a survivor and said so, and his stomach was acid with wine. He wanted to go dancing and they hunted for a nightclub, but it commenced to rain and they were exhausted and went instead to bed; he slept on top of the sheets.

He dreamed of Guanajuato and picking his way through cactus on horseback, the cacti waving in wind. He followed streambeds that became the Vatican; he wakened Jean and said, "Make love to me. Please. Please."

She drove him to the airport and they lost their way again and he felt, purely, rage. He trembled, lit a cigar, stubbed it out; he buckled his shoe three times. They reached the airport and it was not busy; he checked in with time to spare and disliked the entrance hall, and they walked outside.

"I could meet you in Paris," Jean offered, "or Brussels, on the fifteenth."

"No. I'm no sort of yo-yo, strung out across the Atlantic. If I go now, that's that."

"If?"

"When. When I go now, that's that."

"You could come back, darling; if you wanted to, you could."

"Eight hundred and thirty-six dollars round trip," he said, "not to mention meals. That's an expensive lay."

She slapped him, and he her.

"It was worth it, though," he said, and emptied his pockets of lire. "Here, you keep the change."

Magnificently, she kissed him then, said, "Darling, let's not squabble or turn the whole thing foul."

They had argued once, as to the distinction between martyrdom and sacrifice; Jean maintained the former was insane. "What did Sebastian accomplish," she said, "except a painting in his honor? And a history of pillage, maybe, and that ain't sacrosanct."

Jean bought a Waring blender, and she drank quantities of

cocoa which she mixed in it with cinnamon, and she could identify trees.

"I'm sorry," he said, "I'm sorry. It's just that I did have such hope."

"Don't lose it; it can't be all gone."

"Yes. One doesn't take the same decision twice and not mean it one of the times. Good-bye, my love."

"It's not good-bye."

"It is," he smiled. "Eat a reality sandwich, as Knuckles Horwitz used to say. Fingers in my mouth."

"You won't get me to say that; it's simply not good-bye."

"Not farewell, perhaps, but fare forward, voyager. Christ, but we're urbane."

"I need you very much."

"Let's have a Campari," he said. "I've got this ridiculous lump in my throat. No worse than pollen fever was in May. But it's bad enough."

She clung to him, retaining: "It's not good-bye; you won't get me to say it. I love you very much."

(Andrea, married to Simon, became a practical nurse. She worked at Mount Sinai and then at Bellevue and studied to be a registered nurse. She had had, Nicholas assumed, affairs with doctors and had worn only garter belts with her white stockings. She would have slipped her skirt up and been naked, in the dispensary, at lunch. "How many bedpans did you empty since I saw you last?" Nicholas greeted his sister. "How many slops did you slop?" The doctors would be married also and brandish hypodermics at her and, operating, would whisper, "Nurse, forceps, sutures, let's screw."

When nineteen, he visited her at Bellevue, and the image shattered; she wore her hair up and was fat. She showed him the Intensive Care Unit. A man did smile at her, then shut his mouth—and Nicholas could see, through the man's closed lips, teeth. "We'll keep that date at Rockefeller Center," Andrea said, and plumped the man's pillow, "we've got some ice-skating to do." Leaving, she took her brother's arm and whispered, "He's got lupus. He'll be dead next week."

Simon and Andrea were to have two children, sons, Nicholas's nephews. One was called Abraham and one was David. Abraham would move to Tampa, Florida, and go into the junk-metal business; David would attend Haverford College and be a social worker in Philadelphia for three years. He also would marry a woman called Andrea, and they moved to Denver, Colorado, in 1961, and David worked as a salesman in an Indian Rug shop. Simon died in 1963. With his father's legacy, David bought a share in a dry-cleaning business with three branches in Aurora and one in Colorado Springs. Abraham was mafia, Nicholas thought, and brought his mother to Florida for six weeks each winter; she disliked it there, she said, but would depart aglow. Nicholas drove her to the airport; she streaked her hair and discussed her varicosity and asked if he also had varicose veins.

"Not that I know of," said Nicholas, "not yet."

"It's all those years of standing at the stove," she said, "or working in the hospital. You're lucky, sitting down."

"Who do you think will win?" he asked.

"What? The elections? Nixon."

"No," he said, "not again."

"Certainly," she said, "Nixon. Certainly."

He helped her with her single suitcase and she carried a satchelful of presents for Abraham's children. "Give my love to all of them," he said.

"I will," she promised. "You're kind to bring me here."

She bustled to the crosswalk and pressed the button for the pedestrian light. No single car was coming, but she waited for the green. There was a cold wind, and snow eddied at their feet. He shifted the suitcase from his right hand to his left and back again. "You've got eighty pounds," he said, "in this one case."

They crossed, and she went ahead of him and stepped on the rubber carpet for the Exit Only door. "The doors don't work," Andrea said, "nothing in this airport works." He hit the Entrance carpet, and the doors swung open. "Yes," he said, "things work." She checked her ticket and luggage and swallowed one Librium capsule. She kissed him good-bye, blue-haired, myopic, and spiraled to go; "Give my best to everyone," she said.

"I will," he promised. "I will."

Legions of the dispossessed would follow her, he knew. She maintained pen-pal correspondences; she adopted a child in Nepal. She took a special interest in tuberculosis patients; she went to synagogue sometimes; she liked bratwurst and mustard and sauerkraut and liked refried beans. She learned to drive, badly, but drove.

Simon, dying, had left Nicholas two thousand shares in his company. At the time the will was drawn up, eight years previous, one share in Simon's company had been worth forty cents. "I'm glad he thought of you," Andrea said. "That was a generous thing." In 1964, there was a two-for-one stock split, and Revlon purchased the company, and the shares were worth eighteen dollars apiece. "You've always been the lucky one," she said, "even in that recession. You've always been the sunshine child around here." He bought the property in Cossayuna and promised her that she could stay there whenever she wanted, and forever if she so wished. This generosity, he knew, was also counterfeit. He knew she would not wish to visit, hated the country, was terrified of cows and prowlers and poison ivy and cats.)

Nicholas drank two Camparis and soda, and they waited for his plane to be announced. Jean recognized John Thompson, and called to him, and they said hello. Nicholas felt murderous and squeezed his glass and John Thompson wore thong sandals—but John Thompson was polite.

"Good-bye," he said, "my friend. I wish you an excellent trip."

"Thank you," Nicholas answered. "Thanks very much."

He turned to Jean again.

"This is good-bye," he said.

"I'll write you," she said. "I'll telegram. I'll call on Monday. Where will you be next Monday? At the apartment? I'll call."

"Don't call," he said. "I won't answer the phone. I won't be there," he said.

He saw her as through water, and her face was washed. "I'll call." She wept; "what an orgy; don't weep."

"I can't not weep," he said.

He walked away from her and into the locked gate. He gave his passport to the official and received his segment of the boarding pass. He put the boarding pass in his pocket and then in his wallet and then extricated it. He turned and skirted the booth and touched her on the elbow and walked through the open gate; he latched it carefully. He moved to his left for departure gate six, then saw it to the right. He shook his head to clear it and, knowing she would watch, rubbed fists into both eyes. He turned, eyes blurred from rubbing, to see her leaning at him, hear her—"Nicholas, come back!"

He shook his head and walked away and wondered how he looked; he had intended to purchase a watch. He wanted an Omega, solid gold, with a black band, with the day and date. He hunted for the counter and felt, as not since thirteen, that he would, after all, weep. He commenced to cough, and cry, and leaned against the window of the dignitaries' hall.

No dignitaries were within. He chanted, "Jean, Jean, Jean." The choking, however, did not continue, nor was his plane about to leave, so he hurried to the gate where she had called, "Come back."

She was not there, nor could he find her in the hall, though he stood on tiptoe, swallowing. Soldiers passed, and then he felt the reality of loss, and stumbled, and started in earnest to weep. He made his way back to the window and put his head against it, sobbing steadily. He blinked his eyes and bared his teeth and whined; he rubbed his eyes again. After a few moments he looked through the blurred crescent and saw her moving, in the middle distance, past. He spoke her name and wept and she could not see him and he felt for his dark glasses and retained the memory, for years, of that red suit, her hurtling progress to the car and what would be oblivion; he wept for hope defunct, its utter completion, her hair. He wept unstintingly and noticed a Greek Orthodox priest and a girl with a cat-case at his plane's gate, the girl's breasts excellent. He turned his back and wondered how his back appeared and blew his nose, deciding not to bother with the watch. He wept and aped control and could not contrive it and wanted to telegram, telephone, drive to her, adjusted his dark glasses and did not. He wept as not when gassed, the gas tear-gas in Baltimore, the canister exploding where he walked. He cried as not when wounded, the wound a shattered shoulder when he was flung at a telephone pole—as not since, when thirteen, his father had ordered him in from the street for stringing obscenities in football. Pride turned to self-pity, then, he had howled for the ignominy of it, and was not contrite. He wept and traced a spiral in the window and bisected it, then traced a cone. He wept at her weeping and love and incessant exile and retrieved his boarding pass from his right vest pocket and, shivering, embarked.

XI

AUGUST 26

His book was books; his books were sentences. He could not sustain time, place, nor the naming of names. He began a novel that was not his, mine. August 26. A plastic whale that costs nine hundred lire to touch. A comic and cheerful exchange with a cabdriver, full of imprecations and the invoked madonna, traffic impossible, and when I offered French or English—why in that order, I wonder, and never would offer German he said, no, *sono Romano*. Left at four to meet K. who had stormed off at eleven, and who missed the meeting. My attentiveness. What: guilt that mocks, masks the essential indifference within. Anger subverted to solicitude. In an apartment with a shower-stall that locks: this the definition of the anal, yes. And if I ever went mad, the madness would take, I think, the form of taking nothing for granted. So that each task would have to be relearned, each decision weighed.

And shaving would take forty-five minutes, whereas, with efficiency, it can be dispatched in four. And the choice of food, or clothes, or how to enter bed would be deliberate and difficult and freighted with significance. A ritual behavior that comes upon most when alone; attention paid to each pipe smoked, so that it lasts an hour. Madness, therefore, seems situational; it's possible, when alone, to take two hours to tie shoes. Myself on the terrace and it growing cold; gnats. I suppose it comes to this: that over time and with application one comes to credit the fake. That enormous breach pity blasts through integrity; it's noisy, beneath, in the park. A bad traveler, I take myself scuttling through streets. The hermit crab. Which is to say I travel well and easily and am readily adaptable because I notice nothing, give us a wipe *per jesu*. And hold to this journal as guidebook, the seven hills of Rome as yet simply shapes, and peopled with my terror's nation, and therefore I reread these notes and am in Cossayuna truly—at the table made from a flush birch door, rubbed twice with linseed oil and turpentine, set, temporarily, on orange crates. No, am underneath the pine trees in Wellfleet, Heidi's firs, which I should like to trim; at the Hotel Bella Vista Milton, fourth floor, third room on the left, what sort of story to write. Question: how to achieve reconciliation? Answer: by trying. Question: what? (A pretty diversion.) Question: what might a man slough off like skin? Answer: habit. Question: how? Use, in this novel, seven metaphors.

AUGUST 27

You know what saddens me? she said just now, and I stopped typing; what? That I'll never be a convert to anything. A long cheerful walk along the Tiber back from St. Peter's, via the fortress; my birthday today. Have been chopping trees. The first time I wielded an axe, it was with N., for whom it also was the first. But I did not admit it, pretended competence. As also with S., when we disembarrassed each other of virginity. Pretending ease. Why? The pine falls cleanly now, and I wasted, therefore, all that beginner's elation; the youngest dirty old man on the block. My birthday unannounced, and I suffer loudly this elected absence— that someone should have known. Resolutions to return to physical labor. As I age. Typing even in bed. The ostentation, in St. Peter's, of those lines of demarcation; which nave stops where inscribed on the floor. To prove it the largest enclosed area of worship; the toes of St. Peter rubbed smooth, shiny from the kissing. What ceremony else. A quick flight to Catania. What to report of this island; initial disappointment, though we sleighed down Etna's slope. The airport peopled with faces from Lampedusa, Germi, men selling rosaries and chocolate, shining shoes. The drive to Siracusa fifty-three kilometers, refineries throughout. Happy Birthday.

AUGUST 28

Further information from *The Cultivator*. "My wines of all kinds are always clear enough to bottle off the lees by March, except my grape wine, which I then rack into a sweet pure cask, in which I first burn a little sulphur—(say, a bit of paper one by six inches coated with sulphur, for a half-barrel cask)—as soon as the paper, ignited and hung into the bung hole by a thin wire, is properly burning, the bung is put on tight so as not to impregnate the wood of the cask with the sulphuric acid, and in 30 minutes I put the wine into the cask, and fill with clean pebble stones to make the wine come up to the bung hole, and bung up air-tight—then leave it at rest."

AUGUST 29

One of the taboos of romance: calling your lady by another's name. When mating or sleeping or drying the dishes, whenever. Yet it seems to me a compliment; the husband is not, after all, going to confuse his second wife and first. And that he call her by a name which once ratified love need not be nostalgic nor signify betrayal. Am reading in the Cabala: the reader with wisdom will see what lies behind these numbers. 596-42. A fort with a dynamite chamber underneath, so that they were leery of letting us through; we had to request permission of the colonel, wait inside the waiting room for a military escort, nor take pictures nor go to the toilet. And the Ear of Dionysus, where, the story has it, prisoners were kept and overheard by Dionysus in his palace, two miles distant. A wind tunnel acting as tape. The cream of the Athenians, Nicias's brave remnant, dying there. And a guide snapping paper in order to impress us with the echo, extract tips. The temple of Apollo in a central square. Think what it would mean to speak through a megaphone-mask, to have the audience surrounding, circular, and the sea behind. Must see Taormina and, if possible, Cefalù. (*I have moved back, darling, into your downstairs room. Am typing in the very bed I tiptoed to mornings ago. And wonder where, how you are. It's late, I miss you, need you, come back.*) A curious waiter who capered and simpered and giggled at us, but whose face in repose was that of a separate man: lined, lonely, even austere.

AUGUST 30

Siracusa was contained by walls once; twenty-seven kilometers of rock. Five towns within; one where the old one still stands, one beneath the castle Euralia, one in the new town, one by Dionysus's Ear, one directly at the shore. With a secret passage and drawbridge and pincer walls to trap the enemy and rocks cut so that you can shoot up from underneath, but not the reverse. That broke the Athenian Empire's back. What an image. Then Rome succeeded via betrayal, someone in the town who let the drawbridge down. End of nursery rhyme. A drive through Avola famous for what I understand are nazis and almonds. On inquiry, they prove to be nuts and almonds, benign. Rotten squid; swam by a ruined house surrounded by cacti and wire, the door painted green. A motorbike rammed off the road; workmen asking were we *tedeschi*, germans, who earlier than anyone, arrive to swim. They make cement molds with poles, and wire slings. (Make him a script writer maybe, set to work on some young man's novel, your fantasy his fact.)

AUGUST 31

This January 23 and K.'s birthday and celebrated with display. This August 27 and N.'s birthday and celebrated with display. You tweak earlobes as many times as there are years; a meal in Catania by the shore; spaghetti *alla cozze*, and Vincenzo saying *basta* as he held his plate out for fifths; now in Taormina with the Greek amphitheater and Roman surrounding, and Etna in the background, always, hovering. The Hachette allows as how the last significant eruption was 1951, which makes this both the largest and most active of European volcanoes; I plucked a lemon from a tree by the church we'll use, the street signs taken down, the chapel almost empty, an excellent cove discovered for swimming where once was a tunnyfish factory. We should stay here ten days, complete the rough draft of the island sequences, then to Rome for a week, then to Istanbul. We passed a field of fennel, much heavy humor as to the insult of its name, and the strong smell of licorice; ways to offend with the hands; *che te dice la patria. La Patria Viva.* As the commendatore offers hands to Don Giovanni (that old "finocchio"; is he still in show business?) he too sends the letter's last bleat: *Rispondimi.* M.O.S. meaning "mitout sound." And short-ends mean the extra two to two hundred feet, depending on the size and extravagant nature of the film company. With the viewfinder in hand I begin to see what screens contain; pillboxes throughout. Rough fighting here to take the land back from the Germans; vendettas rampant still. The front doors, tongueless, clamped, declaim lost fathers, cousins, mothers-in-law; the black-rimmed cards recording loss. I've bought five tent-pegs and we smoke them, hawking, in lieu of cigars.

SEPTEMBER 1

This is Sunday the twenty-fifth and the second in a sequence of Etna-dominated days; much morning sun, with the single cloud-wisps those coming from the cone, and smoke, and images of Tartarus beneath. Condensation gathers till the peak be wreathed, and the afternoons cloud-ridden, and this morning the sun starts as haze, but each of the nights have been completely clear with the volcano spouting, that broken tetrahedron, flame. John has no fear of heights nor balance but an inordinate fear of fire, keeps a close watch on this surrogate Popocátepetl, instant yang, with Ixta underneath. Three years since I drank my-self wooden in Amecameca, with S., and shattered my watch. This afternoon inserted feet in sea, and saw the boot of Italy, and identified myself as a Sicilian for the maid. Prose worked up as paragraph depends en-tirely on the spacing, and the way words edge; these scenes won't live till on the tongue, not page. They have to be gesticulated, not made sonorous. Title for an Existential Polka, with the Kierkegaard Six as Swing Bund. Hey hey hey/ Shut your eyes/ cross your fingers, snap/ and do the Dialectical Leap.

(EDITOR'S NOTE: The following pagination refers to the transcript of *In the Middle Distance*.)

EDITOR: I dreamt that you and I were in a store in the Village, resembling Gyro West on Bleeker off Sixth, to buy some pants. We each picked out a pair and went off to the dressing rooms. I pulled mine on, felt that they fit, maybe did a knee-bend or two to test, and then wondered what you were up to. I called you over the partition between us. You didn't respond. So I chinned myself up on the partition, there being a space between its top and the ceiling, and I, still smiling at my acrobatics, gazed down at you, crumpled against the far wall, your throat slit, blood around. My dream must have created its own defense, because it im-mediately shifted to a future time in which it was clear that your wound was not fatal. But the only other picture I had in the dream was of myself, walk-ing down a dark street, near a corner, a razor in my own hand to ward off attackers.

AUTHOR: I too (and probably concurrent with yours) had a strange sorry dream. Having to do with lunch with you at Le Pavillon (at long last, though I was there in sweater and corduroy only) and suddenly delivering you a lecture on the evils of intemperance; get, good friend, neither too drunk nor too often. A plywood soapbox, at best, but my dream's message: Hide Park.

EDITOR: p. 77, penultimate line: Should "still" be "fill"?

AUTHOR: p. 204, line 6: Substitute "background" for "distance." No use offering false leads. There's blood enough for hounds. "background, always, hovering. . ."

SEPTEMBER 2

Suitcases, and the car to sell, and all those things to pack. As we came from the hotel, she was surrounded again; each time she walks down the hill, it's off to some alternative. But I'm willing this separation, and witting it, and have long since decided it needful. Therefore the unraveling rends. But it's best accomplished cleanly, and like this. Rather like the notion that I ready a house for a bride long since left. And publish these poor testimonials, *ex voto* Notre Dame de la Garoupe. Thank you, blessed virgin, for my miraculous if engineered escape. Whilst all around me lieth bleeding. From the Big Guns. Donkeys tethered to lampposts, beneath us, make a circle round the staking-place, and the lampposts shake. We're so strong a cross between dissolution and resolution, the Resolute-Dissolute-Hop. Though there's no true analogue, I'm beleaguered by comparison with 1962. The starting of that year, though it more properly March. As if I've returned on myself, or as if, ten pounds fatter, one Alfa Romeo the less, am still incompetent to keep. That which I don't fully want. And withdrawn into daydream and mountain walks and work. Feeling bloody elegiac every time I face these keys. The waiters here simper and grin.

SEPTEMBER 3

(Darling, can't we be kind to each other? I love you and really don't want to pain or give pain. Be pained, I suppose I meant. You must know that. You can't simply cut yourself off and refuse to communicate on any level; that's not fair to either of us. This is terribly hard on me too. Really. You leave me no choice but anger. Or disdain.) The gloss on this to be provided by event. The interlinear later provided, or forgotten, for that too instructs. What the hell does she, did she mean; where are those letters; how could I, pathologically producing words, not have written these? Those. That. All of fiction resides in the definite article. The city of Messina was destroyed in thirty seconds in 1908. Six o'clock, and I'm sitting on the balcony, and there's a general strike, it appears, or something has immobilized the shore of Sicily; straight down the series of headlands I see, even blanking out the lighthouse, the lights alone of cars, fireflies hurtling down the mountain's screen, and in snake-file. (Gertrude said these things. That she ran the Casa Esmond as a low-class boarding house, but only for friends. Light-fingered gestures still; her hands that paddled and were perfect, dominating lunch.)

SEPTEMBER 4

Trains pass. What kind of character-amalgam have we here, how send them shuffling through the decky-dance? Odysseus's ship was wrecked in the Straits of

Messina, which, the restaurateurs have it, represents Scylla and Charybdis for certainty, sir. Today another parody: the phone ringing and the man at the desk howling *pronto, pronto,* but the connection distant, and John, outraged, holding his stomach, shouted at last, "There's nobody here." Hanging up. And I witnessed Polyphemus hurling his acidic wine, those rocks; dreams of duplicity, F. in the house, or simultaneity rather. Gertrude said these things. It is not safe to tell confession to the priests here, because they sell the secrets. One has a Maserati and nine children and no wife. The gardener is devoted, however, to the kitchen's papier mâché christ. Since once, while sitting beneath it, he set odds and won eleven horses out of twelve. Tales of a cousin who left her, of his great wealth, only a silver teaspoon. The cousin shot up in trenches in the First World War, and desperately nervous thereafter, but kept by fear to his regimen, and away from preference. One year he would journey south, one year west, one year east—the direction east his favorite—and desperately, every fourth year, he would journey north. We hear for the eighteenth time the tale of Harry's drake, which gender he mistook and named duck, and Massimo's rented auxiliary teat. The goats are slaughtered here at six months of age, since they make deserts of hills. Have been clacking at these keys three months, the progress a snail-pilgrim's at the best.

SEPTEMBER 5

A ceremonial beneath; tables spread with olives and potato chips, Giuseppe and his minions greeting each other, a wedding, but solemn, a band in rehearsal, the terrace wreathed with crepe. February 5. Antonello da Messina painted, on his master's fresco, that mosquito which, biting the master, had occasioned disease. And, after a slow recovery, when the master witnessed what his journeyman had done, he exchanged caps, saying, "Antonello, you're the master now."

XII

Nicholas first fell in love, and was reciprocated, when twenty. He had a large collection of bowties and matching socks and handkerchiefs and considered that appearance did somehow mark the man. He attended Columbia College and lived in the maid's room of his aunt's apartment on Riverside Drive. He lived behind the kitchen, and there was a bathroom also, but the pressure system was faulty; he could hear the plumbing cough and spit all night. Later, on a camping trip, he slept beside a stream and woke to think himself returned to One-hundred-and-first Street, and the stream the upstairs toilet's rush. Mr. Bemelmans, a widower, lived in 9B, the apartment above. Nicholas would always know if he slept well, or poorly, and if he entertained.

His closest friend was Greek, and they played tennis together and talked of jumping freight trains from Chicago to Los Angeles, or from Maine to Georgia, or the Rock Island Line. Iorgo worked in a pizza parlor his family owned.

Nicholas would take the IRT to the end of the line, then traverse Broadway and sit at the counter and order a pizza and watch Iorgo twirling crust. Iorgo would draw cokes and curse the mozzarella's quality; he attended Columbia also, and wanted to go into real estate. "The only thing as certain," he would assert, "as death is life. There'll be a glut in the market; keep them condoms on."

"I've practiced rolling them," said Nicholas. "I can do it one-handed now."

"Which hand?" Iorgo sliced green peppers and tomatoes. "The left?"

"Either hand," said Nicholas. "I'm ambidextrous. See?"

Iorgo said, "Pretend you're a girl. And say, 'I'm perfect,' see?"

"I'm perfect."

"I'm practice," Iorgo roared. He loaded the pizza into the oven with his wooden loading paddle. He shut and fastened the door. "Practice makes perfect, see."

Iorgo's father was a furrier and branched out into the glove business and wanted his son to speak Greek. Nicholas and Iorgo bought a Chevrolet for one hundred and seventy-five dollars and laid a plank across the rear seat and covered it with blankets and pillows and drove about looking for girls. They had little success, but one night they met two girls and drove them up to Riverdale, and Iorgo, to rouse the neighborhood, leaned on his horn. They were immediately surrounded by police and searched, and the police told them there were two prison inmates escaped. There was a roadblock on Delafield Avenue, and one on Grosvenor Avenue, and one on Fieldston Road. "You don't answer our description, boys," an officer said. "Run along home anyhow. You're out late, anyhow."

Nicholas's aunt would reproach him sometimes, for neglecting his studies. "All you do," she said, "is sit there, in that bar, or drive around."

"*Tante*," he would answer, "I'm an architect. Almost. I'm going to be an architect. I have to study shapes."

He moved his hands in an hourglass pattern, and wolf-whistled.

"You know I'm color-blind," he said. "I have to study form."

He met Sarah at a sherry party for the sophomore class. She attended Barnard and was the daughter of a man who owned a music-publishing company; she wanted to learn to make cellos, and was a pacifist. "This is rotten Amontillado," she said. "Whoever walked these grapes should wash his feet." She was as tall as Nicholas, and he improved his posture in the three years that they spent together; he shared initiation, with her, into sex. Her parents had an estate in Amagansett, and Nicholas would visit each weekend, lying in the guest-room till she judged the family asleep. Then Sarah would come to him, carrying candles, and he would light them and pull off her sweater and squeeze her till she whispered, "Hey, quit that, you don't know your strength."

He did push-ups and sit-ups and leg-raisers every morning; once, he did sixty push-ups, inside her, on the bed. They sang love songs and showered together and he was convinced of permanence. "No matter what happens," he would say, "I'll love you forever, you'll see." They deliberated over marriage and the problems of the concentration camp; they copulated endlessly, in bathrooms, on beaches, and on the back-bench of his Chevrolet.

"I've never loved," said Sarah, "anyone like this. Tommy Ratner had a Studebaker, and I guess I had a crush on him, but never," she massaged his back, "anyone like this."

He was jealous and delighted and maintained decorum with

her family. Sarah had two sisters and a younger brother, who was friends with Nicholas. He liked photography and wanted to be a professional photographer; he was twelve and five-foot-four and had a harelip. Sarah made a salad dressing with garlic and ketchup and Worcestershire sauce and olive oil and mustard; they would sit in the kitchen till dawn, eating lettuce and discussing isolationism. He wondered if he should have volunteered for the army, rather than attend Columbia; she was delighted, she said, that he was right there, right then.

Sarah's legs were long. She was a graceful dancer and had the remnants of a childhood stutter; she had visited a therapist whose name was Mrs. Sykes. She entered Freudian analysis with an analyst named Manfred Goering; she labeled him "Manny," and laughed.

On weekends they took trips to the Berkshires, and to Newport; Sarah's family was generous to Nicholas and paid for his room in the Lenox Inn. Sarah came to his room; she was wearing an orange halter with a design of doves.

"What do you think," she asked, "of free love?"

"Fine. Who wants to pay for it?" he said.

"No. I'm being serious. And the I.W.W."

"Workers of the world," he said, "unite. You have nothing to lose but your belts. Garter belts, chastity belts. Girdles."

"You're impossible," she said.

He felt eloquent and devious and tried to smoke cigars; he told Iorgo later, "That one. She's a superb animal. Yes."

Her father laid a brick wall in their house in Amagansett. He was sloppy with the mortar and let it lip over the bricks. Nicholas liked the effect, and they did a section of the wall that way on purpose; the wall looked like cake with rich, gray filling, and Sarah's father said, "This way we won't need to repoint. Not for ten years, at least."

They had a poodle called Laurie that they kept unclipped.

She was ten years old and silver and enormous—but Sarah said her fat was coat, and denied, though Nicholas asserted it, that Laurie stank. They also had a poodle named Bascom, who was epileptic, and whom the family kept clipped. Heat contributed to his seizures, the veterinarian said. They played charades, and sang madrigals, and painted portraits of each other; Sarah's mother loved to organize picnics, and rounds of rummy after supper, and she would drink creme de menthe from a plastic flask. Once she took Nicholas up on the roof, and they lay back, discussing the artist as pariah or saint, and the futurist-architect's role. She massaged his neck and scalp and said, "Darling boy, you're tense," and he thought that if he kissed her she might indeed respond.

The house was gabled and had an extensive wine cellar and a tennis court; he felt an imposter throughout. Laurie came when he called, and heeled, and slavered over him; he bought a Lacoste shirt. Sarah said, "You know, when the school-car used to come, I'd walk down the driveway to get it. And the kids would call me 'Princess' because of the size of the house. But I never knew about that kind of envy. Really. I never realized we were rich. Having to wash the dishes."

They discussed, interminably, selfhood and dignity and how much they loved each other and how much they needed sex. She left notes beneath his pillow or pierced by his belt-buckle, or on the seat of his car; the notes were in praise of his penis, or generosity, and warned him to drive carefully, driving away.

"Good night, sweet princess," he would quote, "and flights of angels sing thee to thy rest."

She closed the front door on him, gently, and reset the burglar alarm. She flicked the lights off, on, off until he started the car. Then he, in turn, would flick his lights and coast down the driveway and nose into the avenue and start for home elated, reverent.

They had many such routines. When finished with the kitchen, he would shut the door and say "Bye, kitchen." She sang to the tune of "Row, Row, Row Your Boat"—and her name and address and telephone number, and they made a round of "I love you." He thought that time would not diminish need, nor desire, nor trust. He thought that his children would cluster to her like grapes. He would build buildings for her, and the name of their boat would be *Sarah*, and all manner of thing would be well. She had what she called "Dry feet," and disliked walking barefoot on sand. She had, also, what she labelled a "worry lump" on her right collarbone; she rubbed this when nervous, or sad.

Nicholas read Marx and Shakespeare and admired Taliesen greatly; he sang "Barney Google" and learned to drink creme de menthe. Sarah's mother liked espresso and had the cook ready espresso by seven. Later, Nicholas would stare at espresso pots and scour them and have the past intact. The house in Amagansett had been owned, previously, by an eye doctor. He had saved the sight of a Ceylonese prince, halting interstitial keratitis, and effecting a corneal transplant, and the prince was very grateful and sent back Ceylonese wood. The house was paneled, therefore, in excellent wood, and Nicholas lay beneath teak, carving his initials, and Sarah's, minutely by the bed.

She left Barnard after three semesters, calling it irrelevant, and moved to the East Side. She worked in concert management and embraced, he found, a succession of pastimes; she studied haute cuisine. "The reason for this art," she said, "is really the reason of waste. Let's say you had five hundred widgeon and no intention of giving them away. You and your noble friends have slaughtered them for sport. And no way to preserve them, there not being ice in France at the time. So you toss them to a chef and he brews up a stock from it. Eighteen birds go into sauce Béarnaise."

"Poacher in his lordship's forest," Nicholas said. "Pass the salt."

He argued with his aunt, at breakfast, as to the virtues of virtue; he said, "It comes from the Latin for strength. From that root, anyway. Give me your tired and poor. I'd a lot rather feed the hungry than the fat."

He discussed mortality with Iorgo, and what the Comintern might hope to accomplish and whether art would be, of necessity, henceforth, agit-prop. Iorgo's uncle was the godson of a man who rehabilitated tankers, and they got passage, therefore, on a freighter to Marseilles. It was the summer of 1946, and neither had been to Europe before. From Marseilles they hitchhiked to Paris, and from Paris to Madrid; Iorgo had no need to visit Greece.

"We're students," he said, "we're privileged observers, so to speak."

Nicholas said, "No. Participants. We're all participants."

"Guilt by association," Iorgo said, "I refuse. Later, maybe."

They sang "Barney Google" together and clicked glasses and were, they asserted, brothers in the wide fraternity of man. Nicholas combed his hair forward and considered an earring and was, a waitress said, very gypsy-like. "*Ach, du schwarzer zigeuner*," she said.

They traveled from Madrid to Venice in two weeks, and met the freighter in Genoa and returned to New York at September's start. Nicholas was frightened of the clap and wrote long, fervent letters to Sarah, and Iorgo contracted the clap in Nice. "Some privileged observer," Nicholas reminded him, "some participant."

They saw Jean-Paul Sartre on the Rue de la Paix, scurrying in front of cars. Nicholas was moved by Chartres more than by Notre Dame. He argued for commitment; "Life is a sin of commission," he said.

He kept a journal of the trip, pasting in entrance tickets and timetables and menus; he analyzed himself at length, and with derision, and compiled a sketchbook of the Romanesque.

"Darling," he wrote Sarah, "we're intertwined more closely than ever, I think. Read Donne on the subject. You are the point of my compass. Someday we'll spend a winter in Grasse, or in the Seychelles. I dream of you each night."

He dreamed of otters disporting themselves in mud, and of Don Budge missing his half-volley; he attempted to gauge, wherever he lay, whether she was lying in the same direction, and at which of his flanks. Sarah preferred to sleep on the side of the bed farthest from the door; if they lay in a room with two doors, she lay farthest from the entrance door. He dreamed that Ted Williams was french. He dreamed that Esther Williams swam the catafalque, and did a swan-dive from some gargoyle's snout.

"You are part of me," he wrote to Sarah, "and you are the part I need most."

They went to Monaco and lived in a *pension* with a girl called Kate from Boston, and her lover, Michael; they attempted roulette, but were not twenty-one.

"The main thing," Nicholas wrote, "is that I can't forget you. And won't. Kiss those initials by your pillow. Please. I will always love and want you. More than anything."

Nicholas and Sarah traveled west. They borrowed her family station wagon and had three weeks for the trip. They spent the first night in Pennsylvania, in a meadow; he had bought a pup-tent and interlocking sleeping bags. She wore a wedding ring, and he had purchased four dozen prophylactics; they stocked the car with books and beer and Sarah brought her flute; she practiced "Green Sleeves" and "Bist du Mein Lieb." He found a stream and filled the canister with water and considered pataphysics; he built a fire and laid out the campsite and felt competent, protective; Sarah played "You'll Never Walk Alone."

"This is"—she smiled at him—"nirvana." She practiced fingerings.

"This is the life," he intoned.

"This is peachy keen."

They left the tent flaps open; it was July twenty-eighth.

In Aspen they camped at Maroon Lake and hiked, beneath the full moon, at midnight, the trail to Crater Lake. Sarah was frightened of snakes, and bear, and the ragged, jutting edges of rock. "I know it isn't logical," she said, "I know it has nothing to do with reason. But it terrifies me all the same. You can't imagine the things I imagine; you can't."

Deer startled her, and the few, far birds; he thought of her as a deer. Clouds ringed the moon, but the trail was clarified, and he quoted her his single memorized speech.

"The moon shines bright," he said. "On such a night as this, when the sweet wind did gently something the trees. . . ."

"What's that?" she said. "That's beautiful."

"In such a night stood Dido with a willow in her hand upon the wild sea banks. . . ."

"The green mantle of the standing pool," she said.

"And waft her love to come again to Carthage."

"There you go," she said, "again. Those Punic Wars."

He shone his light at her. "Listen, white woman, you die. Me heap big Arapaho person. You listen to Shakespeare or die. Crazy Sitting Duck."

"All right," she said, maintaining cheerfulness. "Bill. Buffalo Bill Shakespeare. Speak your speech."

"On such a night as this," he said, "when the sweet wind did gently kiss the trees, that's it, did gently kiss the trees, and they did make no noise. . . ."

"Extract your pound of flesh," she said, "O merchant,"

and they kissed. He felt witty and handsome and brave; he skirted a rockslide with ease.

Later, that winter, as they discussed what had gone wrong, and when, and dissected failure, Sarah said, "I did love you that trip. Truly. You and your flashlight and, what shall I call it, your preening recitatif."

They drove to Seattle and San Francisco in order to complete the loop, but could not stay more than one night in each town. Nicholas was timid about hotels and did not like displaying Sarah; he tested the phrase, "My wife." He used it elaborately, and with emphasis, and more often than needed. "My wife and I," he would say to the clerk, "have never been here before. But she's the boss and says we ought to stay. Whatever she says," he said, "goes."

Sarah moved without direction but with certainty; she was ambitious but, Nicholas said, aspecific; her father wanted her to model so she modeled for two years. "You're living out your father's fantasies," Nicholas complained, "Electra. It doesn't make sense."

Her analysis went well. "I was rejected," she said, "as a child. So I'm hungry for assurance now. And praise."

She modeled hair dryers and he saw her in the Sears catalog with a vacuum cleaner; she had albums of photographs on the coffee table, and photographs pinned to the kitchen corkboard, and on the bathroom walls.

"It's a lack of identity," Sarah said, "see? I have to have these mirrors in order to prove I exist."

He had little sympathy; he thought a problem recognized should be a problem solved. He thought her analyst a rival, and her photographs ridiculous and himself demeaned; he wished she were not rich. "You're living on the past," he said, "and for those fifty minutes a day." Later, he blamed the affair's collapse on tradition and a self-indulgence he claimed not to possess.

Nicholas's father disapproved of Sarah; Nicholas's mother had been killed by a truck, in 1931. She was crossing the Concourse, holding packages, and the bottom of the bag broke, spilling tea. She always purchased tea in triangulated bags, the man at the counter measuring, sorting them, and he subtracted the weight of the paper from the total weight. Nicholas's mother was killed as she stooped, and the truck rounded the corner in third.

He had few memories: her hair pulled tightly back, her dislike of the telephone, her way of holding glasses, once dried, to the light. She used yellow rubber gloves to wash. She sorted the dishes and rinsed them; she used a scouring brush. Nicholas learned, in the funeral eulogy, that she had been a union organizer and had helped establish the hatters' union. He later tried to picture the picket lines they spoke of, and work camps, and the trouble with passports; he had considered his mother inert.

He remembered, also, her habit of sherry at noon; his father gave her, the final Christmas, a case of Dry Sack. She died in April and had emptied eleven bottles and replaced them, empty, in the case. She was devoted to his father and would take her glasses off whenever he entered the room; she liked and read for solace, Mrs. Menendez said, the sayings of Boethius. "Such is life," Mrs. Menendez repeated, "such is life."

Sarah found his father romantic and wondered what he did, at night, sleeping with grief and the dialectic. "Historical awareness," she teased him, "should never close its eyes. Your dad must snore 'class consciousness' and exhale 'The Internationale.'"

"That's better," Nicholas said, "than what your father

whistles. Which must be 'Yankee Doodle Dandy' or 'Hail to the Chief.'"

"Let's introduce them," she said. "Let's wave the red rag at the bull."

"Bull market," he answered. "Let's love each other all the time," he said. "All right?"

When Nicholas was graduated from the Fieldston School, his father took a trip to Cuba and padlocked the apartment and Nicholas moved to Manhattan, to his aunt's back room. He studied torque and heating and ventilating and problems of linear space; the function of the architect, he said, is to marshal signposts and point the time's direction and organize shape's shape. "What does that mean?" Iorgo asked. "That's gibberish."

"You'd be surprised," said Nicholas, "at how much we take for granted and how much it matters if we live in a round room or square. Which part of a street do you walk down, for instance, the sidewalk or the middle of the street?"

"Depends on the traffic," said Iorgo.

"Not at all," said Nicholas, "it only depends on the street."

"What do you see," he would ask Sarah, "when you see me?"

"My hero. My lover. My man."

"Wrong. A shape that's yellow here and brown on the top and has a red swatch, I think, in the center. Even calling it a shirt is making an assumption; you see what you see, and that's that."

His innocence, he decided, was intact; he had a spoiled boy's way, he said, of looking at the world. He wanted to see it unencumbered; even color-blindness served to clarify. He wanted to preserve surprise, and joy, and the sense of selfhood as receptacle; he exalted energy.

"That's why I love you," Sarah said. "You bounce a lot."

179

"Yes ma'am, the old up and down."

She calculated the number of orgasms they might achieve, together, in a quarter century. "By 1970," she said, "assuming we continue at the present pace, allowing a slight decrease for the last decade, but only slight, because I'll leave you otherwise, allowing intervals for pregnancy and trips and etcetera, we should have come, give or take a thousand, let's say fourteen thousand times."

"That's not enough," he said.

"I'm limp," she said, "already."

"I have not," he said, "begun to fight."

Her apartment had beige carpeting and rattan furniture, and she wanted velvet drapes. Her bathroom had a row of glazed bulbs lining the mirror, and pink tile.

(There was a broad, flat meadow with what Nicholas learned was alfalfa. "I thought that hay was bird's-foot hay," he said. Sparrows chittered as he passed, and birds he could not name, and a clothesline arced between two ponderosa pine. Diapers were slung on the clothesline, and pillowcases, and a hooded sweatshirt and three pairs of khaki pants. The meadow stretched as far as he could see, would walk, although its width was not more than two hundred yards. Inexplicably, a beer-keg lay before him; he skirted it and came upon a tent, a mining shaft, barbecue grill, a girl. She was seventeen, she said, and in the fourth grade, and fucked. "I never took no trouble," she said. "I never wished to be beholden to the law." The mining shaft extended, he learned, for two miles. Fifty feet from the entrance, however, it had caved in on itself. And the best guess was that silver, since William Jennings Bryan, was not worth the mining any more. Even with the rubble cleared, she mouthed, that shaft would still be shut. Birds complained, and the hunting season was bow and arrow only, and he thought he saw an elk. "The sky," the girl informed him, "is an abalone's gut." "Some metaphor," he said. "Yes," she said. "Them cumulus clouds make me sexy; want a beer?"

He continued on his pilgrimage and came upon, with heaven-aspiring heart, his sixth-grade mathematics teacher twirling a baton. "Roosevelt," she said, "goes round and round like this." His feet were caked with mud and he could not understand how women walked in heels, and the horses, though hobbled, had left him and it might, she said, commence to snow. "Have yourself," she said, "a banana daiquiri; have a peach melba; have you learned your long division yet?" She translated, "Peach, that means fish. Also sin. Them magpies is talkative birds.")

Sarah bought more clothes in a season than Nicholas wore in a year. "It's ego-support," she announced. "Besides, you like me changeable. Custom cannot stale."

They went ice-skating, and to Harlem for jazz; he felt himself inviolate. His mother had told stories of John L. Lewis's cigars, and how the rank-and-file would send him ashtrays, and how he would always return them with a handwritten letter of thanks. Sarah resigned her job in concert management and went to work in publishing, as a children's-book editor. Her job, to begin with, was layout, and which illustration went where.

("It used to be potato country here," his mathematics teacher said, and was his aunt, "before they opened Idaho. And there's a deal of oil-shale left, and the Mormons used it for oil. And we get a foot of snow, maybe, and no rain."

"Even our poor," he said, "are richer than what's left. In the rest of the world."

Dogs followed where he went, and assented to the journey. Though querulous and whimpering, and careful of the horses' hooves, Sarah was the tent-girl. Clouds lifted, and she lifted legs on the mattress, and his world was roseate, would be. "Amortization rates," he heard, "on five hundred acres is more than the horses can stand. You got to have this truck, and Cat, to run a ranch."

Sopris rose straight above them, clouds belting it, and the eye of the mountain was snow. Nicholas would walk, he said, forever with the chittering magpies, and the beer keg ahead. "Them other horses," she moved against him, "bite that quarter horse. Who's flat-out fastest at her half-a-mile.")

Iorgo woke him. "Your turn to drive," he said.

Nicholas stretched; they were on the Merritt Parkway, coming from Boston, heading south. The road bellied out, and down, and they were at Wilton, Connecticut; Iorgo stopped the car.

"It's your idea," he said, "this trip. Your turn to drive."

Sarah had telephoned. She said, "I need to see you badly. Please come back. I need you very much," she said, "you've no conception. Please."

It was ten o'clock at night; Iorgo and he had gone to Boston for the Yankee-Red Sox game. "And for whatever we catch," Iorgo grinned, "on the fly."

"The game's not till tomorrow," Nicholas complained.

"You don't understand," Sarah said, "I mean it. I need to see you. Now."

"All right," he said. "We'll drive back. Just leave the door unlocked."

"I'll be waiting," she said, "baby."

Returned, however, he saw no reason for returning, nor would she explain. She welcomed him, and they made love and slept, but she had released the horror, she told him, and would not discuss it. He dreamed of hurtling, headlong, repeatedly, into the front left fender of a Pontiac.

"That woman's got you on purse strings," Iorgo said, "so long that she hauls you from Boston; some tug."

"Don't you call Sarah a tug," Nicholas said.

They drove back to Boston in the morning, and Ted Williams went three for four. Nicholas bought the gas and food and Allie Reynolds was wild. Oil-shale, he had dreamed, slicked the engine block.

His father feared tuberculosis, and the tests were positive, and he went to a sanitarium for observation and rest. Nicholas drove to Purchase, but his father was not sick. "They're only taking blood away," he said, "they're not giving anything back." His father introduced him to a nurse called Harriet, and said, "Harriet and I will leave together. Next Monday. Please pick us up at three."

Harriet was fifty-two and fat and careful of Nicholas's father; she came from Hartford, Connecticut, and compared the Concourse to it favorably. She installed herself with curtains and plates and liked to hook rugs. The plates had a hunting motif: deer drank from streams and leaped ditches on the rim. Nicholas took Sarah for a visit, and they commented, at length, upon his shoes.

"Here, let me shine them," Harriet said, "I've got shoe cream here."

"And besides, they're covered with mud," Nicholas's father said.

He was graduated from Columbia in 1945. He walked to the ceremony from Sarah's apartment, carrying his robes. She had refused to go with him; "Come back afterwards," she said, "we'll celebrate."

It rained, and he was welcomed to the fellowship of educated men. Sarah had two chilled bottles of Taittinger, and he thought about popping them, and aiming for the lightbulb; she had paper Chinese lanterns on the overhead lights. He would propose to her, he decided, when she completed therapy, and when he could earn five thousand dollars a year. He felt manipulated, often, by her style and will. She used almond lipstick and owned one fall, two wigs, and plucked the hairs of her nose. "Congratulations," she toasted him. "I'm so glad you made it through. Even if I couldn't manage Barnard; let's drink."

He wondered, would he have the strength to vanquish her, and in what sort of arena, and what would be the stakes? She gave him a series of sketches by Le Corbusier. Her analysis cost more than he could hope to earn; she hated mosquitoes and the cold and was, he told Iorgo, too high-strung.

Nicholas received no summons from the draft. He thought, perhaps, with the apartment in the Concourse locked, the letter had been misdirected; he thought, perhaps, his course of study made him draft-exempt. Sarah said, "Let well enough alone. Just let them come to you."

Five of his friends left Columbia; four died. The fifth had been a paratrooper and had landed in France. "Some liberation," he said. "I stayed in a haystack, it looked like, for two days." He had hoped to be an architect also, but he had witnessed too many buildings exploded, he said, and too much beauty blown up. He drew, for weeks, drawings that were hallucinations only, with men in segments, tanks with eyes. He attempted Nicholas's portrait, and submerged a minefield in his cheek; the teeth were carious and the eyes were planes.

Planes delighted Nicholas; he could gauge the holding patterns for La Guardia. He planned extended trips with Sarah, and she said, "Yes. But I've only got a month. That's all I can afford."

"What do you mean?" he asked. "Once we're there, it won't cost anything to stay. We could live a week in Srinagar for what one lunch costs here."

"That's not what I meant," she said. "I mean in terms of time."

"I'm playing second fiddle to a couch," he said. "Your doctor takes vacations. Why can't you?"

"I can," she told him. "For a month."

She was in pain for four days every month. "I feel like," she complained, "I'm blowing up inside. You can't imagine it, baby, you just can't imagine the way that I feel. I'd rather be pregnant," she said.

Nicholas drank camp coffee; he put grounds on the pot's bottom and ladled water in and let the water come to a near boil. Sometimes he added cinnamon. He had a theory of sunsets, that they were most beautiful when defined by clouds; Sarah said no color-blind man could afford such a theory; he called it a problem of form. "Form," he suggested. "We've gone ragged at the edges. You and me."

He attempted to meet Le Corbusier, but was not successful. He walked to the site of the UN building daily, and tried to find an outboard motor so that he might see it from the river side. Le Corbusier said, "All architects are either boastful or peevish," and Nicholas thought the characteristics twinned.

He had, sometimes, a sense of outer limits, and that growth was not ascent. He would attend architecture school in New Haven and amass credentials and sever, haltingly, from Sarah; they aped intimacy and knew it long since gone. He was tentative about betrayal and kept a need for possession after the desire to possess.

He would see her, eight years after, for a drink; she played him a love song written for her recent lover, Dick. "I'd have a photograph of you still," she said, "up on that bulletin board. The one I love, with you and Laurie on that rock. Only Dick made me take it off." Dick festooned the wall: holding a banjo, a tiller, a drink. "Dick, my song is all sung out," she sang, "my fling is flung."

He watched her—long-legged, patently beginning—and listened and praised it and shifted weight. He was best, he decided, alone.

XIII

SEPTEMBER 6

A lovely pantomime enacted at the airport. Little red-bloused girl persuading swaddled boy to kiss. It is 90 degrees in the sun; he wears a blue shirt, beige leggings, a hat. He kisses with disdain—being, at the outside, two—then interest, then delight. The parents, blushing, haul them apart. Balconies throughout this *pensione*, and mammoth standing wardrobes, and a complex, patterned floor. Elegant, lengthy invective from our taxidriver to all those who cross or pass him. Your mother came from the egg of a thousand-year-old ostrich that sucked your father off. Your brothers are policeman in a factory for hens. Your uncle was a shotgun inaccurately loaded (with appropriate, accompanying gestures) and your aunt the ball. Grease on the *saltimbocca* is as flat as is your penis and tastes the same to your dog.

SEPTEMBER 8

A long walk through the zoo, seals disporting brilliantly for fish, and an elephant seeming in heat, and the monkeys picking maggots from fur. The anteater subsists on masticated meal and honey and sugar and milk. Then back through the Borghese Gallery (nine prophylactics counted on a ten-foot stretch of path, this clearly the parking locale, the men no doubt ejaculating them from windows, defying the pope); everywhere superb soccer in progress, and traffic jams. Save a Baby for God. My house could fit with ease in each of the side parlors of the Borghese Gallery, and the house neither narrow nor low.

SEPTEMBER 9

February 12. What further vagaries? These. *(If you still care for me at all, and I know you do, and deeply, please don't force me to relinquish everything I gained. And by that I mean friends and relatives as well as yourself; I can't bear that kind of manifold rejection. Darling, I've not left. I've changed a bit, yes, and journeyed a bit, yes, but by no means disappeared. There are too many things under the skin.)* Such as, he suggests, Harry, Dick and Tom. *(Your letter was in fact cruel, but only, I know, because you feel so profoundly hurt. But there is a way out without damage, I think. Enough said. I am not even vaguely angry about any of this, just melancholic. Misunderstandings, vagaries, and the jumble of our lives.)* These suspicions. That she's thus quickly reconciled because of the car waiting outside, and the gentleman on the rear seat—whose chauffeur wears blinders, then takes his turn. That it's easy to be charitable when victorious. And beneath that ravening, at absolute odds with all else, the conviction she's correct. So that, from this "jumble," and set of interlinears, and refractory departure, he extracts but this: leaving is never singly witted but always reciprocal; two people, when the love is shared, always agree to quit. What else: these shards: the time I turned her diary to early entries, misread my initial, thought she was confessing love for some concurrent someone. And the shame when, finally named, I was merely me. (Reached Bar Harbor by ten, stopped at restaurant outside Ellsworth; weather getting much colder. Felt exhausted and found a cabin several miles out of Bar Harbor for the night; a hot plate and instant coffee. Absolute sleep; awoke, still tired, at 8:30; clouds massing to the north.) Why root hysterically, still, after the past's disintegrated spoor? The Bay of Fundy National Park, the Martello Tower, and Antigonish. A letter I won't send. *A rose lay dying on the dashboard;* in Lunenberg tonight.

SEPTEMBER 11

There are ways, T. thinks, of walking. Ways and ways of walking. Now I stand here, stick in the crowd's current, leaning. Thou hast nor youth nor age. . . .

This data to record. The lava ceased flowing, is a wall, near Catania; lava soil is rich. (Giuseppe comes and, strangely, it matters; we welcome him effusively, with guilt. Wearing his black English hat that he had construed, earlier, as a toreador's; telling his horrific joke about the countryman who asked for the use of the doctor's wife's breasts so that he, too, could cure his neck.) Is mimicry the highest form of compliment, or insult? Those who grow over influenced by habitat or custom seem absurd; just so, however, I mistrust

those who move without inflection from the south to
New England to London and back. A bit of parrot
heralds the noticing man.

SEPTEMBER 15

The habit of asking questions as statements, then deny-
ing intention. So that H. says: Don't you think the
blacks are really inferior to whites? What kind of shit-
eating position, I ask, is that? Who says, he says, I take
that position. Etc. Bernini's self-portrait as David, and
the frieze of heroes in which they dwarf the animals,
or are as sizable, when leading them or bearing gifts.
A lion cub acquires his roar instanter, goes from wheeze
to thunder overnight. How we ready ourselves, flut-
tering, for flight. One of the principal comforts of
anonymity, J. says (and suggests that extreme fame
would undermine him also), is the notion that he'll
soon replace those fat pedestal cats. Flavius Agricola
had a cheerful epitaph. The single writer's privilege,
to compose his own. And when I die, my darling, say
only this of me: he completed the draft. That im-
mortal bunghole stopped up. G. has been smashed at
Kuwaiti state receptions for a decade now. Funny
how much better disposed one feels to the relics of
pagan ruin, and rule. Somehow I can't shake the sense
of all those idiot sons who purchased the papacy, used
it as extortionists, were slain. The sordid past entire
made retroactively just by the doctrine of infallibility,
and that this century's. In the right-hand bottom
corner of the Botticelli, Moses is slaying an egyptian
who slew a jew. *Plus ça change.* All the ingenious
tortures devised, that sequence of armaments shown in
Sant'Angelo—hanging people in parabolas, pouring
in the boiling oil of eighty-four vats. Which had a

secondary use as storage for the garrison. Silos emptied to be dungeons; how much invention went into the first armor-suit? The Bernini statue, aghast, reclining (in the Piazza Navona) in front of the church. And the women on the Via Appia selling, to use T's phrase, love. Fishes scratched on the catacomb walls, and doves, and iron levers only hewed those graves. The summer palace of the pope (this in Castel Gondolfo) surmounted by an observatory; wacky, pleasing, that he should scan for god. Manifold confusion about Istanbul and Athens and the spring; should be a curious time. Cheese sold at the corner of the *autostrada;* plane trees inaccurately pruned. A story from the indian guide (delighted at knowing the area code, though incorrect, of New York City—full of dates, a head for pope's reigns, metrics) as to how the english anthropologist discovered, reverential, the tombs. Then the guard outside, who introduced himself as one of Garibaldi's legion, assured us his uncle would leave bottles in the catacombs to cool. And that he would use the caves when sporting, when a boy.

SEPTEMBER 16

This trip to Athens is elegiac of a long-shelved youth; seven years previous the last time I was here, and no single body-cell equivalent. Not a good notion for transients to return to what they once considered home. Myself the scuttling crab again, with suitcase for shell, connectives snapped. Reconverted landing craft that act as ferries now. Boys with coffee trays; a woman with a tray of pretzels on her head. Shoe stalls with men smoking hookahs: *Eleutheria.* An interminable bus ride taken to Delphi; stops for bread and stops for water and stops for the lady in front. Splendid above all others—this temple—in part for the silence in which we viewed it, the habitat of Phoebus indeed, gigantic pillars placed there by no one records who or what sort of strength. Springs where the pilgrims slaked thirst and were purified; dusk fell; we walked back past donkeys and the final hunters and olive wood's guttering ash. Strayed through the temples of Athena and the Tholos; I tried again to image sanctity, could, almost, in the wind. Of all the memories, this stays; that fissure, the *adityon*, the mist. Sidewalk chapels with olive oil and vinegar and candles and matchboxes to facilitate lighting; stone huts built into the hill.

SEPTEMBER 17

J.'s grandfather ran a woolen mill, then lost it in the Depression, then gained wealth slowly again, and left the business reins to a nephew, this in 1945. And went on his first vacation in eighteen years. After three weeks in the Bahamas, he inquired how his fortunes stood. And found the business going so well he had no reason to return—lay down at forty-nine, therefore, and, to hear J. tell it, lost the will to live. Heart, perfectly sound, just stopped. (*My darling, today you are gone, and only the dog and I knew how much we loved you, wanted you to stop right then and stay. Did you notice that I didn't cry, did you notice that?*)

SEPTEMBER 18

Constantine consulted, they say, the oracle at Delphi. And it instructed him to build his eastern capital "opposite the blind." Abandoning the hopeful, as with all arcana, to inaccurate hope. Operating under the assumption, then, that only the blind could not tell how beauteous was the Bosporus, how logical the site, he chose this spit of land for Istanbul. Constantinople. We are in the Pera Palas now. With only aspidistras absent; Kemal Ataturk took the reins from, the lives of, the government here. Apartments with mosaic fringe, the mosques immense. A certain kind of trepidation; hold me (past, baby, hotel). Neither friends nor language nor history available; the beggar boys, the offered fix, Russian tankers beyond. So that one can image, for the first time, paralysis: what it would mean to remain in one room completely, nor venture forth.

(EDITOR'S NOTE: The following pagination refers to the typescript of *In the Middle Distance*.)

EDITOR: p. 11, bottom: I wish there were some way to establish immediately that the Greenwich you mention here and of this novel is in upstate New York and is not the Greenwich I think most people think of, the rich, commuter Greenwich. *Of course* any careful reader will eventually clarify things for himself. Nevertheless, the novel has enough valuable confusions to make the elimination of this one no great shakes. Perhaps you might, in giving details of the direction in which he drives, hitch the reader right.

AUTHOR: It hadn't occurred to me that this might prove a problem, since I've gotten used to considering it "my" Greenwich, not the Conn's. How would the simple addition of "New York" do? Argal. "Nicholas left Beacon Hill for Greenwich, New York, on June fifth." But I'm not averse, if you can get the copy-editor to do it, to changing the whole thing. "Eagleville," for instance, is a community near by, which could be substituted for Greenwich in every instance. Or "Cossayuna." Maybe that would make the best sense. It would do no violence, might do some good. Rispondimi. (Cossayuna preferred.)

EDITOR: p. 314, line 19: This October sixth is, I take it, the same October sixth as the final journal entry.

AUTHOR: Look, she's too clever, Sarah I mean, by half. So that if I cut "that preening recitatif," I'd have to cut the bulk of the neuroses. And all of p. 222.

SEPTEMBER 19

Men raddled with smallpox, the docks, the arabian horses, the bus, then horses, then bus, straight out of Breughel mayhap, mud-rivulets and the wooden houses that made this so perilous a city, endlessly gutted by flame, the Bosporus mud-brown, the Golden Horn easy to cross. Yowling cats. I can't shake that Delphiwind, nor the cleft's austerity. A rotten supper now, felt cheated with *meza*, and ill. Leeks the size of my arm. Fish stalls, and herbs battened into the bread. Why does a bath exhaust and shower invigorate; something to do with immersion as against opposition; stand to or sink within. Justinian's delirium: Solomon, I have outdone thee at building. The rotary club comes for dinner; we watch from the balcony: one way to root out vanity—let people see themselves only in foreshortening, or with a funhouse mirror. A boy commences to sell postcards; I say no; a leather coat; I say no; change money; I say no; hashish; no; a Mustang for one hundred thousand lire (this about three times the car's value and, I tell him, insufficient; it's an insult to my uncle, Henry Ford); this sets him going and we barter for an unbuilt bridge, then he wants to sell me the Istanbul airport, then, resources unabated, he offers to buy my black hat. No. (L. kept a close watch on her weight, though F. assured her that he liked each extra pound. If he saw Metrecal in any icebox other than his, a shelf of books on quick-loss diets, or calorie-charts in the cabinet, he felt, on the instant, familiar. He admired, though he did not share, the random sexuality of the young. "They never had it so good," F. would say. "Why should they have to get married?") This a frozen currency; superb honey for breakfast; must dominate depression. A sensory barrage.

SEPTEMBER 20

A ferry taken to Harem, the foot of Asia Minor (and muezzins wield megaphones now, are wired for the chant), the Sea of Marmara to the right. Caïques clattering past selling fish. Desperate venality, a razor blade shop with nineteen men employed. Buses stink here (ancient American models, all with muffler trouble and a diesel octane gas; runnels of mud), the maimed and mendicant and children eloquent with english, men bearing their shops in their arms; for twenty-five kurus you can weigh yourself, two men therefore plying this trade, vying for it, the bridge on pontoons (our bar-keep jerking awake, his face in the comics, lighting with competence, to announce, "Brandy, I have"); the elevator man persuaded me at first that he could speak english, but can detail only the number and sequence of his five floors; dead dogs; an analphabet walks through our streets as do I here; red-backed sheep being wrestled from boats, pressed oranges, piles of peanuts, and bluefish boiled amidships; what is it that mocks evocation or makes it, worse, mawkish, agog: the essential distance maintained, the dialogue sought proving monologue only, the courtliness and haste.

Caged dogs in the zoo, with the Latin name for boxer proudly subscribed, and cats, and the fox was blind and the gazelle three-legged, and they fed bread to the bears. An hour spent in the Archaeological Museum, guards bent across heaters, most of the art ersatz, mummies trussed into backflips by time, sarcophagi ransacked for bones, combs sold in the street. Gigantic torsos, all of them imbalanced, with the museum providing the foot or the shoulder in plaster of paris; obscene. A boy in brown walks past, whistling, flips back his coattails, knockkneed, to reveal a pistol. This an abstemious day. The only english language read was on the ferry from Harem—instructions on a truck full of missiles, M-2's. Am full of that self-laceration that is meretricious, not pain.

SEPTEMBER 21

(*Darling now it's one a.m. and I miss you so much. I wish I knew why all this has overtaken us; darling, I don't. You were always so bloody puritanical about us and, in a way, so fearful of other people. In a way you left me no route but the wrong one. So again the pain is shared. Believe that.*) Today a long ferry ride up the Bosporus, through Thrace, docking at the Black Sea's maw; walked through a marketplace with sheep on display, ribbons tied to their tails, horns colored for recognition, some rainbow-like, all various, ate *barbounia*. The Golden Horn was sealed with chains, so they took Constantinople overland, bringing the boats by greased slide. In 1911 this sanitary government rounded up the strays of Istanbul—near one hundred thousand, it seems—and shipped them to the Princes' Islands and exterminated them. Traveled back with bells on, and in the captain's cabin, because the captain and mate were enamored of K., threw *raki* glasses overboard, did us a serpentine wheel-dance, slapping at the windows with their newly-purchased fish. I know now how to shell pistachios with teeth, eight Turkish invocations as to breasts. The jellyfish rampant. The Bosporus has a double current, its surface opposed to its depth, the one notably more saline than the other. I sense disequilibrium again, swaying over this wave-keyboard; how precarious, contrived, our elsewhere stasis seems. Raucous gulls, ah, *hornos*, a prison passed. Chinese food is execrable here; the maoists have all gone home. From the Galata Tower's bar, height, we watched the town go roseate, a bank of clouds careering west, a green smog-line beneath. The difference between wooden wheels and rubber on a cart. Men who shape old inner tubes as shoes. Those arthritic arabian horses, lumbering up hills; men ladle cheese from buckets, and women haul their purchases on rope. Huks. Gone to Ialova and back. The engine screw shearing as we pitched, women baying, sick; pashas with retinues; pashas holding court on the fore-deck, under umbrellas, hearing suits, dispensing grace. It snowed.

XIV

Living on the Concourse, Nicholas had to walk fourteen minutes to reach the IRT. If the weather was very bad, and he had the time, he took the bus and transferred from the IND. He then walked up the hill and was at Fieldston fifty minutes after leaving home; Peter Sim's chauffeur made it, from Park Avenue, in forty-six. After soccer practice, sometimes, Nicholas would go to the Sims' for dinner. The chauffeur awaited them and they went against the traffic and made it to the Sims in thirty-five minutes; Peter said he got most of his homework done in the car.

Their teachers warned them against cliques. "Cliques are a form of insecurity," they said. "If you've got an inferiority complex and show it as a superiority complex, then you're likely to be in a clique."

Nonetheless, Peter and Leland and George and Nat called themselves "the fellas" and they considered it envy when the mathematics teacher labeled them "the fellahin." Nicholas could never decide whether he was or was not part of the clique. "To the outsiders," he confessed to Sally Rieb, "I'm in; to the insiders, I'm out."

"You move in a lot of cliques," she told him, "you're in the intellectual clique too."

He took a course called Ethics and debated social distance. "Why should it be," he inquired, "that the deaths of three thousand Peruvians in a landslide bother me less than a traffic accident outside my house; what does that imply?" The Ethics course was compulsory but he enjoyed it; he pondered the problem of ends versus means. In the Third Form, when he was fourteen, he published an essay in the school magazine called "What We Mean by Means."

His first experience of farming was in New Jersey, at a farm connected with the school. The farm was called Hudson Guild, and they went there in the Second Form, taking the school bus and singing "Marching to Pretoria" all the way down the Henry Hudson Parkway to the George Washington Bridge. Sally Rieb was musical, and she tried to teach Nicholas a round. "I shall arise," she sang, "and go unto my father, and shall say unto him, father I have sinned against heaven and before thee and am no more worthy to be called thy son." Nicholas came in on "say unto him . . ." but they could not find a third person to complete the round.

At Hudson Guild they helped harvest corn. "This is cow-corn," the farmer said. "We use it for silage." "What's silage?" Leland asked. "Silage is cow-corn," Nicholas explained. They cleared a field so that it could be seeded in the early spring; they ate home-grown vegetables, and eggs from the farm chickens and milk from the farm cows. They played football in the cleared field, and Nicholas was left halfback and passed to Nat for a touchdown on the second play. George Stearns, who was on the other side, insisted Nat caught the pass out of bounds. "He's way out," he yelled. "He had both feet over all the time."

"Kiss my ass," Nat said. "That was a perfect play."

Nicholas got Millie Neuborg's picture (in a lace blouse, grinning, with braids) and they played mumblety-peg after dinner, and he shot the moon. It was the first weekend in October, and not cold; Nicholas considered sleeping on the cabin's roof. He was afraid, however, that he might roll off in his sleep. George told a joke about the fleet in port, with the whorehouses filled, and the final customer taking his girl to the roof.

"Just as they're coming," George said, "they lose their balance and, still locked in love's embrace, roll off and over and smash to the pavement below. So a drunk is passing by, and he goes up and knocks on the door and says to the Madam, 'Lady, your sign's fallen down.' "

They slept six to a cabin; Nicholas imagined horses neighing on the hill. He told his joke about the king who lived in a glass house and found out he shouldn't stow thrones; Leland told the joke about an alligator and Huey Long and which was the bump on which log. " 'Very funny,' the elephant said," said Leland, "as the alligator bit his nose off." Leland held his nose. " 'Veddy fuddy.' "

They considered sneaking into the teachers' cabins and puting warm bowls of water underneath the teachers' hands and making them pee. "It works every time," Leland promised. "Watch out, Nick."

He dreamed of dutch women in clogs and cowls who offered prayers for his soul for twenty florins; he had studied Martin Luther and Erasmus the previous week. Stately, he bicycled to mass. Nicholas would grow a beard and fix watches and the women would address him as "Your Reverence." He was naked, on Eighty-second Street, and George operated a lumber shop in a basement apartment. George told the joke about the doctor, examining his patient, who said, "Big breaths." "Yeth," she answered, "and I'm only thixteen."

He woke and watched the dawn and dressed. The sun surmounted mist, and the near pine trees were a lattice on the ceiling; he walked through the meadow and was soaked. He startled what he took to be a badger; he wondered, were there bear? He wondered, what was a woodchuck and what was a groundhog and what was the difference; he decided there was none. The moon became a shadow-crescent, and Nicholas breathed deeply for the count of eight. He held his intake for eight, then exhaled for the count of eight, then held himself vacant for eight; he crushed pine needles in his hands and smelled the sweet pine smell. When he returned to the cabin, he found Leland propped on one elbow on the upper bunk. "Hey." Leland pointed. "You pissed all over yourself."

"It's beautiful out there," Nicholas said.

"Yeah," Leland whispered, "I'll bet. What were you doing: beating off with Millie Neuborg? Or a bush?"

"Fuck off," said Nicholas, "fuck off into a lake."

He studied Latin and translated the story of Mucius Scaevola, who, to assert his loyalty, put his hand into the flame and let it burn witout wincing. "*Civis Romanus sum*," Nicholas said, "*civis Concursus.*" In French, he tried to translate Nat's phrase, "*Pas de leur Rhone que nous.*" "I bet you can't tell me what that means," said Nat. "It means something," said Nicholas, "like this. 'Not of their Rhone but ours.' Maybe a part of the sentence is missing; maybe it's only a phrase. Or, 'Steps of the Rhone which we. . . .' "

"It means," said Nat, "paddle your own canoe."

They conjugated verbs together, and Nicholas practiced Latin declensions and read that it was useful to recite declensions to prolong the act of love. The male partner should restrain himself, he read, in order to achieve simultaneous climax. He imagined touching Millie Neuborg on the breast, as if by accident. That would make her passionate, and she would let him do anything he wanted to her, and he would make her take off all her clothes except her socks and he would enter her, reciting *"Amo, amas, amat."* At *"Amavi,"* he would touch her breast again and that was a mistake because the magic would reverse. She would freeze and be sane and furious and he would have to touch her breast before she would permit him, magically, to continue. He knew her secret, therefore, and contrived to brush against her breast each day in the hall, and she would drag him, while George and Nat and Leland and Peter watched, into the girl's bathroom. And they would lock the door. "You can call me Marilyn," she would say.

Nicholas had to take one semester of cooking, and his first dish was glazed carrots; he put too much honey on, and the carrots stuck to the pan and burned. He took one semester of printing and printed up informals with his name; fourteen years later, he had not emptied the box. He studied his name and tallied thank-you notes unwritten; he had used black ink and gothic lettering. He was not barmitzvahed, though nearly everybody else in Fieldston was barmitzvahed. "Either you're a practicing jew," his father said, "or not."

"Why can't I be both?" Nicholas asked. "I could use up thank-you notes for presents."

"Stearns," his father said, "that's Stern. I know. His father changed it for business reasons. And don't tell me Bobby Rosenzweig isn't jewish. And don't tell me what's-his-name Wertheimer isn't a jew."

"OK," said Nicholas, "I won't."

He printed, "The quick brown fox jumps over the lazy yellow dog." He printed a set of cards with the following prayer. "Lord permit me to know the difference between wisdom and stupidity and to speak only about things I know about and at other times to Keep My Big Mouth Shut."

Andrea was graduated from high school when Nicholas was in First Form. She studied ballet and said that Fieldston was not real; she teased him, singing *"Iam cantate, iubilate,"* which was the Fieldston school song. She sang it to the tune of "My Country 'Tis of Thee," and sang it out of tune. "Why don't you stay home on Founder's Day?" she asked. "Why don't you play hookey—or ain't that ethical?"

"Swift as an eagle, strong as a vulture, rah rah rah for Ethical Culture," she sang.

He studied biology, later, and hurt his left leg at soccer and made a habit of vanilla egg creams at the bottom of "the hill." Students from Manhattan College passed him, climbing it; he shifted his briefcase, was cold. His right leg was his takeoff leg for the broad jump, and he could do kazatzkys easily. He did kazatzkys at the mixers, and the bunny-hop, but he could not Charleston well and talked to Richie Silber by the Cokes. His practice with his sister's friends paid off, and he won a lindy contest once; Millie Neuborg watched. His partner was Alice Metzger and she had red hair and halitosis and a dislocated pelvic bone; she wore falsies by the Fourth Form and, Leland said, put out.

Peter Sim's father's partner's brother owned the Stork Club, and they went to the Stork Club for Peter's fifteenth birthday. Nat was there, and Leland Harris, and George Stearns. They drank Coca-Colas and had tournedos with sauce Béarnaise and Leland had brought rum to add to the Coca-Colas. "Yes, we have no bananas," he announced.

Peter had two rooms in his New York apartment, because he played the drums. The room not facing Park Avenue was soundproofed, and he would sit there, chewing his tongue, practicing riffs; the rear wall had signed photographs of Jean Harlow and Rudy Vallee and Michael Dennis Browne. "I once met Hedy Lamarr," he said, "but she was too busy getting drunk."

"To busy to do what?" Nicholas asked.

"To give me her autograph. Or screw."

"Sounds like Claudette Colbert," Nicholas said.

They collected autographs of baseball players also, and Mickey Cochrane came to consult with Peter's father, once. Peter's father was an ear-nose-throat specialist, and had separate offices in the same building; he had, Peter asserted, a willing nurse. Peter had tropical fish and could name the various species. The maid fed them every morning, and if Peter remembered to feed them, they were fed twice. Peter knew the doorman at the Stork Club, and knew the first name of the hat-check girl. He claimed to know her telephone number but would not divulge it to Nicholas or George or Leland or Nat. "You don't know her number," Leland said.

"Sure, I've got it," Peter insisted, "but no one's going to share a thing like that. It's too much of a good thing," he said, "to share."

Nicholas dreamed of dogs, and space, and a mother who was thirty, slim, dressed by her private couturier, alive. He created ancestries—an uncle had committed suicide in Monaco, and Nicholas ascribed that to a gambling debt. Aunts wearing white skirts, twirling parasols, rose from lawns to greet him; the hall porter took his suitcase and admired the leather and reblocked his hat. "How good of you to come," his aunt said, fingering silk. "How delighted we are that you came."

By Fourth Form he had acquired a Boston accent and a habit of referring to himself with the impersonal "one." "One wishes for some sort of privacy," he said. "How else ought one to live?" He parted his hair in the middle and used eau de cologne on his handkerchief. "Don't put eau de cologne on your back," his doctor warned him, "it will aggravate the skin." Nicholas had pimples on his neck and back but no prominent pimples on his face; Leland did.

He told his father, "Look. One must attempt to grow. And most of man's history is imitation."

"You imitate false gods," his father said.

"What does that mean; you're not religious?"

"You're ashamed of your past," his father said, "our past."

"That's not true." Nicholas aped exasperation. "That's unfair."

In the telling, later, Nicholas made of his father a hero, holding back battalions of Franco's picked troops, drinking with Hemingway and Dos Passos and George Orwell. "He made it in a banana crate," Nicholas boasted, "and there were tarantulas all over the bananas."

"They didn't ship bananas from Spain," Nat said. "They don't have tarantulas there."

"What do you know?" Nicholas asked. "The boat came from North Africa."

"There's a blockade at Gibraltar," Nat said. "No commercial ships got through."

"This happened," Nicholas persisted, "before the blockade."

"When were you born," Nat asked, "in 1924? Must have been a long time before the blockade."

"He went back. Five years ago. Not everyone made money off the dole."

"What are you talking about?"

"Not everyone bought houses in Katonah for free."

"We paid thirty-seven thousand dollars for it," Nat said, "cash."

"My father," Nicholas said, "lost his estates in Spain."

Nicholas's father had been to Denmark, and he spoke of

how the danes hid jews at Elsinore. "Right across from Trävemunde," he said, "a short day's row away. They drink too much aquavit, but they're excellent people, the danes."

"What is't to me," said Nicholas, "but a foul and pestilential congregation."

"What?"

"Of vapors," he concluded.

He studied Hamlet and felt intelligence awakening and scored in the highest percentile on spatial relations tests. He professed himself a modern man, a mass of contradictions. He was pubescent at thirteen and five-foot-two-inches; he shaved twice weekly, then three times a week. Nat Kott could do forty chin-ups; "It's all a question of balance," he said. They had to hang from the bar before chinning, so as not to utilize the momentum of the jump; Nicholas, in First Form, could manage only three.

His mathematics teacher had a summer house in Nova Scotia and was adept with an axe. He would fell dying trees and lop off branches and quarter the trunk; he provided firewood for his apartment house, and for the apartment of the French teacher, Monsieur Laporte. Monsieur Laporte insisted on pronouncing the final "e," but the students called him "Door." He would bring his wife to the mathematics teacher's house, and they would get drunk and argue as to appeasement strategies, and Munich, and Daladier. "Take Chamberlain's umbrella," said Monsieur Laporte, "and stick it up his ass. Then open it," he said.

Nat Kott wore turtlenecks. "I've got sixteen in Katonah," he said, "not to mention the ones in New York. They're all of them cashmere, besides." Nicholas borrowed a purple turtleneck in exchange for his blue wool cardigan, but Nat pulled him to the mirror, laughing. "You look like a turtle," he said, "with your no-neck. You'd better give it back."

Late afternoons, after practice, Nicholas would wander to the near birchwoods. He stripped birchbark and used it for letters or tried to locate owls or hid beneath the mathematics teacher's window, listening. Sometimes he would fall asleep, watching the leaves shift with wind and release and settle; he slept beneath a maple once and woke with leaves on his eyes.

Returning to the Bronx was difficult. He spent weekends with his friends as often as possible, and sometimes he stayed over weekday nights. On Wednesday afternoon before Thanksgiving, Nat Kott invited him to Katonah; they would have, Nat said, both turkey and goose. Nicholas telephoned his father to ask permission; he had never invited friends to his house; his father asked him why.

"What's there to do on the Concourse?" Nicholas said. "There's no basketball court, really, or anything."

"Of course there is," his father said; "you could play at Fordham."

"It's not only that." Nicholas wrapped the line around his finger, then unwrapped it, then wrapped it again. "There's no place to go horseback riding."

"What about Van Cortlandt Park?"

"Or movies."

"You've never been on a horse. You hate horses, you said."

Nicholas sneezed, twice. "One could change one's mind."

"You're ashamed of your father," his father said. "Why not admit it; why not tell the truth?"

"No, that's not it, not at all. It's just I've never been to Katonah, and Nat's family asked me, specially."

"Well, bring him here first, I'd like to meet him. This Nat."

"It's not on the way, Dad, it's exactly the wrong direction. We're getting picked up by the driver; I can't ask him to come all the way to the Bronx."

"Which driver?"

"Nat's family's driver," Nicholas cradled the phone. The booth was airless and hot; he opened the door, not enough to be heard but enough to get some air.

"When will I see you next?" his father asked.

"Don't be that way," Nicholas ventured, released. "I'll come back on Sunday. I'll try."

"We've got a lot of yams," his father said. "Would you care for me to send you some?"

"No, papaito, thanks."

"Well," his father said, "have a good time. Think of us."

"Yes. Happy Thanksgiving," Nicholas said.

"Yes."

"Good-bye." He cradled the phone, then, ten seconds later, lifted it, then cradled it again. He wiped his face.

When he was sixteen, Nicholas went sailing with Leland Harris and Leland's second cousin Jill, and Jill's friend Mary-Anne. Leland was an expert sailor and his family had a home in Truro, on Cape Cod; Nicholas went there for Memorial Day. The Harrises owned a forty-nine-foot sloop that could be oceangoing, Leland said, and could sleep six. "Sleeps four more easily though," he said. "We sailed it down the inland waterway once. All the way to St. Thomas. My family."

Nicholas was a junior life-saver and an adequate swimmer; he knew nothing, however, about boats. Slow-fingered, he followed Leland's instructions, and the boom slammed his shoulder as he winched it up from the boom-crutch. Leland showed Nicholas how to raise the jib; "I want Mary-Anne," he whispered, "OK? She's built like a brick shithouse." "Like a masonry defecatory," Nicholas answered, trying to coil rope. "Like this," Leland said, and curled the rope around shoulder and elbow and, twisting it, made perfect loops.

Jill had been sailing often, and she pulled Nicholas around with her when Leland called "Ready about." She wore short white shorts that she had rolled up twice and a blue shirt with the tails tied together. "That looks like donkey's ears," Nicholas said. His shoulder ached. "Asses' ears, you mean," said Leland, and Jill and Mary-Anne laughed.

They tacked across the bay with Leland giving orders and took, he said, two tacks too many to make it; "Some crew," he said. "Some crew." They anchored at Jeremy Point and lay in the sun, deciding it was far too cold to swim. White-caps roiled, and Leland said, "I'll bet the small craft warnings will be up."

"Does that mean we shouldn't go back?" Nicholas asked. "Should we wait it out?"

"Can you think of anything else to do?" Leland asked Mary-Anne.

"No, what else could we do?" she asked.

"I've got a suggestion," he said, and lunged for her and kissed her and she put her arms around his neck, and Nicholas watched them, aghast.

He walked to the shoreline and watched the sandpipers and called Jill's attention to the sandpipers. "I wonder if the anchor holds," he said, examining the boat.

"Let's take a walk," she said.

He took her hand in his and massaged it, using each of his techniques. First, he took the whole hand as if it were a handshake and squeezed it softly, then hard, and rubbed his thumb across the back of her hand. Then he shifted position and let each of the fingers interlock. Swinging his hand, and hers, he could brush the back of his hand against her leg; he dared himself to do that, and he did that, twice. He next extricated his fingers and held her by the wrist; he rubbed his hand along her wrist and squeezed her forearm, hard. They rounded the cove's corner. "You can kiss me now," she said.

He kissed her, feeling the fabric of her shirt with his left hand, and squeezed, and had an erection. "You can kiss me again," she said, "if you'd like."

"If I'd like," he whispered, "Jill!" He fell on her as he had seen Leland fall on Mary-Anne; she grazed his erection with her legs.

He put his hand on her breast, which he had never done to any girl before, though Leland said he got bare ass and bare tit all the time. Nicholas wondered if, on the next kiss, he could open her lips and french-kiss her and if he had halitosis. "You could take your pants off," Jill said, "if you'd like."

Each fantasy outstripped, he stared at her. She had reddish hair and freckles and there was a line of his saliva on her cheek. She was compliant past believing and would marry, he learned later, Dennis Humphries and move to Santa Fe and die there, of leukemia, in 1953. She had a mole above her elbow and a mole above her knee and her pubic hair was, he told Leland, like the tail on Porky Pig. There was a strong wind, and they lay on his shirt, and Nicholas aped competence; a dog shark, washed to shore, stank. Gulls ravened at it and flew off when Nicholas moved and settled, pecking, again.

"I don't have a safe," he nuzzled Jill, whispering. "I left it on the boat."

"That's all right," she told him, "it's not that time of month."

"I won't," he promised, "make you pregnant. I'll finish outside."

"Don't worry," she said, "about that."

He had read chapters on the danger of preliminary ejaculation and of timed withdrawal; she inserted him and lay back, wiggling. He wondered would his acne show and how was Leland doing and if he could describe Jill, later, as a brick shithouse.

He pumped and gathered himself and felt a doubling distance, as though he alternated open eyes and the image leapt left, right. He touched Nicholas touching Jill and pictured her as Mary-Anne and the images were units and Nicholas exploded, making them one. Sweat was in his eyes and streamed down his chest and he left droplets on her breasts. She said, "We better get back."

Leland was impressed. He taught Nicholas the difference between a controlled jibe and an accidental jibe. They hoisted anchor and Nicholas held the anchor off from the boat's side. Leland said, "When she sashayed down the beach, I thought, you got a good thing going there."

Nicholas would work as a pinboy that summer. He could bowl one free game for every five games he set up, and the tips were adequate, and he got a base pay of twenty-five cents an hour. He liked the clatter of the pins and the combinations they described and the ways they slammed against the wall. If a pin came head-on, two out of five times, he learned, it would carom back and stand. For the first days, Nicholas gathered the pins and reset them, one at a time; later he could handle three pins with his right hand and two with his left. First, he waited till he set the pins and then sent back the ball; later, he sent back the ball and set the pins and jumped back on the bank and raised his legs. Jimmy Pontresino got hit by the eight-pin and had a broken knee.

Nicholas had a strong left hook, so he started to bowl down the extreme right edge; if he uncurled his wrist, he guttered the ball. He began with an average of ninety and had advanced, by September, to an average of one hundred eighty-two. His best game was two-forty-four, and he had a run of seven strikes. The work was sporadic and, as his speed in setting pins increased, so did his boredom. If a customer complained that the pins were unsteady, or fell, he said, "That helps your score."

Jill smoked and he lit her cigarette, sheathing flame. They ran before the wind and raised the jib, though Leland said that was not necessary. Nicholas put his arm around Jill's waist and said, "Maybe we could see each other soon again." She lived in Orleans the year round, as did Mary-Anne. She grinned at him and flattened his nose with the palm of her hand and said, "Maybe." He never saw her again nor wanted to; he wanted, he told Leland, to screw Mary-Anne.

(When Eve was four, in 1962, he took her to the airport to watch the planes land and leave. She was fascinated and went to the airport, thereafter, whenever she could; she waved good-bye, strenuously, from the observation deck. She insisted on going to see him off and to collect him and she went with him to meet cousins and business friends. When she was eight, therefore, he gave her a birthday present of a trip to Washington. Eve was terrified. On the plane she was repeatedly sick, rigid, and so short of breath they gave her oxygen. Nicholas told the steward, "I can't understand it. She's watched planes all her life. She's always loved them; she knows about flying."

Eve cried. "When do we start to get smaller? Planes get small. When"—she screwed her fists into her ears—"when do we disappear?")

Nicholas read about the Bauhaus and Paul Klee and admired futurism; he wanted to learn how to fish. He did not try to kiss a girl for three weeks after sleeping with Jill; he had been repelled by her sucking hold on him, and the shared fish-stink. Leland exhorted him to try for Mary-Anne. "She's got a six-inch clit," Leland said. "She'll be grateful if you rub it. Try."

Nicholas wanted to train his hair the way Leland trained his hair, with a curl behind each ear. He turned seventeen, and his father sang him "Happy Birthday" in Spanish, his voice still resonant. He received a purple blazer, a copy of Plato's dialogues, and a compass set inlaid in velvet, with a leather case.

"Hitler's given up on England," his father said. "He's going for Russia. He'll lose."

"What makes you so certain?" Nicholas asked.

"Napoleon lost. He'll lose."

"How can you be sure? He might beat Stalin or make another truce and have that whole land mass. All the way to Japan."

"The war is over," his father said. "You mark my words. It's only a matter of time."

"Which matters pretty much," Nicholas argued. "We'll never join the war."

"Hitler's a lunatic. He'll lose. He has to lose."

In September, 1941, Nicholas set his broad-jump record against the broad jumper from Horace Mann. He came to admire George Stearns; George studied lettering and copied an entire *Book of Hours* for practice and told Nicholas about Freud and Adler and Jung. George was burly and took boxing lessons and taught Nicholas the use of a left jab and check, then hit him, open-handed, with a right hook. He was on the track team also and threw the shot put, and the Locust Valley putter beat him by nine feet.

"Say something interesting," Nicholas said.

"Something interesting," George said.

Nicholas won the broad jump against Locust Valley also, but the track team lost. Inexplicable, this gift, the single authority offered, legacy of some ideal engendering self—"They broke the mold when they made him," said George about Leland, said Alice about George—as if in compensation for his elsewhere inadequate prowess, and cowardice, and envy, and all attendant mediocrities, and greed. They walked through the Locust Valley streets subdued; they had twenty minutes before the bus would come. The houses were imposing; "Strange Interlude," George said. "Desire Under the Elms."

They followed a long yew hedge and came upon grass tennis courts, a country club, two men in whites and one girl watching them. She sat in the driver's seat of a red Excalibur, with Gabriel mounted at her left-hand side, his trumpet the horn. She had nail polish, Nicholas saw, and inserted a cigarette into a cigarette holder, then licked the cigarette holder and lit the cigarette. "I'm in love," Nicholas whispered. "Come on, Nicky," said George, "this is second-rate Fitzgerald." Nicholas asked her the time.

"I haven't got it," she answered, "and wouldn't give it to you if I had."

"That was a kind of sexual foreplay," he assured George as they left. "That was a kind of advance. Really." He blushed, scanning the streets for the bus. Nicholas learned tennis and learned about lawns and, his second year at Columbia, slept with Alice Metzger in the back seat of her father's Mercedes; he later read *Les Déracinés* and decided that he also was uprooted, dispossessed.

He argued with Richie Silber about anarchy and passive resistance. "Wouldn't you kill Hitler," he asked, "if you had the chance?"

"That reasoning," said Richie, "is as porous as the Maginot Line. It's specious. It's teleological."

"I would," said Nicholas, "if I could get away with it. I would. A sufficient change in quantity, says Marx, becomes a qualitative change."

Richie was the class intellectual and they played chess together and Richie won four games out of five; he let Nicholas win the fifth, he said, in order to keep him interested. Richie volunteered for the O.S.S. and was killed in Buxtehude in 1944.

Peter Sim received a Pontiac for his eighteenth birthday; he would career down the West Side Highway, taking both lanes at the turnoff for Ninety-sixth Street. He kept a copy of *The Confessions of Jean-Jacques Rousseau* in his glove compartment and pulled it out to read at traffic lights. Nicholas said, "You should get *Lady Chatterley's Lover*. That would really stop traffic."

"OK, John Thomas," Peter said, "anything you say."

After graduation, they had drinks at Millie Neuborg's house and then a graduation dance, to which Nicholas took Millie Neuborg. She was beautiful, he thought, and had long black hair and would, they said, let him get hot. She had, however, broken her leg ice-skating, and it was still in a cast, and so they hopped about together, she on crutches. Not knowing what to do with his hands, he held her shoulders, then waist. Next they went to City Island for a drink on Leland's uncle's boat, and next they drove to Orchard Beach for a dawn swim. Millie could not go swimming because of her cast, and Nicholas lay next to her, hand on her cast, caressing it, wanting to sleep.

"I'm going to be an architect," he said. "I'm going to be a monk."

"I'm going to teach kindergarten this summer," she said. "You know, painting, stuff like that."

"Don't say kindergarten," he hissed. "Zat's a Sherman vurt!"

"What sort of monk," she giggled, "will you be?"

"What sort of fun will I have," he said, "nun."

On Pearl Harbor Day he had suspected Roosevelt; he would be eighteen in two months. Peter Sim had been eighteen in October, 1941, and Leland had turned eighteen in the beginning of May.

"One will pursue," Nicholas said, "one's ecclesiastical studies. Ain't going to study war no more."

He studied American History and did his final paper on the Reconstruction period; he focused on the Georgia Sea Islands and Sherman's Special Field Order #15. By this edict, every single "freedman" was to receive forty acres and a mule, and Nicholas projected what would happen had the land-grants held. Tunis G. Campbell proclaimed himself, he found, president "by the grace of God and General Saxton." Nicholas had one black friend named Mel. Mel was the son of a Pullman car porter and Fieldston offered him nearly a full scholarship, and his picture appeared with frequency in *The Fieldston News*. He was elected Student Council President and was elected valedictorian also. Mel was right halfback for the varsity football team by Fourth Form, and he was double-teamed and broke his collarbone. Everybody signed the cast, and Nicholas signed it with a purple crayon. "To Mel," he wrote. "Scatter back."

Nicholas concentrated on track. He ran first leg of the relay mile and slapped his palm with the baton while running; it was a bad habit but he could not break it, and he ran no faster without the baton. He was first-string broad jumper by Fifth Form, and, when there were standing broad jumps, he also standing broad-jumped. He had to compete in three events, and, if the meet had no standing broad jump, he entered the hop, skip, and jump. Evenings after practice, he would sometimes get a ride to the subway with Harry the track coach; Harry lived in Mount Vernon and he bred Pekinese. He had been married three times, he told Nicholas, and he preferred Pekinese. "They shed about as much," he said, "but they eat and argue less."

Nicholas wore flannel pants; he kept his hand against his thigh when walking, or climbing stairs, and he felt the muscles flex. He flexed his calves for Alice Metzger, and his biceps, and his pectorals. He had no noticeable triceps, and he determined to exercise his triceps. He used Wildroot Cream Oil, though Leland said it smelled. His father said his values had gone bad, and Nicholas responded, "That's haywire, papaito, that's ridiculous. What does that mean?"

"It means," his father said, "what I said."

"That's ridiculous."

"Now you're insulting me," his father said, "Q.E.D."

"*Quod erat demonstrandum,*" Nicholas intoned. "*Quod licet Iovi.* I know."

"You used to be so sweet," his father said. "And now. Look at your room."

"One sees it," Nicholas said.

His father spoke about the factory and Asturias and his ear and his wife's death. Nicholas interrupted. "Maybe I should go away," he said, "once and for all. Maybe then you'd appreciate me."

"Go then, the prodigal."

Nicholas wanted to weep. So adequately on his own in Riverdale, or on the East Side, he shrank in front of his father and would, when at Columbia, not live at home. He had entrance to the Stork Club yet had to wax his floor; he raged at the indignity and frenched his sister's bed.

She woke him at three o'clock. "Hey," he complained, "I've got to get my beauty sleep."

"Did you do that?" she asked. "You little fucker."

"Don't swear," he said. "What sort of language is that?"

"You little fucker," she said.

Nicholas yawned. "I'll have rings," he said, "under my eyes."

"Fix it."

"Fix what?"

"It." She advanced to his bed and pulled the covers back. He had an erection.

"I thought maybe," he pulled the blanket up, "you'd like to get cozy. That's a big bed, I thought, she doesn't need all that space."

"Very funny," she said, "ha-ha. I'm dying with laughter. See."

She wore a white skirt and a white wool sweater with little puffballs at her neck; she had six buttons and turned the room lights on and was luminescent, furious.

"OK," he conceded, "Miss Good Humor. Turn around."

She turned, and he labored out of bed, and his erection refused to subside. He retied his pajama pants and shifted the pants to the right.

"Where have you been," he asked her, "anyway?"

"None of your business," she said, and opened the door to her room. "Fix this."

The bed was a shambles, blankets on the pillows, sheets wrenched back. He bent to work. "Boy I'll be glad," he said, "when you get married."

"Not as glad as I'll be," she promised him, "to get out. Out of this inquisition."

She was not wearing shoes.

XV

SEPTEMBER 22

The bayram is a holiday for all. A holy day, and the sheep slaughtered at dawn. Their carcasses slung onto trucks, the meat distributed. For days there had been more sheep than cars in this town, now nothing left; red snow; the rain making rivulets of blood, the rain again, this the tenth day of rain. A man at the restaurant, having ordered six dishes, sat there immobile, smoking, staring at his absent partner, her hand, whatever; for the two hours we ate he touched nothing, smoked, was misery incarnate, paid and left. Ten minutes spent watching the elevator man attempt to get out of his cage. Tonight in the music tent, this endless celebration, reminiscent somehow (if only in the sideshows provided, and smoke, though as far as I could tell no drugs in evidence) of the Fillmore West. The hooves and heads of sheep. Some attempt at reconciliation; eating mussels with K. Am in the only corner of the room where I can't see myself (four mirrors quartering the space), and not a pleasing prospect, this.

Womack came from Arkansas and was six-foot-three and, when he was seventeen, traveled to Richmond, Virginia. He played the slide trombone; he painted the Provincetown Airport. His uncle was a railroad engineer and let Womack handle the controls; when he was seven years old, Womack hit a cow. He married and had two sons and his brother, Mickey, had rheumatic fever but survived.

There are twenty-seven plots. What's Hecuba to him? Employ as leitmotif, perhaps, the following expression: "Set fire to his cakes." Or, alternatively, "Love."

SEPTEMBER 23

R. saw, in 1956, a public hanging here. The man simply standing on a chair, and then the chair pulled out. Return to Rome. There's something about the system of *cinéastes* that pleases even less than that of poetasters; easy name-dropping, the studied gesture, the immaculate conception. Each tempest rehearsed. Routines wear less well now, this the disengagement. Statuary like K. Socks that keep slipping. The Barone P.P. Sixty at least. Recruited during the Italian-Ethiopian campaign. Lived in Ethiopia nine years. With time out for a prison camp after El Alamein, and three journeys back to Italy to visit with his parents. These trips taking fourteen days by boat. Had a family chauffeur called Ferrara who went out on his own to make cars. Wears, for reading, half-rim glasses; wrote and acted in "Paysan." (At the Excelsior Bar

the magnates enter in procession, all of them precisely
placed, as if by instinct, pyramidal, the head at the head,
the flunkey at foot, the pecking order between.) The
Barone P.P. takes us to dinner, bearing I., a Finn.
Whom he describes, and correctly, as, how do you
say it, a bottle of milk. Loves, just between men (this
said slightly lower as the ladies were powdering noses
which, in America, he says, takes three hours at the
least), to go down on her, since she has only feathers
for hair. And is not troublesome. The mullet come
from the Adriatic, not the roman waters, where
there are more plankton. Avoid the inaccurate parallel
construction and, where possible, parataxis. What is
syntax but the art of subjugation; after every course,
to clear the palate, he nibbles parmesan cheese.

SEPTEMBER 25

*But there is a rather dashing sixty-five-year-old mil-
lionaire who wants to take care of all my problems;
Rome is crawling with these men, I think. He's really
quite sweet and drives a gold Bentley and speaks to me
only in French and called me up before he left for
Easter vacation (the rich take two weeks off for
Easter) to say that he'd rented an apartment for me
and wanted to leave me some cash. After I'd seen him
once, and very casually at that, for dinner. And so it
goes. (And so it went.)*

SEPTEMBER 26

A man in front of the Baths of Diocletian, rearranging
tires and boulders and haranguing the *signore, signori,*
dressed in a sweatsuit, no hair beneath his arms but

heavily fleeced on the shoulders and back, sweating, soliciting applause, the children vaulting fences as he whirled; then, more forbiddingly, outside of Hadrian's Villa, a man in an overcoat, toting a briefcase, his hands begrimed, the grime gunpowder, screaming that he had a license and worked hard, the children attentive but terrified, and he came to us and showed his tablets, canisters really, then flung one at the pavement, one at the wall, and asked for payment, went muttering on; someone shot his head off while demonstrating, to his girl friend, the principal delights of russian roulette. Madness; the breasts spewing water in Tivoli; A., habituated to insult, cannot receive praise with grace. I tell her, and it's true, she's looking well; how can you say that, she answers, I must look horrible; this is a fright wig, this wig.

112. CHRYSANTHI: Philippos and I were just talking about autobiographies. And he maintains that, just as novels try for truth by lying, so autobiographies do the opposite. PHILIPPOS: That's not what I said at all. That's not the point. The point is, if Philippos writes, 'I walked down the street at 3:37 PM,' you'd believe me. And if I wrote, 'Alexandra walked down the street at 3:37 PM,' you'd think I made it up. Yet the fact is she did and I didn't. And that's what I mean by authority's confusion, its duplicity. CUT TO 113: CS Chrysanthi's eye. She meticulously applies eye-liner, then mascara to her eye. With a pair of tweezers she removes one black-caked lash. CUT TO 114: TOP OF THE GALATA TOWER. BALCONY. CHRYSANTHI: All this author-ity nonsense. What I want to do is learn about the person, isn't that so? PHILIPPOS: Why should I believe Lord Russell any more than I disbelieve Proust? Who can really remember what happened when he was four

with his nursemaid in the park? CHRYSANTHI (reaching for Sotiris's hand): This is fun. We ought to do this more often. CUT TO 115: SOTIRIS: Those delicious grilled shrimp, for instance, that we had at Sariyer. CUT TO 116: TOP OF THE GALATA TOWER. LS PHILIPPOS: I'll give you an example. Conrad's *A Personal Record* is the least revelatory of any of his books.

SEPTEMBER 27

These habits of accumulation. Avarice. Cunning. Deceit. Infidelity. The lack of compassion throughout. If cunt is *frauenzimmer*, why should not the head be house? This slow winding up for release. G. is vain but not self-conscious. Which gives him no notion of other people's response, yet a fascination with their opinion. The man who has sequestered himself for forty years in an apartment, spends ten thousand lire a day on food, reads voluminously, neither gains weight nor grows pale. And has not stepped outside of it since 1931. Rubens is the Mozart, say, of painters— between conception and completion no sort of tension exists. Did the Athenians, facing Syracuse, attach as slight importance to it as we did, once, to Hanoi? Were they sucked the same way out, like the innards of an egg, the fructifying part blown, so that the shell remains?

(EDITOR'S NOTE: The following pagination refers to the typescript of *In the Middle Distance*.)

EDITOR: p. 305, line 1: The phrase "under god" was not added to the pledge until 1958; and, damn it, I remember when they did it, making me blush. I was in, I think, the 10th grade at the time, and God was my enemy; it was all tits and soft lip fuzz for me then, obsessed and not to know of God's glory until woman's pale curse was lifted from me on the day of my wedding to Sister Patricia, guardian of our Lord's holy candle, digital virgin (a vestal virgin with smooth hands; not what you're thinking, pal).

AUTHOR: If that's the way it's gwine ter be, howzabout: "One Ray shone in de vestibule." (One nation indivisible.) Wisht I'd a been smart enough, hand on me heart, to thunk it then. Not to mention when in hell "God Bless America" was written. Not to mention when it became popular, and when the rhyme. . .

SEPTEMBER 30

Back in New York, one way station, eleven to go, have a fever of one hundred and three. Again, the cosmic egg, and Christ; select henceforth only those comparisons that do not aggrandize. Am frightened of cholera; strange, how the body rebels. She said "nightmeg" for "nightmare," had a butting head-punch, loved to wrestle; uncertainty tied to conviction, argumentative. I can keep these portraits, the secondary ones, and some of the description, and the self-reflexive prose. But there's no organizing principle as yet; no way to shape a book, time. Who, except those I include, might be moved at all? (*"I love the country. I am a city and country boy. My grandparents had a big place and places up in the country and there was everything a boy can wish. But love. But the summers were good there and my memories are rich. I have never forgotten a thing and they all wonder how I remember. I remember everything and I often am being kept awake, reviewing in my mind all. And I have not seen enough.*") This Friday, March thirteenth, the kitchen derelict, the cesspool defunct. For the first time I see D.'s dilemma, and his hesitation, and that he may be right; why publish if only to wound. We're all created characters with self-esteem as author, and that does trick illusion up in Sunday clothes. Those hunting traps where you cover a hole in the ground with false ground, a lattice of branches; sometimes, only rarely but sometimes, the quarry does plummet through. Must do taxes. Must not repeat myself. Must shovel into the garage. Say Grace. Grace. Read. Have a fire. Learn restraint. It snows, still. Stop. Hoist by a witting petard. It's easier, I suppose, to sever in some new place than to be so whelmed by memory. Roads filled with feet. The dogs yapping; elms. Photographs. Anent this snow. I'm writing nonsense. Reader, this page contains the genuine misery absent elsewhere. Include letters. Maybe. Yet with no hint of fact. Maybe.

OCTOBER 1

The coffee-maker stinks of M. This procedural integrity, the notion of shucked shelves. The shock of molting, really, when lobsters rise to the sea's surface, sink. Fire in the lake/ the image of the Revolution/ Thus the superior man/ Sets the calendar in order/ and makes the seasons clear. Transition inevitable. (March the thirteenth survived. We cleansed the cesspool. Maybe I'll make him an architect; perhaps he'll have the farm as summer house. New definition of delight: with one toothless idiot called F., and one toothed half-wit called H., the former wielding a pick, the latter a broom, myself the shovel, in a snowstorm, the snow two feet deep, the stench surrounding, try to find a septic tank. Their coffee mugs untouched, and set in snow, they regale me with tales of shit they've elsewhere pumped. H., the boss, has to take his honeydew wagon to a processing plant now, not like it used to be, he says, got to pay more than town taxes, state too. He sifts through shit for leavings, finds nothing, concludes it the drainage at fault.) N. lives, in a muted way, off the venom the morning's mirror provides—his face. Sodden goddess his wife; call her, mayhap, Aurore. Wears tab collars, does N. Summered in Easthampton; read McLuhan once, daughter goes to Dalton. Fifty-three years old.

OCTOBER 3

M. misses appointments, S. creates them, and neither matters much. (*Darling darling it's ten pm and I'm watching television and drinking a bottle of something red and dry from normandy and feeling dissolute and mostly mainly lonely and in love with you. I've been this way all week—terrible state of affairs. I'm feeling very sorry for myself, miss you in whatever the adverb is for an anguished way, and have regretted all week my decision not to monkey with, or monkey-wrench the divorce. Been bitching steadily, and nobody to hear me, bitch bitch bitch. Am I sounding melodramatic. No matter. These couples strike a sad chord, really; my stiff upper lip keeps getting soggy with tears. So there's this wine, and it's a far more festive way to get to sleep alone.*) N. unplugs the hotplate and the coffee curdles on him and he wonders, looking at the groundhog, how best to scatter waste. Interested in garbage disposal. The sap runs now. I have wasted, he thinks, hunting for the antecedent, its echo, my life.

March 12, 1971

Mr. John Crowther
RHM Productions
Via Tagliamento 9
Rome, Italy

Dear John:

The photographs of Nick arrived some time ago, but I haven't written you to acknowledge them because I've been waiting to consult about them with our art director. Consultation having been accomplished this morning, I can now write and say that I think the photographs are beautiful in themselves and just perfect for our purposes. And our own preferences seem to agree with yours: we shall be using the close-up that you mentioned in your letter on the front of our jacket, and on the back of the jacket we'll be using the photo of Nick at the table. There will be copy on both front and back, but it won't obscure the photographs.

Suitable pictures were a long time coming. I'm grateful for these and happy about them.

Take care, and come by the house when you're back in New York.

All best wishes,

[Signed]
James Landis

JL/jp

OCTOBER 5

Strange story S. tells of an umbrella flown from a shinto shrine and become recalcitrant lover to a widow in a bamboo hut. Moral: don't wait, he says, upending Scotch, for mail from an umbrella. That surly delight functionaries take when protected by rules. Am tempted to call his wife Aurore and daughter Astrid; one renders justice only via catalog, the accretion of detail made metaphoric. A wet snow, branches break. Plague Year. I make good coffee. I can clean the kitchen. I make excellent salad. Marry me. A girl here sprayed De-Icer in her eyes, attempted to remove her hair with candles, hearing with pins. N. wears muttonchop sideburns, is frightened of mugging, is muddle-headed about time. Habitually late. Neck-twisting exercises meant to forestall age. Insomniacal. His wife bakes bread. It does not rise, but he's appreciative nonetheless. Will leave his monies to some pension plan. We never really had those lengthy parting conversations which find their simulacrum only in the starting. And where sex grows bittersweet, gestures too studied for truth. D. says, and he's perfectly right, that the whole is inevitable, therefore there's little credit in the acquiescence. Christ, but it's hot on this freight. Groddeck's bawling baby called the "It." Things pursue him; people; I painted the upstairs study today.

OCTOBER 6

This Easter Sunday, and the snow impassable; myself running the joy number, as R. says. He lectures on retribalization, is convinced, except that we might blow ourselves up, and that no small exception, that tribal man once more assumes hegemony. Friends' wives exploded inside. Indifference shakily mustered; no, I am not happy, yes, remain intact. Jealousy, says R., is a western attribute. Unknown to eastern toxicologists, or, at the most, released in a ritual fashion and without despair. This trip a rite of passage; the plants Christine will kill. What if the journal were to leave its persona behind, to take tangents past his comprehending, out of his control? So that the grief resound, and without the frame. Let us, says D., float opposing moralities, juggle the standard at will. His prick bent out of shape with screwing, his hands reek, and still he shrieks fidelity, something of a joke.

October 6. The house again carapace now.

XVI

A soft rain fell; Nicholas played basketball on the concrete court. He was good at left-handed layups and good at jump shots but not good enough at set shots; he practiced set shots. He wanted to sink seven out of ten. His father always showered in the factory and came out, friends said, looking like he owned it; he was foreman of the shipping department and could wrap packages, friends said, faster and better than any of his employees. He would have been, he told Nicholas, a professor like his father, and his father's father before. "Excepting for these wars," he said, "we would still own respect." He had emigrated to America in 1921; Andrea had been three.

Nicholas walked Betsy Lang back from school. "Do they call you Niccolo? At home?" she asked. She wore a brassiere by the sixth grade and giggled when he asked her what magazines she read; she read the ones with woman-ads, she said. In the summer his best friend went to summer camp, and Nicholas did not; that winter they had played "sock baseball," playing inside. His best friend was Harry Burten, and Harry lived in the same building, three stories up. Harry threw a sock, and Nicholas would take a half-swing, and if Harry caught it he was out; two outs completed the inning. If it landed on the bed that was fair, and a double; if it landed underneath the bed it was foul. The mirror was a home run, and bouncing off the ceiling counted and the radiator was a single, unless the sock got caught in the radiator ribs and that was a ground-rule double. "We sure do pound the stuffing," Harry said, "out of that sock."

It was a low-scoring game, though they played for fifteen innings or until supper, whichever came first; the winning score was six runs at the most. Nicholas pitched sidearm and, sometimes, underhand. "I'm Christy Mathewson," he said, and Harry was Walter Johnson. Harry was fat and had bowlegs and liked Babe Ruth best.

(Nicholas would, later, divide his father's life. There were times, he knew, when walking was sleepwalking, when conversation, food, work, worry all become habitual; satisfaction, also, was merely matter-of-course. Then his father reached a kind of climacteric, would wake and stay in bed or exit from the house illuminated, rapt. For days he noticed everything, was moved by everything, made changes, resolutions, would not die. He was easy with machines and regulated them; carburetors held no mystery for him, nor fuel lines, nor toasters. Nicholas would watch his father fix switches or spackle the ceiling; he could nail a nail above his head. When what his father called "the fit" took him, however, all inanimate things were enemies. Driving, his tires flatted, and did so in sequence, and the jack would not work.)

Nicholas had wooden Civil War soldiers, and he built an apple tree out of pipe cleaners and cotton; the gray soldiers sat roan horses, and the blue soldiers sat white. He built an exhibition of Appomattox and had Lee presenting swords; he affixed a white cotton-wool beard onto Lee. He built the courthouse at Appomattox. He used popsickle sticks and wire and a bandage that his mother used for her ankle; he painted it brown. He went to the movies with Harry every Saturday. His father liked Greta Garbo and took Nicholas to see movies with Greta Garbo and John Garfield, but Nicholas preferred Adolphe Menjou.

Nicholas could hurdle hydrants and he put pennies on the subway tracks and he watched them spread. A penny dropped from the top of The Empire State Building, Harry said, would go right through your head and shoes and pavement and six feet down. "Which falls faster," he asked, "a pound of feathers or a pound of lead?" Nicholas said, "A pound of lead," and Harry said, "Let's put it this way; which weighs more?"

(He would be sent to Fieldston in the seventh grade. Fieldston was an Ethical Culture School and called the seventh grade First Form. "I want you to have the things," his father said, "I would have had." Nicholas took entrance tests and was awarded a scholarship that was the second largest in the class; Benjamin Dupuy had a bigger scholarship, they said. "Do you know enough Latin," his father asked, later, "to translate this? *Alea iacta est.*" "The die is cast," said Nicholas, who commenced to study Latin in Third Form. "Do you know what this means?" he asked his father. "*Quod licet Iovi non licet bovi.*" "What is permitted to Jove is not permitted to the cows," his father said. "*Ad astra per aspera.*")

"What is black and white and red all over?" Nicholas asked.

Andrea knew the answer. "A newspaper," she said.

Nicholas ate quantities of raisins, because his father thought them healthy, and he could only eat one chocolate bar each week. "Besides the fact that they're expensive," his father said, "they ruin your health and your teeth." His father believed in grated apples also, and in the nutritive value of beans. "There are nothing like beans," his father said, "to aid the digestion and to nourish growth."

He had many such theories. He lectured the children at length about the positive and negative effects of diet; raisins were a sugar-substitute and had concentrated energy and were, he said, Asturias's best crop. Nicholas wanted a bicycle and dreamed of an English racing bicycle, all black. It would have three forward speeds and a reverse and a horn and bell and two separate sets of reflecting lights. Andrea had a bicycle, but it was a girl's bicycle, and Nicholas did not like riding it; he even preferred his tricycle, and, when they went for bike rides in Fort Tryon park, he could go almost as fast. He thought that if his mother had lived, he would have had a bicycle for his eighth birthday, or for Christmas that year.

They went to the zoo each Saturday. Andrea liked the monkey cages and she used to watch the gibbons and baboons and orangutans with attention; of all the monkeys, Nicholas liked gorillas best. He preferred the lion cages to the Monkey House and sometimes he could stay there, watching lions and tigers and leopards and jaguars and cheetahs and ocelots, while Andrea and his father visited the Monkey House. He admired, mostly, the cleanliness with which they ate, and the way leg-sockets shifted when they sat.

The radiators sounded, Nicholas thought, like guns. Sometimes he would fall asleep to the clanking and chatter of heat, and it would fit completely with his dream. He would dream of Natty Bumppo, noiseless, startled by guns. He painted watercolors and poster paint pictures of Natty Bumppo and of his cousin's house in Montclair, New Jersey; when he pulled the pictures off the wall, the tape left marks. He had a history chart that he taped above his bed; it started with the pyramids and ended with Queen Victoria. It went by century and country and emphasized England; it was made in England, certainly, his father said. Philip the Second received one line, and so did the Inquisition, and the defeat of the Armada in 1588 received, under England's entry, seven lines.

Nicholas's father believed in cold baths and that they helped the circulation; he let Nicholas choose if he would take his bath in the morning or at night. But he had to take at least one bath per day, and afterwards his father rubbed him with the rough side of the towel. "There," he said with satisfaction, "you're healthy and you're clean." He would spread the towel, to dry it, on the radiator, and the towel dried in lines.

They owned one of the few phonographs in the neighborhood. It was a black-shell phonograph and had a swivel-horn and black and red and silver mesh across the speaker; it sat on a table by the window in the living room. Nicholas felt like the dog on the record label, listening; his father insisted that they learn about the opera and symphony and forms of devotional music. They sat and listened for three hours every Sunday morning; "This is," his father said, "instead of synagogue."

They sat and listened to Wagner, therefore, and to Verdi and Handel and Haydn and Bach; in summer it was worse, because their father opened the window and Nicholas could hear, between movements or during recitatives or when they changed the record, sounds of the street beneath. He hated opera. He hated it, he said, because it stank. "What does that mean?" his father corrected him, "things that you smell stink."

"Whose language is this anyway?" Nicholas asked.

Andrea liked the music and she developed a crush on Caruso and she argued with her father as to the respective merits of Caruso and Chaliapin. Beneath, Nicholas could hear the stickball games, and handball, and games of Capture the Flag.

Nicholas's father believed—as his mother had believed—that walking was exercise and that children should not be beaten. The Italians in the neighborhood, he said, were wrong to beat their children, and would live to regret it, and soon. He left for work at seven thirty and came home at seven; the apartment had five rooms. There was a living room and dining room and his father's bedroom and study. Nicholas and Andrea shared one room till Nicholas was six.

"What's green and has eight heads and claws?" Andrea asked.

"I don't know," Nicholas said. "I give up."

"I don't know either," she said, "but it's crawling on your shoulder."

Nicholas remembered wanting to die, the nightly sweat and terror, flashlight beneath his pillow, scanning the wall for shapes. At five he learned to swim, then fell in the Coney Island breakers and, wallowing, was sick. For two weeks he woke gagging, tasting salt, heels over head in the bed. "I want to die," he whimpered, "and nobody cares. Nobody cares if I die."

His mother held him in her arms but was no true comfort. "Hush-a-bye-baby," she sang, "in the tree top. When the wind blows, the cradle will rock." He imagined breaking branches, and the hurtling collapse of his bed, her arms. "When the bough breaks, the cradle will fall, and down will come baby, cradle and all." He imagined forests falling, deer breaking loose from flame, the crush of it incessant, irretrievable, the floorboards splintered, upended and their apartment falling into the incinerator, gone.

He made exhibitions of soldiers, mounting, as accurately as he could construe it, the Battle of Bunker Hill. "What if the english soldiers wore sunglasses," he asked, "or if they kept their eyes shut running, or if there was too much smoke to see?" His father read him an english history book in which the American Revolution was referred to as the Revolt of the Colonies; he dressed up as Kit Carson for three straight Halloweens. He went trick-or-treating with Richie Steers and Harry Burten and Bob Bollinger; Bob Bollinger was Wild Bill Hickock and Richie Steers was Eddie Rickenbacker and Harry Burten was Chief Sitting Bull.

Later, he made exhibitions of the Civil War. He called the english the South and painted gray poster paint over the redcoats; it rubbed away as he arranged the battle scenes, but the South looked tattered enough. Some of his American Revolutionary soldiers had coonskin caps and leggings, and he made them scouts. He studied Antietam and Bull Run and Shiloh; he asked his father, "Who's the Rock of Chickamauga?" and his father did not know. "Who's Stonewall Jackson?" he asked, and his father did know that.

His family was jewish but not orthodox. "We're not even reform," Andrea said, "we're reform reform." Sephardim, they had been assimilated in Spain long since, and Nicholas was proud of his family tree. His father threatened synagogue as punishment, but Nicholas only went twice. "I believe in something like God," he would say, "but don't think he had a white beard."

(Later, with Hitler, his fervor was to increase. He wore a yellow star of David as a sign of solidarity; he would proclaim himself a Zionist, was not.)

Richie Steers and he and, sometimes, Harry Burten, stole bubble gum and chocolate bars and water pistols from Elman's Variety Store. One of them would ask a question about magazines or baseball to Mr. Elman, and the other would pocket the pistol or chocolate or gum. They took turns asking questions. Nicholas preferred discussing baseball because he could also mention weather then, and if the game would be held.

Mr. Elman was a friend of his father's, and very tall and thin and knew about their stealing, Nicholas thought, all along.

The world was sizable. He visited Monticello and Washington D.C. on a school trip. "P.S. 33," they sang, "rah-rah, turds and pee." His sixth-grade class photograph showed Harry Burten twice. It was a time exposure, and Harry had had time enough to run from the back left row to the back right row; his face in the back right row, however, was blurred.

Nicholas felt he played roles. When his mother died he played the grief role; when he walked Betsy Lang home he played the thoughtful friend.

"You're not stuck up," she said, "no matter what they say."

Richie Steers said, "I defended you this morning. They said you weren't fit to eat with pigs, and I said that you were."

"Thanks a lot," Nicholas said. "I'll do the same for you some time."

"I'm kidding," Richie Steers said.

Sometimes Nicholas feigned rage and, shaking someone in the school corridor, would howl, "Don't ever do that again!" He would hold his breath and go scarlet and trembling, and the guidance counselor tried to discuss it with him, but that was also a role. Andrea went to Elizabeth B. Browning Junior High School; he went to the Fieldston School but would have attended, otherwise, Creston Junior High. He went to see the guidance counselor and promised to behave and said it was only a game. "You said one time," she said, "that you wanted to die."

"Not now," he told her, "not any longer. I'm very happy now."

(Nicholas's friend Sam went places with him that no one else could go; Sam was not afraid of closets or the incinerator or the roof. Sam was tall and tough. He had yellow hair; he disappeared when Nicholas was seven. Sometimes he would not want to sleep when Nicholas wanted to sleep, and then they would argue underneath the blanket till one of them won. Sam liked the Yankees best. He liked chocolate too, and could wrestle a rhinoceros with one hand behind his back. Sam had to have a chocolate bar on Wednesday, and Nicholas got his on Sunday afternoon. But he had to listen to three hours of opera first.

Sam would face the door while Nicholas would face the window, sleeping; that way they could cover every entrance to the room. Sam went away on trips to Antarctica or the Pacific Ocean or to Washington, D.C. He would write letters back or telephone or send a carrier pigeon announcing how he liked the trip, and what sort of people he met. He generally sent the pigeon during dinner, and Nicholas would listen and thank the pigeon politely and offer it something to eat. Most times the pigeon refused, but it had a fondness for beans. Nicholas did not like beans, so that worked out all right.

Sam went to school with Nicholas and helped him beat up Sandro Cavalcante. When Nicholas had won and was kneeling on Sandro's arms, he taught Nicholas a trick of rocking back and forth upon his knees. Sandro howled. Sam was one year older than anyone else in the class; he had trouble remembering dates. He disappeared when Nicholas went into the first grade, and Nicholas decided Sam was visiting his, Nicholas's, mother, and would not return.

Sam was excellent at baseball, and the New York Yankees' farm team would be interested in him someday soon. Miller Huggins watched him swing; Sam was a pinch-hitter and never broke his wrists on a bad pitch. Miller Huggins said that he would probably be ready for the sandlots; Connie Mack, regretfully, agreed.)

Nicholas remembered dates. He closed his eyes and could

see dates above his bed, in rows, on the historical chart. "What happened in 1492?" Nicholas would ask. "Columbus sailed the ocean blue," was the answer. "What happened in 1776?" Nicholas would ask. "The American Revolution," was the answer. "What happened in 1215?" Nicholas asked. This was harder, but some people knew, or Nicholas would prompt: "The Magna Carta" was the answer. Then Nicholas would ask, and this was the point of the joke, what happened in 13 A.D. Nobody could answer, and, when they gave up, Nicholas answered the riddle himself. "Christ was barmitzvahed," he said.

Nicholas took piano lessons. He went every Tuesday and Friday to Mrs. Lehman's house, and she made him practice scales and play "Long Long Ago." He also practiced the melodic line for Schubert's Unfinished Symphony. "This is the melody," it went, "that Schubert wrote and never finished." He hated piano lessons and they did not own a piano so he rarely practiced. He was glad when there was not enough money for piano lessons, and Mrs. Lehman moved.

His mother, he remembered, told this story when he was sick. Once upon a time, she said, there was a little boy called Nicholas who was, let's say, seven years old. He wasn't feeling well. His tongue had spots, his arms had spots and they were called the German measles; he had already had the mumps. When he had the mumps he stood in his crib and pushed one cheek out of the crib between the bars and was a sort of hippopotamus. Or an elephant. Except that he had forgotten the mumps already and therefore couldn't be an elephant because elephants remembered. Now that he had the measles he wanted to be a leopard, because that was an appropriate animal; if the measles had been stripes he could have been a zebra. But instead he would be fierce; he would cry so loud and roar so long that everyone in the apartment building would be frightened; he would tie his red pajamas in the back and that would be his tail. His bed would be his cage.

Nicholas-leopard got into adventures, and the adventures were different every night. Once he stopped a forest fire by running faster than the wind to tell the fire chief and lead the fire engines back and got a medal for not moaning about how hot he felt, or thirsty. Once he met Dr. Livingstone in the middle of the jungle and Dr. Livingstone was very kind and introduced himself and they took a canoe trip down the Nile. Once he met President Hoover who said chicken soup was just the thing to make the country and Nicholas-leopard all well.

It was while he had the measles that his mother died. She was thirty-one years old and thin and Nicholas was also thin because he didn't eat. She had been born in Cadaqués and had always, she said, loved the sun; she did not like the Bronx.

Nicholas and Andrea campaigned for Roosevelt in 1932. Andrea rang the doorbells and did most of the talking, but Nicholas would hand the buttons out. He had a favorite shirt with fringes and mother-of-pearl buttons and buttons on the pockets and fringe lining on the cuffs; he did not take his holster but he wore that shirt. He learned how to read by himself; before that, he would memorize the page and turn it at the proper time. When he was nine, his father gave him *The Outline of History* by H. G. Wells. "I know you can't enjoy this yet," his father said, "but soon."

Nicholas learned table manners from the sitter, Mrs. Menendez. She taught him which hand to hold the fork in, and to wipe his mouth before he drank and to cross the cutlery when he was done. She taught Andrea how to set the table and Andrea set the table every night. Nicholas learned by watching and would help fold napkins and could bring the salt and pepper if he was very careful about the kitchen step; he broke three glasses by mistake.

Mrs. Menendez had blue hair and wore black dresses only; this was, she explained to Nicholas, in honor of her husband and her son. She lived two streets away, and came to visit every day and helped Nicholas's father when he lost his ear. She had been to New Orleans and told Nicholas stories about New Orleans; people there wore iron grillwork on their hats and skirts, she said.

His father admired Floyd Dell and Leon Trotsky and Ida Rauh and read *The New Masses* with care. Nicholas learned in school that Henry Ford was very important, and his father said that was true but was a shame. "We have to change the world," he told Mrs. Menendez, "so that the lumpen-proletariat perceives."

"Perceives what?" Mrs. Menendez asked.

"These systemic evils," he explained. His father lectured friends about the lumpen-proletariat, and Nicholas was proud of pronouncing the word.

His father had many shirt-collars and always took an extra collar when he went to work. "You will," he told the children, "live to see things better. This country had the first real revolution, and it will have the next. Men won't sell apples much longer; mark my words. Just read the Bill of Rights," he said, "and see how little of the Bill of Rights is real."

Nicholas read the Bill of Rights in the fifth grade, and he mumbled, "One ray shone in de vestibule," when he pledged allegiance to the flag. He and Harry Burten sang this song to the tune of "God Bless America." "God Bless my underwear," they sang, "my only pair. I wore them, and tore them, on the back of my old rocking chair." He was best friends with Harry Burten by fifth grade. They would walk home slowly, playing "Who do you like better?" Nicholas would name two people (not counting himself, since Harry Burten liked him best) and Harry would rank them, in order of his preference. Then Harry's turn would come and he would do the same, not counting himself. This way they would rank everybody in the class and they would remember the order and see how it changed every week. "You wanna fight me buddy?" Nicholas would ask of Sandro Cavalcante. If Sandro said yes, Nicholas would point to Harry and say, "Here's me buddy. Go ahead."

If someone boasted they could lick him anytime, or with one hand behind their back, Nicholas would answer, "Yeah, you and what army; yeah, you and how many besides?"

When it rained, or snowed, Mrs. Menendez brought an umbrella which she left in the hall; it left puddles there. They lived on the seventh floor and sometimes Nicholas would race her downstairs. She would press the elevator button and he would take the staircase; if the elevator came quickly and made no stops, Mrs. Menendez would win. If she had to wait for it, or if two other people got in, Nicholas would win. With one stop, it would be a tie, and he would reach the elevator door exactly as it opened. Sometimes he ran up the stairs, and then he always lost.

When it rained and Nicholas did not want to go out, Mrs. Menendez asked him, "Do you think you're made of sugar; do you think you'll melt?"

"The lumpen-proletariat," his father would proclaim, "sooner or later. Sooner or later they'll fix Henry Ford."

Mrs. Menendez liked flowers and grew many flowers in the house and had, she explained to Nicholas, a green thumb. He could not tell the difference between the color of her thumb and the color of her fingers, but he liked the plants. She watered some every day and watered some every three days and some she watered once a week. She wiped their leaves. "That lets them breathe," she said. She always drank one glass of wine at five. She commiserated with the children at their mother's death; Andrea wept and Nicholas wept also and Mrs. Menendez, weeping, said, "She's gone away. On a very long journey."

Nicholas's father interrupted and said, "That's not true. She's dead. She's not traveling and you can't expect her to come back. Except in memory," he said.

Nicholas had little sense of the Depression. He ran errands for food and wore shoes till the soles gave way and shopped, with Mrs. Menendez, at the designated shops. Sometimes he waited, for a long time, on line: Mrs. Menendez went shopping and made him keep her place. He could not have a bicycle, his father said, because of the high unemployment rate. Yet he felt deprived of nothing, troubled by nothing, intact. His sister was laid off from her part-time work, after school, and she reported friends getting pregnant for clothes.

Nicholas remembered visiting his cousins in Montclair, New Jersey, and that his youngest cousin had a belly grown air-big with hunger; he heard of freight trains left in the desert and eighteen men that baked to death inside. The engine slipped its couplings, and the engineer took two days correcting the problem. He returned from Omaha to find a straggle of corpses, and one survivor in the flatcar's shadow.

Nicholas had study rituals. Before tests he crossed himself, then touched his forehead to the wainscoting three times, then picked up his pencils and did a fencing lunge. His sister baked popovers; she promised him a popover for every point above ninety, and if he scored a hundred he would get a dozen bonus popovers. "I guess you'd call us," Harry said, and he included George, "the three musketeers."

Paul Waner came to school one day because he had a nephew there, and he demonstrated fungo hitting and how to throw to the plate. Nicholas caught one throw on the short hop and thought of keeping the ball; Paul Waner called, "That's it exactly, fella. But get down lower, use your body as a back-up; you've got to be prepared to block."

Andrea had friends who were sixteen when Nicholas was ten. They discussed *The Well of Loneliness*, sharing the book. They practiced dancing and used him as a dancing partner, making him lead. If two friends came, Andrea would dance with one of them, taking turns as to which was the man, and Nicholas would always be the man. They smoked cigarettes and studied for exams together; they tried to anticipate questions, and Andrea got good grades. She wanted to attend Bryn Mawr, and Bryn Mawr accepted her but did not offer enough scholarship money; she went to New York University instead. She was short and dark and had, Nicholas thought, enormous breasts; she made Harry Burten sit on her lap and she called him cute. She wanted to go into fashion, or landscape architecture.

"Why landscape architecture?" his father asked. "What's there to do in that?"

"You can change the way the country looks, papaito," she said.

"What do you know about trees?" he asked. "Name me ten kinds of trees."

"Poplar, ash, maple, oak, birch, beech, elm, that's seven, pine, apple and tupelo tree."

"Tupelo tree, what's that?"

Andrea had boyfriends that she lay down with on the couch, and Nicholas would listen to her giggle and low laugh; in the morning he would sniff the pillows, smelling where she sat. Stephen Leavitt was Andrea's boyfriend and was nice to Nicholas and did push-ups in Nicholas's room.

"Keep your youth," said Stephen. "That's important. Really. You have to keep fit."

Nicholas protested. "You're seventeen. I'm ten."

"You'll never have it," Stephen said, "I promise you, this good."

Stephen ate sparingly at dinner, though Mrs. Menendez cooked well. "Once your stomach expands," he explained, "it never shrinks again." He drank carrot-juice cocktails and had twenty-two-hundred vision in his left eye. He refused to wear glasses, however, claiming it weakened the muscle; twenty years later, Nicholas learned, he lost the sight of his left eye. Stephen worked for General Foods and he lived in Australia and shot his son by accident, hunting wallaby.

"Twinkle, twinkle, little stink," Nicholas sang, "what the hell you am, I think. I'm not under the affluence of incohol, like some people teep I am, for I only had twee martoonies."

Nicholas's father taught him how to manicure nails. His father had an ivory-handled manicure set and he taught Nicholas to keep the half-moon rising from his cuticles, and to use Vaseline. Nicholas bit his nails; his father said if he continued with that habit he should sleep with gloves. He promised, "Next month, if you've learned this, I'll teach you to pedicure feet." Nicholas continued, till he was sixteen, to bite his nails.

(Andrea had developed breasts before the other girls in her class had breasts; she had been proud of that and had bought a brassiere. But the boys had pinched and teased her, she said, and the girls were jealous, so she had worn an undershirt over the brassiere. She wrote a report on pasteurization and Louis Pasteur that got three golden stars.)

His father spoke spanish with friends. Nicholas did not learn spanish but later found he could understand it with ease. When, later, the Battle of the Ebro was concluded and con-

244

clusively lost, his father got drunk. He was lean and martial and, his friends said, a great patriot; whenever Franco's name was mentioned, Nicholas's father would spit. Mrs. Menendez said, "He's spanish too, after all. Perhaps he will improve with time."

Nicholas's father replied, "If you value my friendship, if you cherish anything, do not speak that way in my house." Mrs. Menendez complied.

Nicholas's father was never out of work. He maintained his job in the glove factory when the glove factory had only a skeleton staff. In 1935 he was promoted to foreman and he received a raise. The glove factory diversified and they also opened a haberdashery shop. Nicholas's father received, as a Christmas bonus, three silk scarves and a cravat and one dozen socks. The socks were gray and black with a white circlet on the ankle; Nicholas admired them very much. When he got three golden stars for his report on Benjamin Franklin, his father gave him a pair. "Benjamin Franklin," Nicholas said, "was a statesman and inventor and printer and a man, in Thomas Paine's phrase, of great common sense." His father had told him the phrase.

"Thomas Paine," said Nicholas, "lived in New Rochelle."

"And was stoned there by the *canaille*."

"What's *canaille*?" asked Nicholas.

"Rabble. Boys."

"Why?"

"Why did they stone him? Why what?"

"Why did they stone him?"

"For his independence. For his hating cant. For being an old man, alone."

"Why the boys, I mean. What's cant?"

"Nonsense. Reasons that aren't reasons. Falsity. Because their parents let them, I suppose."

245

(Later, Nicholas would mourn the constituted hero and consider truth betrayal and embellish fact. Of a professor's son, his father, he made a near-professor; of an intermittent marxist he made the cadre's core. His father spoke excellent english and with very little accent; Nicholas construed him as a linguist, lied. He would describe intolerance as ideology and his father's bitter fastidiousness as love. Love and shame were counterbalanced; shame engendered praise. The cravat was legion and the flight from Spain enforced. Only with his father retired, living on Social Security, fierce, his pose became the habit of integrity, each protestation proved, did Nicholas learn—and luxuriate and wallow in—respect.)

Mrs. Menendez smoked. She said ashes were good for the rug. She dropped ashes on purpose and ground them into the rug. They had rugs with circles that went into squares and triangles that went around the squares and eagles in between; Mrs. Menendez dropped ash into the eagle's eye. She said prohibition of any sort was bad. She encouraged Nicholas to read. He played checkers with her and always won if he cheated and sometimes won if he played fair; "If you cheat," she said, "you're only cheating yourself."

He drank milk from his favorite mug. It was tall and cold and had teepees on the outside and a campfire on the inside; he would uncover Indians as he drank. At the bottom of the mug, inside, there were coals.

(Later he would hunt through notebooks, letters, tracking in that bric-a-brac growth's trick. Photographs convinced him of some inner innocence, the boy he'd been deflected in the man he was. He kept *I and Thou* on his bedside table, at the farm, all summer long. "I've always been becoming," he said, "never simply been." He felt resolute, recorded, defined. He did not finish the book.)

His room was pink and white because it had been Andrea's

room first; the pink paint, fading, looking white. He had a rocking horse called Silver and a bear called Teddy Bear; he stuck toothpick-claws in Teddy Bear when Teddy Bear was mad. He learned to whistle; he could whistle two ways, by sucking breath in or by blowing breath out. Andrea said she didn't want to whistle, anyhow.

(Nicholas split logs. He splintered logs for kindling and decided he would have to hone the axe. He lamented possibility erased. Each aspiration, he said, had entailed concomitant defeat. "I would not," Barbara said, "be a kid again for anything. I'm so very glad that's done." Nicholas did not agree. Some part of him, he said, trailed clouds of glory once. He formulated the phrase, "A tin can to time's tail" and used it frequently. Burning leaves, or pumpkins, or a corner football game set him adrift; "Time's mooring," he said, "slipped."

They drove to New York City and drove, immediately, back. The Palisades at night had seemed the Palisades he saw when young; the river, though sludge-slimed, persisted. Nicholas considered middleage a holding action; he had bought *Up the Down Staircase* for its title and he thought of youth as going down an up. Barbara brought tea. They would remain together and would remain in Cossayuna for the fall. "You and I, my love," he grinned at his wife, "are programmed for collapse. Half the population's under thirty now.")

They learned the Virginia Reel in gym, and how to do-si-do. Nicholas could whistle "Turkey in the Straw," and he learned it backwards and made people guess what tune it was, and nobody could guess. They also played slam-tag; in slam-tag you hit a person with a basketball and then he was out. Nicholas could not tie his sneakers with a bowknot until the third grade, but he invented knots. He wrapped the laces many times around each other and then tightened them by pulling underneath and making what he later learned was a square knot. He would pull the sneakers off, after gym, without untying the knots; then, slowly, with a pen or pencil as lever, he could unravel the knots.

("What happens," Barbara asked, "to the man in the gray flannel suit?"

"He wears it out. Or throws it out," Nicholas said. "Or keeps it till the fashion starts again."

They were in the attic of the farm. It was October sixth.

"When he gets sentimental," Barbara asked. "Or self-conscious. What happens then?"

"These are the seventies," he said. "Autoanalysis. Regret."

"Why, Mr. Wilson," she said, "Mr. Sloan, I do declare. Personal pollution, is that it?")

They also did tumbling and he did not like tumbling; they did a rope-climb and he did like that. Nicholas was bad in citizenship and penmanship but he was a good speller; he and Harry Burten won the partners' spelling bee. He could not understand syllabic division, however, and he remembered wanting to cry, in fourth grade, about where to divide words. He never understood the rules of syllabic division, but he did not cry.

(He rummaged in his work and college mementos and grade school looseleaf books. A wasps' nest was by the window; when the frost lasted past ten, he resolved, he would remove the nest.

"People are their data's sum," he said. "Especially us anal types. I don't believe in mood. It's my body hair I've got here, not devotion."

He wondered if his journal might have value, if he should buy a Mosler Safe or use a safe-deposit box; he decided, no.

"Build your buildings, master builder. Mister my husband," she said.

"You do want to stay?" he asked. "Nonetheless?"

248

"Nevertheless."

"And need?"

Christ, he thought, this first-person pronoun, this trio, this me and myself. . . .

"And need." Barbara finished the tea. "Foul rag and bone shop," she said.

Christ, he thought, it's endless, it simply doesn't end.

He organized the letters and the journals and the photographs. His journal was no novel, he decided, nor would be. He put the whole in boxes and aligned the boxes. He covered the boxes against leakage, with a sheet of six-inch insulation that remained.)

There was a drinking fountain that was too high for him in first grade but too low for him in the fifth. He was a traffic monitor from fourth grade on. He wore a red and white armband and had to get to school twenty minutes early and stay twenty minutes late.

XVII

NOVEMBER 12

Grasse. (V., the photographer's assistant, kept copies of the photographs of cars and girls and houses he admired; he superimposed himself on Christmas trees and patios and breasts. . . .)

H. had the habit, after love, of complimenting men's backs. This was effective, ambiguous, unusual. "Praise their pricks," she said, "and they'll think it's only that you want their clientele."

I believe these things. I believe our nation cannot long continue without change. The people are manipulated daily and, where not complaisant, outraged. Democracy is not the chance to juggle party hacks. Democracy is not this glut and starvation and waste.

I believe the ruling class, as constituted, will not gladly suffer change. They are fools in the long run, not foolish in the short. They have planned their obsolescence, though unwittingly, as surely as the nickel-plated car's. If this prove inaccurate, and the ruling class survive, this nation as we dreamed of it will not.

The military nexus is self-perpetuating, I believe, and I believe it evil. Madison Avenue is its civilian equivalent. Men grow rich in office, or via the office once out. When the republic was constituted, and for some time thereafter, the best were politicians; now, by and large, the worst.

I hate this rhetoric. I believe it necessary now. Nor can the artist survive if only as court jester, though he might have earned the jest. Things are not amusing any more.

About the Author

Nicholas Delbanco's previous novels are: *The Martlet's Tale*, *Grasse 3/23/66*, *Consider Sappho Burning*, and *News*. He lives with his wife on a farm in upstate New York and teaches at Bennington College.